in
this
moment

AUTUMN DOUGHTON

Autumn Doughton
In This Moment

Ebook Edition

ISBN: 1492167762
ISBN 13: 9781492167761
Library of Congress Control Number: 2013915544
CreateSpace Independent Publishing Platform
North Charleston, South Carolina

Contents

For my family.
Because, let's face it, there's you guys
and then there's everyone else.

You're all nuts. Really and truly.
But you're my kind of nuts and I like you just fine.

Prologue

"**D**on't think, just do."

The wind sliced up through the air teasing the thin strap of my tank and whipping my hair up around my face. I gathered it in a messy bundle at the nape of my neck and squinted down. A long way down.

"It'll be quick," she assured me, gripping my wrist and tugging me closer to the edge. I let go of the railing and tipped forward. The blue waves that tossed against the cement piers stirred up a swell of unease deep in my belly.

"You should go if you want to, but I don't know..." My voice trailed off like a draft of thin smoke. I pictured myself plunging feet first into the fast-moving water, the shock of it hitting my nostrils and closing in over my head.

Her gaze was level, drawing me in as easily as a moth to the light. I knew that she'd use the familiar words before they were out of her mouth. "I will if you will."

I moaned and rolled my eyes in protest. "That's not fair."

She laughed triumphantly and pulled me so close that I could feel the heat of her body and the rumble of breath moving in and out of her chest. "It's the code of any good friendship."

"Or blackmail."

She ignored me and began counting the numbers out slowly. "One... Two... Three..."

A flutter of wings lifted behind my ribs as I squeezed her hand and jumped into the void.

One

Aimee

I had forgotten what it was like. That first moment—the one that cracks me open like I'm nothing more than a flimsy piece of brittle, dried-out plastic and spills my guts all over the ground.

I had forgotten the way it slams me hard, the impact vibrating against my skull, rattling my teeth. One second I'm breathing oxygen and the next, my windpipe seals off and I'm thrown sideways in my own body—gasping and choking on my swollen tongue as I sink below the surface of her reflection.

It shouldn't seem so foreign to have the warm tones of her voice inside my head, or to see the golden brown hue of her eyes, or to think about the pattern of her laughter and the silky feel of our feet entangling as we kick through the water, but it is.

For the briefest instant, I can't translate what's happening, and then I get it…

I've forgotten to remember.

I swallow back the bile building in my throat, clench my fingers into my sweaty palms and focus on each thud of my heart. One. Two. Three. I feel queasy but I refuse to have a panic attack or throw up on my shoes. *Not here. Not today.*

I'm okay. I'm okay.

The words rush through me—settling in my chest and weaving themselves through my ribs. One. Two. Three.

I'm okay.

I just need to get my bearings and shake off this fog. Squinting my eyes against the glare of the sun, I step off the sidewalk and hang on to the hope that with the mess of students pushing past, my face will remain lost in the gauzy shadows.

My right foot hits something solid and I tumble backward, my arms flailing in front of my body for balance, a flurry of dark hair catching in my lips, and—

The tsunami whooshing around inside me seems to stop all at once as a firm band wraps round my waist effectively stopping my descent.

"Oh," I huff. "I-I—"

I realize that there's a set of wide-fingered hands on my stomach and that there's something digging into my back. Just perfect. It's a knee.

"Are you okay?" A deep voice hums in my ear.

Self-consciously, I uncurl my fingers and dare to peek to my left. Strange deep green eyes—like leaves submerged in water—are blinking back at me. With a jolt, I realize that those green eyes are attached to a face—an absurdly attractive face.

Oh my God.

I glance down quickly to confirm what I already know. Yep. I'm limply sprawled out in this guy's arms like some kind of storybook damsel in distress.

"Hi," he says as a slow, knowing smile transforms his full lips.

Horrified by the way that my heart bucks and spasms, I jump from his grasp—fumbling for my fallen bag as I try to get my feet under me. "Wow. I'm s-so sorry. Thanks, I—uhh… "

"Walk much?" The acidic question bites off my apology.

Still half in the guy's arms and half on the grass, I crane my neck around and see a beautiful girl sitting on the ground with an open notebook in her lap and her lunch spread out in front of her. I note with dismay that a few students have stopped on the sidewalk and are watching the entire exchange with open curiosity.

Great. In my play to remain invisible, I've become the most conspicuous person on campus by tripping over this hot guy and literally falling head over heels (or flip-flops) into the middle of his romantic picnic. Score one for Aimee.

I open my mouth to apologize, but the hot guy speaks first. "Polite much, Kate?" Turning back to me, his face tightens into a mask of concern. I have to bite back the shiver that slides down my spine as his eyes skim my body. "Are you sure that you're okay? You really wrenched your ankle when you fell. Let me see."

His fingers graze the skin of my calf and it's as if the gears in my head chug to life all at once. I regain my balance and mumble, "I'm fine, uh, but thanks."

Keeping my back to him so that he can't stare at the angry jagged pink line that runs from my right ear down to my collarbone, I wipe my clammy palms on my shorts and pull my long hair over my shoulder.

"Well, it was a pleasure to catch you. My services are always available for pretty girls like yourself."

I blink twice. Is this guy seriously flirting with me in front of his date after I just fell on top of him? And did he just call me *pretty*? Is this supposed to be some kind of a joke or is he really that arrogant?

I twist around and see that he's standing now, his head bent slightly to one side like he's considering something. He's tall—definitely topping six feet—with a body that brings a flush to my cheeks. It's the kind of body you normally see on TV—long legs colliding with a broad, chiseled-out torso and tanned arms that put the stretchability of his t-shirt sleeves to the test. God. And that face... It's a mosaic of angular planes: straight brows falling away to intensely green eyes, a narrow nose, and a severe jawline. His hair seems to be the softest

3

thing about him—a tumble of disheveled sunshine, just long enough that it begs to be touched by female fingers.

Handsome isn't the right word. It sounds too bland and average and this guy is anything but average.

As if he's reading my thoughts, he shifts his weight to one hip and smiles at me. It's a doozy. Dimples, teeth… the whole shebang. He moves his arm to grip the back of his neck and in the process he exposes a slice of his bare stomach. Wow. I have the sudden urge to walk over and skate my hands over his wide, powerful shoulders and up to his hair and… *God. Get a grip, Aimee.*

Still on the grass, his girlfriend—Kate, I think he called her—is glaring at me with open hostility and I can't say that I blame her. I'm sure that people try to steal her boyfriend all of the time. Bitchiness must be her conditioned response to any and all threats.

"I—uh, I…" What is wrong with me? It's like my entire vocabulary has been completely swiped from my brain.

"Once I heard someone say that a simple hello could lead to a million wonderful things." The angle of his chin deepens and his gorgeous smile goes lopsided. It's clear that this guy is enjoying my embarrassment. "What's your name? I think you owe me that much."

Seriously? Flames lick up my cheeks and tickle my earlobes. I suck in a breath and try again. "Thanks for the help but I don't think I owe you my name."

He laughs. "You're not going to tell me your name?"

"Is that going to be a problem?"

"No. Not a problem, just a shame." He furrows his brow in mock disappointment. His index finger waggles between our bodies. "I've really enjoyed this."

Who the hell is this guy? I'm tempted to say something snarky to put him in his place. I rub my tongue over the bridge of my teeth and open my mouth and—

"Aimee?"

I automatically turn to the sound of my name and see my sister standing about ten feet away. She's under a low, slanted overhang with her mouth slightly ajar and her eyes flared wide.

I think that the guy says something else, but I've stopped listening. Dodging a few students, my gaze zeroes in on Mara's thumb, which is poised precariously on the screen of her phone. I really do not need her to call our mother right now.

"Don't call Mom." I adjust the strap of my bag and pull on the bottom of my blue shirt. "Please."

Tucking her phone into the pocket of her linen shorts, Mara darts a shadowed look at me over her shoulder and starts to walk. I keep pace beside her. "What. The. Hell."

I let air whistle through my teeth. "I know…"

Mara's head juts forward, her blue eyes full of intention as we continue down the path toward the Student Union. "Aimee, I leave you for exactly thirty seconds so that I can drop something off at the Bursar's Office, and you go and trip over Cole Everly? Of all the thousands of students that you could have encountered today…"

"Cole Everly?"

"Yes. Cole Everly. You know, the perfect specimen of manhood that you just trucked."

Cole. Instinctively, I turn and look behind me, but the grassy spot where I fell is already deserted. Cole Everly—or whoever—seems to have packed up his girlfriend and moved on from our run in. "Oh, that was nothing. I just lost my balance and he happened to be there."

"Lost your balance? Aimee, I watched the whole thing. You looked like you had seen a poltergeist and you practically jumped into his lap!"

The imagery replays in my head and I cringe. "I-I…"

"What happened?"

Sighing heavily, I move my hand over my forehead to gather tiny beads of sweat between my fingers. "God, it's hot today, isn't it?"

5

Mara rolls her eyes. She knows that I'm deflecting. "What do you expect? It's Florida and it's August. You're avoiding my question. What happened?"

"Mara…"

My sister stops walking and turns her head to look for whatever it was that set me off. Her gaze finally settles on a stocky figure casually chatting up a girl. He's got on a grey t-shirt with bold red fraternity lettering and a backward baseball hat that hides his dark hair.

"That's Caleb Oster over there, isn't it?" She asks me.

My breath is thin and shaky. I feel a wisp of the earlier panic sneak up my spine. "Yes."

"Hmmmm." Mara lifts her eyebrows and takes a small step toward me. "He went out with her, didn't he?"

I swallow. "Sort of. He took her to the Homecoming Dance sophomore year. He wanted it to be more, but you know how she could be with guys. She blew him off and I don't think that he ever talked to either of us again."

"That sounds about right. You two were always a package deal." Mara shields her eyes against the sun and shrugs her shoulders dismissively. "Well, Aimee, you knew when you enrolled here that you'd eventually be seeing familiar faces. We're less than thirty minutes from home so there are going to be people who know you. People who knew *her.*"

My face is hot. This isn't a discussion I feel like having right now. "Look… This was just the first time so it threw me off guard, okay? And please don't tell Mom anything because you know that she makes a big deal out of every single thing that I do. God, she considers it an *episode* every time I hiccup or sneeze. I can't imagine what she'd think if she found out that I've been going around jumping into strangers' laps before classes have even started."

Mara winces at my pitiful attempt at a joke and takes me by elbow. "Come on, slowpoke. I won't tell her anything if you promise not to fall on anyone else."

"Fair enough."

"Anyway," Mara crinkles her forehead and bends her mouth to my ear, "I think Caleb missed out on your little show. He seems too preoccupied by that girl's low-cut shirt to even notice you."

I scoff because Mara is right. Caleb doesn't even look up as we move past him toward the hulking Student Union.

The building is five stories high, surrounded by a fringe of young palm trees and crepe myrtles. Blunt concrete pillars bolster the corners and dip down to form a low-slung wall that circles the front walk. Beyond the pillars, the exterior is mainly composed of panels of blue-grey mirrored glass that remind me of calm water on a cloudy day.

Mara flashes an encouraging smile as she pulls open one of the double doors, releasing a cool gust of air conditioning and the abrasive sound of students reengaging after the summer separation.

She steers me through a towering, glass-ceilinged atrium past a large campus bookstore and a string of counter-style food places. Against the farthest wall, I pick out a small coffee shop sectioned off with narrow tables and comfortable looking stuffed chairs.

"My best friends, Lindsey and Jenn," Mara whispers in my ear as she points out two blonde girls sitting at one end of a rectangular table. "Don't be…"

She doesn't finish the sentence but she doesn't have to. I already know what she was about to say. *Don't be weird, Aimee.*

I could act offended, but considering what just went down outside, I don't think that would be entirely fair. It's Mara's junior year and I know that she's worked hard to fit in at college. My sister is the type of girl who participates in life. She's in a sorority. She goes to parties and bakes oatmeal raisin cookies and joins clubs. Mara Spencer is a girl with a life and an image. The last thing she needs is for me, her unfortunate little sister, to screw things up for her with my special brand of emotional drama.

Returning her gaze, I pull my long hair over my right shoulder to cover the scar and murmur quietly, "I'll be fine."

Mara blinks and her expression flattens out. "Just remember that this is the beginning of a fresh start. That's what you told Mom and Dad that this was going to be. It's what you promised."

The words settle around me. I can feel the weight of implication in them.

You promised.

I guess that I did call it a "fresh start." I'm not sure if it was ever the truth, but after more than a year of not understanding who I'd become or what I expected from them, I knew that it was exactly the sort of statement that my parents and therapist wanted to hear. And maybe it was what I wanted to believe.

I take an exaggerated breath and nod my head. For my sister, I can do this. I can steady my heart and act the part for the two girls that she introduces me to.

Lindsey and Jenn are exactly what I expect Mara's friends to be like. Pretty, popular, polite. With matching lip-gloss enhanced smiles, they squeal like meeting me is the greatest thing that's happened to either of them in the past year. It's excessive. It makes my stomach turn over, but when Jenn—the blonder one—asks me if I'm coming with them to the recruitment fair to check on their sorority table, I swallow down my uneasiness and say brightly: "Yeah, of course I'm coming."

I don't miss the approving smile on Mara's face, or the way that her shoulders relax.

Keeping up the façade, I smile back and I listen to their stories and I laugh in all the appropriate places because I know that this is what everyone wants—a normal college freshman. They want me to be like Mara. They want me to talk animatedly about hair products and get excited about recruitment fairs and parties and nail polish colors. Nobody wants to know about the nightmares or the riptide of memories constantly trying to drag me under. The world doesn't want to be forced to look at my scars.

• • •

"The sorority table is over there!" Mara shouts, grabbing my hand and almost pulling me off my feet. She tugs me toward a wide courtyard nestled between the football stadium and a cluster of brick-faced dorms. The space is open and bright—bursting with tart greens and gemstone blues.

Looking over her shoulder, Mara points out a large fountain in the center and some picnic tables and I nod absently—my eyes bouncing off the unfamiliar buildings and the smooth planes of nameless faces.

Classes don't start for three days but today there is some kind of informational event on campus and people are everywhere—looking into clubs and fraternities and sororities before Greek Rush next week. The recruitment tables are set up in tiers that spiral outward from the fountain in three large loops. Lindsey is trying to explain to me the dynamic of each of the student groups, but I'm not really paying attention. I'm focused on keeping up with my sister as she weaves determinedly through the crowd trailing me behind her like a limp flag.

We stop in front of a waist-high booth decorated in a blitz of pink and green glitter. Mara, Lindsey, and Jenn are instantly swarmed with squealing, laughing girls. I let go of Mara's hand and hang back awkwardly—like a strange growth that no one knows what to do about. When I catch a redhead regarding the scar on my neck, I instinctively take a step back from the group and turn away. *Deep breath.* One. Two. Three.

"So you're Mara's little sister?" A lone girl walks up behind me. She's petite with chunky cobalt blue streaks running through her brown curls and a silver stud in one of her nostrils. Her black cutoff jeans are full of at least a dozen purposefully placed holes and her deep purple shirt is cropped so that her tiny midsection is exposed.

I glance at the sorority table and back to the girl standing next to me. It's the ultimate juxtaposition, kind of like looking at one of those *which-one-is-unlike-the-others* brainteasers. She seems to understand the perplexed expression on my face. "Don't ask."

Okay.

"So, you're a freshman, right?"

"Uh, yeah," I answer.

Despite her emo hair and go-screw-yourself outfit, the girl is a ten on the friendly scale and starts to ask me questions. I try to engage, wanting to ease the anxiety coiled in my belly, but every time I attempt to open my mouth, it's like I'm pulled further into myself.

I lift my hair, now damp and heavy with sweat, from the back of my neck and stand on my tiptoes to search the courtyard for a sliver of shade. Beyond the fountain, I can barely make out the outline of a white tent lined with coolers and students selling waters. Turning back to the girl, I say, "Will you let my sister know that I went to grab a water and I'll be back?"

A strange look flickers across her face and I think that she's going to ask me what's wrong, but instead she nods her head and waves me off. "Sure. I'll catch you around campus."

Leaving Mara and her sorority sisters, I push around the east corner of the courtyard by an improv group and a guy handing out flyers advertising the student radio station. That's when I see the sign. It's flat and rectangular—propped up on an easel. Across the top, thick blue letters declare: *SWIM FOR LIFE.*

"Would you like to sign up to support the women's swim team for our annual Swim For Life Relay? We're raising money for Muscular Dystrophy."

I whirl toward the sound of the voice, nearly toppling over a girl. *God. What is with me today?* My hands go out to steady her. "Oh—I'm so sorry. No, I'm—oh, uh…"

My stomach does a backflip and I have to press my fingers to my eyelids to hold on to my precarious balance. The girl standing in front me is tall with long, muscular legs, deep caramel skin, unruly black hair, and familiar brown eyes.

Noelle Melker is a year older than me. We swam together back in high school and had one of those competitive relationships that morphed into a muted friendship after too many hours cramped on the team bus together.

I watch as shock loosens her lower jaw. "Oh my God. Aimee?"

"Hi Noelle." My gaze darts around nervously. *Please don't let anyone else be nearby.* "What are you doing here?"

Noelle is looking at me like ten noses have sprouted up on my face. "What am *I* doing here? The swim team is putting on a fundraiser and I drew the short straw so I'm stuck at the sign-up table today."

"Oh," I say stupidly. "Well, it's great to see you. It's been a long time, huh?"

"I think that's the understatement of the century." She snorts and shakes her head. "It was like you fell off the face of the earth. You disconnected your cell phone number and your Facebook account right after Ji—after school let out, and none of us heard a word from you again. I mean, what happened to you?"

A stream of air leaks out of my lungs and I realize that I've been holding my breath. My eyes drop to the ground. "You know what happened, Noelle."

Noelle makes a strange sound from deep in her throat. "Of course I know what happened, but…" She pinches her forehead and sucks her bottom lip into her mouth as she tries not to stare at the scar on my neck. "Where have you been all this time? Sorry… I just can't believe that you're here."

I swallow against the lump in my throat. "Honestly? If it makes you feel better, I sort of can't believe that I'm here either."

"I did try to get in touch with you. Your parents and your sister wouldn't tell anybody anything. By January, a few of us were convinced that you'd been recruited by the CIA to be the youngest operative or something."

Despite my anxiety, I chuckle. "Uh, not quite."

"The *point*," she says, flicking her wrist and widening her milk chocolate eyes at me, "is that no one knew where you went so we were forced to invent ridiculous fantasies about your life."

"I hate to be a complete letdown, but I'm sure that the reality is less exciting than whatever your imagination came up with." I shrug my shoulders. "My grandparents live in Portland and I went to live with them for my senior year."

"Okay." She blinks. "Not that I'm complaining, but why did you decide to come back?"

I think about telling Noelle the truth—all the complicated things about myself that take up space and fill the dark corners of my brain. I could try to describe how lonely and sad I was in Portland. I might even try to explain how, despite everything it took from me, I missed the blue-green Florida water. Or how I dreamed about the way that the powdery white sand felt squishing up between my toes. If I were stronger, I'd tell Noelle about the night back in June when I hit rock bottom, and how I woke up in the morning feeling lucky to be alive.

What would she say to that? Would she understand?

Sighing and catching the ends of my hair between my fingers, I decide to stick with the well-rehearsed lie that my mother came up with. *Just tell anyone that asks how you hated the awful Oregon weather. This is Florida, the Sunshine State. Everyone will understand.* "I guess that I just got sick of the cloudy weather and the cold."

Noelle chuckles in disbelief. "That's it?"

"Well, no... That's not all of it, but it's the shortened version and the rest can wait while you tell me how *you've* been. You look great by the way."

"Girl, you're too sweet," she says, batting her eyelashes exaggeratedly.

Just then, I feel a presence at my back. I turn and my eyes collide with tarnished green irises so intense and electrifying that the air around me seems to quiver and reshape itself. Recognition only takes another heartbeat, and when it arrives, it buzzes through me with such force that my eyes go in and out of focus and I have to lock my legs so that I don't tip over.

Cole

Fuck. She's blushing and I'm hooked. Just like that.

I've got to admit something. I love a girl who blushes and if I know girls—and I do—this is one of those chicks that blushes all of the time.

My eyes move over the thin scar on her neck and drop to the dark shorts and the loose fitting blue top that does not even come close to doing those eyes of hers justice. I'm used to girls parading around in tight shirts with their tits pushed up in my face, so her laid-back outfit is a nice change of pace. And she doesn't have to prove a point with her clothes because I know that underneath all that fabric she's got a tight body. I felt it when she fell onto my lap an hour ago.

I take a step closer, drawn in to the gentle lines of her face. She twists a coil of her long, wavy dark hair over her shoulder and breathes in through her nose. Her clear blue eyes widen and she does it again.

Wait. Is this chick smelling me?

"Ivory," I say in amusement.

She looks confused so I clarify: "My soap. I use Ivory in case you were wondering."

Jesus. If you had asked me five seconds ago, I wouldn't have thought it was possible for her skin to go even redder, but I would be wrong. Now, she's stammering and her breathing is all funny and I sort of regret the joke. My intention wasn't to make her uncomfortable. I've just been wondering what it would be like to see this girl smile—to be the one to *make* her smile.

Afraid that if I look at her too much longer, she'll bolt or something, I tear my eyes from her face. "Noelle, aren't you going to introduce me to your friend?"

"Oh no, you don't!" Noelle puts a hand on her hip. "I am very familiar with this little game and I'm advising you to go flash that devilish smile elsewhere. If you think I've forgotten about Rachel and Deena then you're mistaken."

I cringe. Clearly I've forgotten about Rachel and Deena because I have no idea what she's talking about. I like to think of Noelle as a friend, but judging from the nasty glare that she's giving me, our relationship status is more ambiguous than I previously thought.

"Noelle, you've got this all wrong. I'm just being friendly."

Noelle's not buying it, which, let's face it, is probably smart of her. "Friendly my ass. Aimee is one of my girls, not a member of the panty-dropping bimbo squad."

Aimee. I let the name roll around my head, making room for the idea of her. "Well, if she's your friend, you should be happy that I'm being so charming."

Noelle shakes her head. "Nuh-uh. I already warned you not to play this shit around me. I declare this one an official safe zone."

I feel my pasted on smile start to slip. Damn. Noelle's not exactly giving me the glowing recommendation that I had hoped for. I rub the heel of my hand over my face and feel my shoulders rising toward my ears.

"What's a safe zone?" A small voice asks.

I look over. Aimee has finally worked up the courage to interject herself into the conversation. Her mouth is puckered up and her light eyes are rounded. She's got this one freckle on her cheek that's fucking killing me.

Noelle gives Aimee a significant look. "That means that you are off-limits and that Cole has to keep his hands and his *slut*-boy tendencies to himself." I think that she deliberately exaggerates the word slut for my benefit.

"Ouch!" I throw my hand over my heart and toss my head back in a show of mock-hurt. "What if I'm trying to turn over a new leaf and by automatically making the assumption that I'm hitting on your

14

hot friend, you're pigeonholing me and effectively halting my growth as a human being?"

"Yeah, I'll believe that when I see it," Noelle replies, rolling her eyes at me.

The thing is that I'm not joking. I've felt it before—that unexpected zing that happens when you check out a particular chick—but this is different. Something about Aimee has my interest piqued. It's true that she's hot. Damn. With all that dark hair and those blue eyes, she's fucking on fire. But I'm not making a play to get her into bed—I just want to know a little more about her. Call it curiosity.

Shit. Even in my own head that sounds like some overused pick-up line. I don't know why I'm pushing this. Zing or no zing, I'm usually not the type to pursue a random. I'm a smile-and-let-them-come-to-me kind of guy.

And maybe that's what's happening here. I can sense the challenge in front of me and I'm craving it—a typical caveman reaction. Aimee doesn't seem completely immune to me, but she's definitely not looking at me like she wants to eat me either. It's been a while since I've come across a chick that made me try, and I'm a guy that's naturally drawn to a fight—on and off the track.

Noelle comes closer and places one of her hands on my chest. She gives me a light shove but my feet are squarely planted so I don't budge even a centimeter.

She sighs. "Look, Aimee and I don't have time to debate your man-whore status right now. We haven't seen each other in a long time and we're trying to catch up, so why don't you scoot along and go annoy someone else?"

Ignoring Noelle's hand on my chest, I turn to Aimee and ask, "So you and Noelle are old friends?"

Noelle doesn't seem to care that the question wasn't directed at her, and she's answering before Aimee can even open her mouth. "Yes. She's a year younger than me and we swam together back in high school. Are you satisfied, Cole?" She makes a shooing gesture. "Now be gone, pretty boy."

I blink, my eyes narrowing in on Aimee's blue irises. "You swam?"

"Yeah… I did, but not anymore." Aimee nods slowly and crosses her arms protectively in front of her chest. I think she looks too small and fragile to be a swimmer. Maybe she got sick and that's why she had to quit.

"She was All-State for the 200 yard medley and the 100 yard Butterfly her junior year," Noelle tells me with a satisfied smile.

This surprises me and has my mind all over the place. *All-State?* That means that she was good. Very good. "If you were All-State, why did you quit?"

The two girls share a look and I notice the way that Aimee's forehead compresses and how she unconsciously touches the scar on her neck. "Other things came up and it was a lot of pressure."

"Huh." I pause. "If you went to high school with Noelle then you must know Daniel Kearns because he went to the same school."

She lifts her chin a fraction and her blue eyes boggle. "Daniel? You know Daniel Kearns?"

I bark out a laugh. "Yeah, of course I know Daniel. He's one of my roommates and we run track together." My gaze swings over Noelle to the sidewalk behind me where Daniel stopped to check out one of the tables. "He was right behind me. Should I get—"

Aimee cuts me off abruptly, her now panicked eyes darting to Noelle's face. "I—I don't understand. I thought he was on scholarship at Michigan." She clenches her fingers and sucks in a ragged breath.

She seems ready to crawl out of her own skin and this awful sensation slithers over my shoulders. Does this girl have some sort of history with Daniel? Did they go out?

Noelle's features contort into a grimace. "I don't know what to say, Aimee. I would have warned you but I just assumed that you already knew. Daniel transferred here last fall after... well, you know. His mom was having an especially hard time and he wanted to be closer to home."

I don't know what the fuck is going on, but I can tell that something is very wrong. Aimee's face looks pained and her eyes are getting shiny like she might start to cry. I touch her arm gently and her warm skin spasms beneath my fingertips. "Aimee—"

She doesn't wait for me to finish. In one fluid movement, she drops her hand, pushes away from us and takes off across the courtyard. Noelle and I are left staring and stuttering in her wake.

Two

Aimee

Luckily, I haven't had any more unfortunate run-ins with people from my past. Mara reminds me every morning that the university is huge. *Chances are slim,* she says and I'm starting to think that she's right.

It's the second day of classes. So far I like all of my professors and the course material seems mildly interesting. I'm even considering applying for a position as an office assistant in the English Department. This, I realize with vague surprise, is what it feels like to settle in—to begin believing that life can be okay again.

With an hour to waste before my next class starts, I turn left in front of the Liberal Arts building and find a patch of summer-green grass to sit down on. Above me, the spindly palm trees buffer me from the pounding rays of the sun. Their fronds whistle in the light morning breeze and fan out across the sky like a web of papery green veins.

The professor for my Media Literacy class emailed the course syllabus out yesterday, so I take my book out of my bag and start to read ahead, taking notes in between bites of the donut I brought on campus with me.

I wasn't always the diligent student that I am now. The first three years of high school I was too busy looking for a good time to be bothered with essays and reading assignments. Admittedly, my best friend was usually the catalyst for those good times. I can almost hear her voice, giddily pushing me toward her open bedroom window while I groggily complained that it was one in the morning.

We'll sleep when we're dead, Aimee.

Shuddering, I remind myself that I've spent the last year cultivating a new persona, and this version of Aimee Spencer doesn't attract attention. She never misses class, she makes the Dean's List, and she reads ahead.

What would she make of me now? The thought is so confounding that I very nearly laugh out loud.

After a solid thirty minutes of reading, I swallow the last of the donut and search the front pocket of my bag until my fingers find the wound-up cord of my earbuds. I jam them into my ears and scroll through my library until I've found what I'm looking for—a mellow indie band that I discovered in Portland. I lean back until the musky smell of earth fills my nostrils and tiny blades of brittle grass tickle the skin of my shoulders.

With the music in my head and my hair pressed out all around me, I follow the twisting pattern of sunbursts darting between the lacey palm fronds. I look until the spanning brightness turns the world hazy white and stings the back of my eyes and I'm forced to close them.

I'll be the bottles on the beaches
You'll be the waves that wash them all ashore

Is it strange that my brain conjures up the image of Cole Everly's face? I only talked to him for five minutes almost a week ago, but like some swoony thirteen year old, I can't stop thinking about him.

Cataloguing his physical assets has become a regular distraction when I want to zone out.

Maybe this is what I get for spending an entire year avoiding any and all guys. Now my suppressed hormones are raging to the surface with a blistering vengeance.

Hmmmm. Cole.

It's definitely those eyes. Sure, the rest of him is gorgeous, but I've never seen eyes like that—green and gold all at once. They blink from his face like two star-bright forest moons. And I remember that his nose has a very slight bump in it that somehow makes his face even better... more interesting.

Sensing movement, my lashes flutter open and I see a figure, back-lit and looming above me. Drenched in equal parts light and shadow, it takes a few seconds for the lines of his body to solidify and for the angles of his face to come into focus. When they do, my heart lurches with a wild dizziness, and my body locks up.

It's like the universe is playing a joke on me. I'm a mess of frozen joints and wide eyes—every single atom of my being seems to be caught in place. After ten beats too long, I manage to reboot myself by sucking in a breath of air and plucking the earbuds out of my ears.

"Hi," he says.

I know that I'm staring like a fool, but I can't help it, can I? Like I conjured him out of thin air, Cole Everly is smirking down at me.

"Is this okay?" He sits down on the ground next to me, folding his long legs into his body and draping his arms over his kneecaps with an easy confidence.

Completely disoriented, I let my eyes roam from the sun-tipped hair sticking out in every direction all the way down to the worn brown leather flip-flops that encase his long narrow toes.

I push myself up on my elbows, feeling the weight of my hair as it falls against my shoulders. "Your third toe is longer than your second toe."

He laughs and the sound of it rumbles through my body and decides to stay awhile. "Of all the things I thought you'd say, pointing out my strange toes never crossed my mind."

"Sorry to disappoint," I reply, glancing down to where my fingernails are gripping the dirt.

"It's not that." Cole closes his eyes like he's searching inside himself for something. "It's just that I wanted to…" He shoves his fingers back through his hair and exhales audibly. "Fuck. I was worried about you the other day and so was Noelle. You freaked out on us and I didn't know what was wrong." He smiles sheepishly. "I was on my way to class from morning practice and I saw you over here and I guess that I wanted to make sure you were okay."

My heart seizes. *Great.* He thinks I'm half off my rocker and has taken pity on me—the broken girl who obviously can't keep her shit together. I feel pulled out and raw under the intensity of his gaze. I fidget with the hair band wrapped around my wrist. "Your concern is appreciated, but why would you be worried about me? You don't know me. You don't even know my whole name."

His laugh is quick and boyish. "Yeah I do. *Aimee Spencer.*"

This flusters me and Cole can tell. His smile gets wider and the dimples make an appearance. Great. There just had to be dimples, didn't there?

"Give me a little credit," he says, lifting his eyebrows. "Did you really think that I wouldn't do my research?"

I push the earbuds that have been hanging from my shoulder into my lap. "I have no idea why you would bother, but if you did your research and are actually Daniel Kearns' roommate, then I'm sure that you already know why I ran away the other day. Daniel and I—" I stop myself and look down briefly. "We don't speak."

Cole's smile falters, but he still pushes forward. "Luckily I'm not Daniel." He kicks back, mirroring my position so that he's settled on his elbows. "So, tell me about yourself, Aimee Spencer."

I shake my head blandly. "There's nothing to tell."

Closing his eyes, he angles his head so that his face is turned up to the sun. "Now *that* I don't believe for a second. How about your family? Start with the easy stuff and we'll work our way up to religion, politics and what type of birth control you're on."

I open my mouth, but there are no words—just thoughts dangling from my tongue. I'm not sure whether I should laugh or kick him where it hurts.

Cole squints over at me. "Waiting over here."

I blow out a shaky breath. "My family is just my older sister and my parents. My dad manages investments and my mom plays bridge on Tuesdays, goes to her book club meeting on Thursdays, and worries about me during all of the in-between times."

His eyes are closed but he nods like he's been listening to me. I wait for him to say something, but after an extended silence that has my brain doing erratic twirls, I break down and ask, "So, ummm... what about your family?"

"I've got a thirteen-year-old sister back home," he says, keeping his face tipped to the sun. "My dad's a lousy attorney in the middle of nowhere-ville, Nebraska, and my mom is out of the picture. She emptied the bank account and ran off with another guy around three years ago."

His tone is so casual that it's obvious that he's joking. I play along. "Oh, like she snuck off in the middle of the night with her tennis pro?"

Cole turns his head and looks at me with serious green eyes. "No, she didn't want to become a cliché so she left on a Sunday afternoon with the her golf instructor. She lives somewhere up north and she calls occasionally, but I haven't spoken to her since she left."

Holy hell. Am I the biggest bitch in the history of the universe? Without thinking, I reach out and brush Cole's hand. Instantly, his fingers curl over mine—capturing me, pinning me in place and sending a hum of electricity up my arm. My eyes snap to his and the world sways beneath us. I notice the hard movement of his throat as he swallows and a strand of hair falling into his eyes. His mouth parts like he has something to say. I shift my body infinitesimally closer and—

"Hey Cole!"

We look up in unison. A leggy girl with light brown hair and pink stained lips is waving at us from the sidewalk. The too-eager look on her face is like a poison spreading through my gut. I snatch my hand back and tuck it underneath my body.

Cole takes a tight breath and nods his head once to the girl before looking back at me with a level gaze. "So, Aimee, there's this thing happening tonight."

I hesitate. "What kind of thing?"

Chewing the inside of his cheek, Cole says, "A party kind of thing. The track team does it every year at the start of school as a sort of way to let loose before practices pick up and we get too busy."

There's no way that I'm going to a party hosted by a bunch of asshole jocks, but I ask anyway: "And where is this party?"

"At a place called Dirty Ernie's."

"*Dirty Ernie's*? That sounds… um, *interesting*."

I watch Cole's mouth soften and everything inside of me rolls over. He pushes himself to his feet so that I have to arc my neck and look a long way up. "Will you come? I know for a fact that Daniel won't be there so you don't have that as an excuse."

I surprise myself with my boldness. "And what if I have plans?"

Cole's nostrils flare slightly. "Do you have plans tonight, Aimee?"

"No, but…"

He quirks one side of his mouth and laughs. "Good. Because I'm going to tell you a little secret but I'd like you to keep it between us."

"What's that?"

Cole stuffs his hands in his pockets and works his jaw like he's thinking over each word before he says it. "It would have bothered me more than it should have if you'd said that you had plans."

My thoughts are moving so fast that I can hardly follow them. *Does he mean what I think he means?*

"The party starts at nine, Aimee Spencer." Then he's gone— jogging after that girl—and I'm left staring after him trying not to notice how nice and round his butt is.

• • •

While I wait for my next class to start, I get lost in my head. Considering that the closest I got to attending a party last year in Portland was stumbling into the middle of a flash mob on the corner of Fourth and Madison, I don't think I'm ready for the party scene. After so many months of keeping myself drawn into a tight ball, I'm realizing that it's harder to make myself unspool than I thought it would be.

A fresh start.

The goal of coming back to Florida was to start living again and I know that if I'm being honest with myself, I'm only partway there. My classes are going well, but other than Mara and a few professors and now Cole, I've barely talked to anyone since I've gotten here.

A noise startles me from my thoughts. In the seat next to me, a girl is staring.

"Hi," she says cheerily.

"Hi?"

I realize that I know her. It's the blue-haired girl from Mara's sorority.

"We didn't meet properly last time. I'm Jodi," she tells me, kicking her head to the side.

"Aimee," I say and take the small, pale hand she holds out to me. She has an awfully strong grip for someone so tiny.

Jodi grins—it stretches across her face like water over dried up sand and exposes a small gap between her two front teeth. "I know your name. Not only are you Mara's little sister, but we have two classes together."

"We do?"

Jodi laughs—it's light and airy and reminds me of another girl's laugh. "Yeah. Are you a Library Sciences major? Because you sure don't look like one."

I glance down at my khaki colored shorts and plain white tank top. If I don't look like librarian material, then Jodi certainly doesn't. With that nose stud and the mesh top and loose linen skirt she's got on today, I think she'd look more at home in front of a pottery wheel than sitting next to me waiting for a lecture on archival access to start.

"Um, I don't know yet. Technically I'm undecided but it's a definite possibility. Or maybe English." I give myself a little shake. "I'm a bibliophile."

"Ditto." Jodi lowers her pointy chin to her chest. "Look," she says firmly, "I have a bit of what you might call 'the sight,' and it's been pretty clear to me since the recruitment fair that you and I are going to wind up as friends so I think that we should both just go with it."

The sight? I'm not really sure what to say to that. I can't tell if this girl is crazy, or on something, or being serious. Whichever way, I'm intrigued. I place my elbow on the armrest of my chair and lean back. "Okaaay…"

That's all the encouragement that Jodi needs to be off. She tells me about her loser ex-boyfriend that showed up at her apartment last night and professed his undying love for her, and her straight-laced mother, who Jodi calls *confounding*, and the yeast infection that she had over the summer, and her thoughts on whether or not cats should be declawed.

Jodi is a sophomore. She's also a Sagittarius who likes reptiles and thinks that Facebook is a tool of social destruction devised by Satan.

She tells me that she's only a member of Mara's sorority because she's a legacy and her mom made it clear that it was either join up or face the wrath of a thousand angry gods.

"They keep me around because of the legacy thing, but I don't participate unless I'm forced. I only went to the fair last week to freak the rest of the girls out." She laughs. "You should have seen the horrified looks that they gave my clothes when I showed up at their precious glitter table. Priceless."

By the time the class is over, my head is spinning and I feel slightly out of breath. Jodi is bobbing two steps behind me in the hall—still talking and seemingly unaware just how out of practice I am at this whole "friendship" thing.

"Okay, I added myself to your contacts so you've got my number now." She hands me back my phone. "I'll look into the tickets for that concert on Saturday and I'll let you know. Do you want to get food first?"

I don't even remember agreeing to go to a concert with her, but my coherent brain function is almost zilch at this point so I just nod my head.

"Great. Chinese isn't really my favorite but there is a place nearby. This one time I ate like eight egg rolls in one sitting and got so sick. Ugh. You don't want the details. Just imagine Hiroshima contained in this stomach." She waves her hand dramatically over her midsection. "Anyway, last weekend I discovered this *amaaahzing* little Indian place off of Connell Street if you're up for it. They have a vegetable pakora that is like—no joke—to die for."

"Um. That sounds great." The truth is that I have no idea what pakora is.

"My next class is this way," Jodi says, gesturing over her shoulder and taking a step in the opposite direction. "Just remember to text me when you get to the bar tonight."

I frown and call after her. "Wait! What's tonight?"

Jodi stops and turns back to me. "Remember that party I told you about?" She blinks and waves her hands dismissively. "I know, I know! It sounds like it's going to be some horrible thing with a bunch of jerk-off athletes, but I went last year and I swear that it was a ton of fun. You'll like it. We'll dance!"

"Sorry," I mumble, trying to mentally backtrack through our conversation. *Dance?* "I missed that earlier. Where is this party?"

"It's at a little place called Dirty Ernie's. Just look up the address and meet me there around ten." She rocks back on her heels and spins away, calling back in a sing-songy voice, "And text me!"

• • •

I'm not going. Not a chance.

The only thing I have in mind for tonight is changing into a stretchy pair of yoga pants, eating a bag of microwave popcorn for dinner, and spending at least four solid hours vegged out on the couch watching bad reality TV. I figure that I'll text Jodi in a little while and explain that something came up. Since she has *the sight*, she probably already knows that I'm going to back out.

When I walk in the townhouse, Mara is on the phone. The guilty shadows under her brow and the way she jumps when I close the front door give her away immediately.

I roll my eyes and stick my tongue out at her. This is our sister-speak for: *I know that you're talking about me.*

"Mom," she mouths as she hands over her cell phone.

To prepare myself, I close my eyes and breathe in and out through my nose three times. It's a technique my therapist suggested utilizing in stressful situations.

Feeling slightly calmed, I bring the phone to my ear and clear my throat. Before I've even managed to get out a greeting, my mother is already launching into her standard *I'm worried about you* spiel. This is what she's like. I swear that every time we talk, my hackles go up and I start pacing and gnawing on my bottom lip.

"No, that's not true," I say, thrusting my hand in my hair and shooting Mara an I'm-going-to-kill-you look. At least she has the decency to stare at the floor in shame because it's clear that she's been reporting every single detail of my unsociable activity to our mother. "I'm doing fine and *no* I don't need you to make an appointment for me." I pluck at the bottom of my tank top and take a deep breath. "I'm actually going out with a friend tonight. Believe it or not, she's one of Mara's sorority sisters…"

That's how I wind up sitting in the passenger seat of Mara's car in a pair of tight jeans and more make-up than I've worn in over a year.

"You sure you're going to be okay by yourself until Jodi gets here?" Mara asks as she pulls the car into a small gravel lot at nine thirty. She's dropping me off on her way to meet up with her sorority sisters. "You can always come out with me instead."

My stomach feels knotty, but I take a deep breath and open the door. "No, I'm good."

"Wait. You have some frizzies." Mara reaches over and runs her fingers over the hair that I've braided and draped over my shoulder. "And would you remind Jodi that if she misses more than three chapter meetings she's going to have a fine? She's not off to a great start."

"Will do." I flash my sister a wobbly smile and step out of the car into the balmy, humid night. The heavy Florida air clings to my skin like a slick layer of lotion that never seems to dry.

Dirty Ernie's is a small brick-faced building stuck between a hipster record store and an artsy coffee shop that I vow to check out later. I slip the strap of my purse over my head so that it crosses my chest and I sidle my way through a few clusters of people standing out on the sidewalk smoking. A big, brawny bouncer checks my ID at the door and encircles my wrist with a neon green wristband that lets everyone know I'm a lame underclassman.

Inside, the bar is pretty much the way that I feared it would be—crowded and loud. I'm standing on my tiptoes searching the sea of heads for one with blue streaks when I'm jostled from behind.

"Oh shit!" Some guy turns his upper body to face me. He pulls his dark eyebrows together and grabs at my bare arm with rough, calloused fingers. "I didn't see you standing there. Sorry."

I shirk from his touch and move away, weaving in and out of bodies in search of Jodi. I pass through a set of glass doors that lead to an open-air back porch. It's hot and sticky but there are wide-bladed fans positioned on tall posts bordering the space and the music and crowd are less intense so at least I can breathe properly. I send Jodi a quick text, find an empty seat near the end of the bar, and ask the bartender for a soda and an order of fries from the kitchen.

Pulling my wallet out of the zippered pocket of the purse draped across my chest, I sort through my cards until I find what I'm looking for. I'm just about to hand over my debit card when an unfamiliar hand reaches over my shoulder and pushes money across the smooth surface of the bar. "Put that away. It's on me."

I twist on the barstool and look up and into a set of almond-shaped dark brown eyes. It takes a startled moment to process that this is the guy that bumped into me over by the front door. He's leaning into my space, a small smile playing at the corners of his mouth.

Before I can even work up to a protest, he places a finger firmly against my lips and slurs, "Let me at least get you the drink and the fries as an apology for almost knocking you over back there."

I wrench away from his fingers. "Thanks, but I'm fine."

"I know that you're fine, baby."

Who calls a girl he hasn't even met "baby"? The needle on my ick radar just redlined. The guy leans in and his breath is warm and moist against my cheek. He smells sour—like a putrid mixture of beer and cheese. I push myself away, shuddering and scraping my fingernails along the bar top.

"Uhhh… Really, I appreciate the gesture, but it isn't necessary."

The guy steps forward, managing to position his body even closer to mine. "Well, this might shock you, but buying that drink was just a way to meet you and hopefully convince you to get out on the dance floor with me." He winks seductively. "I'm Brady, by the way."

The majority of the female population would probably find Brady cute with his glinting brown eyes and flirty grin. He's working a boy-ish, obviously-want-to-get-in-your-panties angle that I guess works on your average college girl, just not on me. I may be out of practice in the dating scene, but I still remember how to read a guy like him and I'm not about to be a part of the one-night stand waiting at the end of Brady's night.

I look back toward the interior of the bar where I can see the outline of bodies grinding to the fast-paced club music hammering through the speakers. This place is not my scene. Not by a long shot. "Thanks, but no thanks. I'm not interested in dancing with you or anyone else tonight." I say in a clipped tone that I hope is polite but still laced with a definite rejection. An uncomfortable knot is starting to form in the pit of my stomach.

"Okay, okay," he says, glancing down at my chest with unguarded interest. "I can see that you're a little firecracker and this is going to be fun. Now," his index finger trails a slimy path down my arm, "if you aren't interested in dancing with me, why don't you tell me what you are interested in? That would be a good place to begin."

Trying to ignore the sexual undercurrent rolling through his words and the jitter of anxiety pumping through my veins, I rigidly pivot my body. "I'm getting less and less interested in this conversation, *Brady*. Does that clarify things for you?"

"Hell," Brady whines playfully as he fingers my braided hair. "You're killing me here! At least tell me your name."

I open my mouth, fully intending to shell out a fake name to get this guy to leave me alone, when a firm grip falls against the nape of my neck. I jump at the contact and the unexpected jolt of warmth that shoots down my back.

Cole

My right hand is balled in a fist. Fuck, fuck, fuck.

"Back off, man. I think that she already told you that she wasn't interested. Now you're just pushing your luck and my sense of magnanimity," I say, stepping forward and squaring my shoulders defensively.

I know how to be threatening when the situation calls for it and this is a situation that calls for it. Brady should be down on his pathetic knees thanking God that I don't have his ass pinned to the ground right now. I saw the scared look on Aimee's face and I heard exactly what she said to him and now a rush of hot blood is surging through my whole body. Maybe it's an overreaction, but I'm fucking furious.

Brady just laughs at me. "What the hell does that mean? *Magnana-what?*"

I feel Aimee shiver underneath my left hand and that pisses me off even more. Swallowing hard, I level a steely gaze at Brady. "Seriously, fuckwad, you need to walk away from this right now."

Brady tilts to his left and I can see that he's had more to drink than I initially thought. "Dude... Cole, I swear that I had no idea that the chick was here with you." He chokes on a laugh and slaps my shoulder. "You never bring girls to this kind of thing. I thought that you liked the room to play a bit?"

My eyes meet Aimee's. She blinks nervously and opens her mouth. "It's not—"

I cut her off by applying gentle pressure to her neck because she does not need to clarify the situation for this asshole. If she does, he'll only see it as an invitation and he'll be right back to ogling her tits and imagining what it would be like to get her in a dark corner. Brady

Samuels is one horny dude. He's like a fourteen year old running rampant in a porn shop.

"It turns out that you don't know shit, Brady, which is why I'm just giving you a warning that she's not available. Got it?" My hip brushes Aimee's arm as I move into the space beside her.

Brady shakes his head and I can tell that he's not going to be a problem anymore. He stalks off toward the inside bar and he doesn't look back. I'm guessing that he's going to find the guys on the team and ask them what the fuck is up with me tonight. That's fine. Let them try to analyze it because I sure as hell can't figure it out.

Breathing heavily, I turn back to the bar and see that Aimee has closed her eyes. It gives me a chance to study her—to soak her in—which is something that I've wanted to do since the first time I saw her. Everything about this girl seems ridiculously delicate. Even the pink scar that weaves across her pale skin looks like it was drawn on her body with a fine-tip paintbrush.

My eyes slowly follow the outline of her small mouth and the slope of her nose and cheeks before moving over to the thin skin of her eyelids. She's got these insane dark spiky lashes that magnify her light eyes like she's some kind of doll or anime character. And that freckle…

"Are you okay?" I ask, yanking myself away from my thoughts. Damn it. Does my voice sound as scratchy as I think it does?

She doesn't answer right away and I worry that Brady really upset her. I press two fingers under her chin and force her eyes up to mine. "I promise that he won't bother you again, Aimee. I'll make sure of it."

"It's not that," she says, sucking her bottom lip in between her teeth. She blinks rapidly and I'm afraid that she's about to cry. What the hell will I do if she starts crying? I'm not one of those guys who understands what it takes to be comforting.

She pulls away from me and squeezes her shoulders in around her body. "I-I'm just completely embarrassed and sorry that you had to pretend to be here with me. What a joke." She grimaces. "Is that guy one of your friends?"

"I wouldn't call him a friend. He's on the track team with me so, yeah, I have to put up with his shit pretty frequently, but it's damn sure not out of choice." I flex my jaw and push my hands back through my hair. What is it about this girl that has my emotions all over the place? "And, Aimee, you have nothing to be sorry about. Brady should have left you alone the first time that you said that you weren't interested."

"It wasn't anything—just harmless flirting. I'm the one that let him buy me the drink and fries so I don't think I can get too angry about it."

My eyes dart to the glass in her hand. I make a low sound of disapproval in the back of my throat. Why did she let that asshole buy her anything? "You really shouldn't go around accepting anything from random guys that approach you at bars. He could have put something in your drink. It's not safe and—"

The expression on her face stops me cold. Shit. She looks like I just ran over her puppy and then I want to kick myself in the balls because I remember who this girl is and what she's been through.

"It's only a soda and trust me—I'm always careful. It never left my sight, and anyway," she shakes her head lightly, "it was an apology."

I take a deep breath and soften my voice. "For what?"

She shrugs. "He bumped into me when I first got here."

I don't want her to think that I'm a dickhead like Brady, but I do want to lighten the mood and I've just found my opening. I brace my elbows on the edge of the bar. "Why didn't you say so? You can buy me a Jack and coke—lots of ice."

"What?" She sputters and her mouth twitches. It's not a real smile, but it's damn close so I'll take it.

I straighten my spine and raise my eyebrows. "Well, you fell on me the other day so I guess by your own logic that entitles me to a free drink."

Aimee rolls her eyes and shakes her head, but she must be playing along because she lifts her hand to get the bartender's attention.

Gently, I push her arm back into her lap. "Not now," I say, leaning in and catching the sweet smell of her shampoo. I don't know what it is, but it has me thinking about fresh-baked cookies and long afternoons at the beach.

"When would you like this so-called apology drink?" She asks, tilting her face up toward mine. She's so close that I can feel the warmth of her breath moving over the cracks on my lips. Her skin is creamy and fucking perfect and her mouth is a delicious pink.

I move one arm and graze the back of her hand. "I was thinking that you could buy me the drink on our date."

Her blue eyes widen and my stomach clenches. I don't know what it is, but there's just something about blue eyes so light and clear that they seem to go on for miles. "Our *date*? Are you joking?"

I don't know. Am I joking? I don't think so. Just because I haven't asked a girl to go out with me in years doesn't mean that I can't, right? "I'm not joking," I say and it feels more like the truth than a lie.

Aimee's words are careful, decided. "I don't date."

I brush a few loose hairs away from her face and bend to her ear. She really does smell amazing. Absolutely amazing. "I don't date either, so I won't tell if you don't," I whisper.

Her forehead creases and I can tell that she's thinking it over. That's probably a good sign. At least she didn't flat-out turn me down which is kind of what I'd been expecting. And then I almost laugh because here I am, happy that some girl I barely know is *thinking* about saying yes to a date with me. *Oh, how the mighty have fallen.*

Aimee stares down at her fingers splayed open on the bar. "I-it's just—"

"Please don't overthink it."

This snaps her eyes back to mine and I can see a change in them. The difference is minor, but I catch it and it makes everything in my chest turn over. I can tell that she's wondering about me the same way that I'm wondering about her.

She starts to speak, but her gaze zeroes in on something over my shoulder and her entire body stiffens. What the hell? I look behind me and see Daniel over by the rear entrance talking to Chad Moody.

Shit.

I thought he had a date with that chick from Colson's class. Maybe it fell through, or maybe he brought her here, or maybe he figured out that she's the raging bitch that she seemed like and he took her home early.

When I turn my head back, Aimee's gasping like she can't get enough air into her lungs. "I th-thought you said that he wasn't going to be here tonight. I can't—"

I grab both of her hands, but she's already pulling away and I'm just clutching the fabric of her shirt like some creep. "Wait. Aimee, please wait! You haven't even gotten your fries yet."

She doesn't wait. Of course she doesn't.

Three

Aimee

I feel her before she opens the door to my bedroom.

"Aimee?" Her voice is hesitant. "Are you okay?"

"Yeah," I croak into the darkness.

The door widens and a stream of pale light finds me. Mara comes into my room and sits on the bed. Her hand finds the shape of my foot through the comforter and she cups her palm around my toes. "You're crying?"

I half-laugh. "Yeah... I saw Daniel Kearns tonight."

Silence. "Do you want me to call Mom?"

"No."

More silence. Mara clears her throat. "Do you want to talk about... her?"

Do I want to talk about her?

I wouldn't even know where to start. "No."

After a few minutes of quiet, my sister lies down beside me and wraps her arm over mine. "I wish that I could make this better for you," she says softly.

"But you can't," I answer. "No one can."

• • •

Sometimes it's easier to think about her in pieces.

She loved Lemonheads. She dipped her fries in ranch dressing. When we were fourteen, she drew a swirling mustache on her face with a black Sharpie and wore a sombrero to her parent's Christmas party and spoke with an accent the whole night. In general, she talked too much, laughed when she got nervous about something, and she never passed up an opportunity to sing karaoke.

She decided that she wanted to be a vet when her cat swallowed a nickel and had to have surgery to remove it. We were eleven.

Her nails were a mess. She bit them down to nothing but would still paint them with glitter nail polish before a big race because she swore up and down that it brought her good luck in the water. On special occasions she tended to overdo it in the perfume department.

Pixar movies always made her cry. She was allergic to scallops. She had a birthmark shaped like Idaho on her lower back.

Those are the things that you don't get to read in an obituary—the memories and bits of a person that make up a whole life.

My best friend, Jillian, was sixteen when she died. If she had lived for another nine days she would have made it to seventeen.

I try not to picture her on that last day—in the blue top with the light purple flowers embroidered around the collar and those shorts that she made from her favorite pair of jeans, but sometimes I can't help it and the memory gets inside my head and my heart and it's all I can do to keep breathing air. I wonder all kinds of things and I want to cry and I want to yell until my throat hurts and I want to pull all of my hair out. But, mostly, I want to go back to that night so that I can grab her hand and lace her fingers through mine, fusing us together.

"Hold on," she'll say to me. "I don't want you to let go."

• • •

"So then I was all, 'you have got to move on because like I've told you a hundred times already—we are done and there's no going back.' And he started whining and sniffling and begging, the big baby." Jodi rolls her eyes dramatically. "I just don't know how to make things any clearer for the guy without completely killing him."

I nod my head as I tear the top of the sweetener packet and dump the powdery contents into my Styrofoam coffee cup. It's Wednesday and Jodi and I are getting coffee in the Student Union before our last class of the day. So far I've seen her hopped up on Indian food and live music, and on a sugar high from one too many Twizzlers, but I've never seen her on a caffeine rush. Just the thought of it is intimidating and I wonder if I should have a tranquilizer on hand. Just in case.

"So, what happened after that?"

I follow Jodi as she navigates through the crowded tables to a set of oversized chairs and a sofa arranged in a sunny corner. She plunges herself into one of the chairs and pries open the lid of her coffee cup.

"Well," she says, blowing on her coffee and looking at me sideways. "After two decent orgasms and a container of Moo Shu Pork, he went home. I haven't heard from him since, but Jason's like clockwork. Even though I keep telling him to leave me alone, the poor guy can't make it ten days without showing up at my front door begging me to take him back."

"Wait." I blink slowly, adjusting myself on the sofa. "You had sex with him? After you told your ex-boyfriend all this stuff about moving on, you had sex with him?"

"And Chinese food." Jodi nods. Today she's got the blue streaks in her hair wound into tiny braids and pulled back from her face. Her eyes are heavily lined with dark kohl and she's switched out the little silver stud in her nostril for a gold one.

"I don't understand. I thought you said…"

"I said that Chinese isn't my *favorite*, but in a pinch I can totally deal."

"That is not what I meant and you know it." I shoot her an exasperated look. In less than a week, Jodi and I have fallen into an easy pattern. She was annoyed with me when I stood her up last week at Dirty Ernie's, but she told me that she'd get over it if I bought her an ice cream cone after the concert we went to on Saturday. Just to be on the safe side, I bought her a sundae with a mountain of whipped cream and three cherries on top.

I look at her hard. "I don't understand why you had sex with him if you want him to leave you alone. Maybe I'm crazy, but that seems counterintuitive."

"Oh." Jodi leans in with an impish smile on her lips. "Well, Jason is too much of an idiot to make for good boyfriend material, but his, umm, *eggroll* is… well, let's just say that it's supersized. So from time to time I make an exception to the terms of our 'strictly friends' agreement."

I flush red. "And that's not confusing? Don't the lines get blurred?"

Jodi rests her head against the wall above her chair and sighs. "Well, yes it's confusing, Aimee, but a girl's gotta do what a girl's gotta do. And Jason can be very persuasive when he wants to be. He does this thing with his tongue and it's so—"

I lift my hand to stop her. "I really don't need to hear about what Jason can do with his tongue. Seriously."

Jodi's smile widens. "Aimee Spencer, are you blushing? Is this conversation embarrassing you? What if I were to… I don't know… tell you that Jason has a name for his penis? And it's very descriptive."

"Shhhh," I murmur, my eyes scanning the nearby tables.

Jodi smacks her lips together. "I can see that you're not a fan of the word *penis*. How about if I were to say… *nipple?* Or *orgasm? Penetration?*" Her voice is dangerously loud and the people around us are starting to look. "*Scrotum?*"

"Jodiiiiii!"

"Aimeeeeee!" She mimics my whiny tone then bursts into her signature breezy laughter. For someone so incredibly petite, the girl can make some noise. "I wish that you could see your face. You're like this." She crumples her forehead and contorts her mouth into a scowl.

I roll my eyes and take a sip of my coffee. It's not that I'm a prude. I'm not. It's just that I haven't talked to another person about this kind of stuff in a long time and it feels strange.

"So," she says, catching her breath and dropping her eyes. "How about you? Any secret *lovahs* to disclose?"

"Nope. No guys for me."

Jodi narrows her gaze. "Girls then?"

"No girls either." I laugh and twist my hair around my finger. "I already told you. I decided over a year ago not to date because I wanted to focus on school and keep a clear head."

The thing about Jodi is that I like her. Being around her makes me feel almost normal. I can pretend that I'm what everyone wants me to be—just a regular college freshman making a new friend. I want to tell her things about my past—about Jillian and why I am the way that I am—but I'm not sure how much honesty is too much honesty. So far she hasn't asked about the scar on my neck, or why I don't drive, or why my mother texts me practically every hour to check up on me.

"I had hoped that was a bad joke because that is possibly the saddest thing I've ever heard. What college freshman doesn't date and wants to focus on *school?*" Jodi bows her head toward me. "Is it herpes?"

It takes me a second to register that she's asking me whether or not I've got herpes. "What?" I shake my head. "No, I don't have herpes!"

"Well, that's a relief." She twists her mouth to one side. "Aimee, you have… you know… *dated* before, right?"

It's true that I haven't gone *out* with a guy in recent memory, but that doesn't mean that I'm Amish or was ever on the fast track to becoming a nun.

I clear my throat. "There have been a few *eggrolls.*" Well, *one* eggroll really… "Just not recently."

Jodi claps her hands in front of her body. "Thank God! If you were going to confess to being a college freshman with her virgin status still intact, I was going to lose my shit over here."

"I am not a virgin." *Not technically.* I tuck my hair back behind my ears and lift my chin. "I'm familiar with penises, scrotums and all kinds of penetration."

"I'll be sure to lock that important information up for a rainy day. You never know when knowledge like that will come in handy." A new voice says.

My heart gives a wild kick. *I know that voice…* I spin around and Cole is there—standing beside the sofa with his head cocked to one side and that increasingly familiar dimpled grin on his face. My mind runs over my conversation with Jodi. *I'm familiar with penises, scrotums and all kinds of penetration.*

A quick glance in Jodi's direction proves that she isn't going to be any help. Her bottom jaw is resting in her lap.

"That was completely out of context," I murmur faintly. I know that every available inch of me is flaming fire engine red.

It's obvious that Cole notices my mortification, but instead of giving me space to breathe, he steps closer and his smile only gets wider. "Of course it was," he replies casually, swinging his backpack to the ground by my feet. When he sits on the sofa next to me, my heart races and my skin prickles. "And I certainly didn't mean to put a stop to such a fascinating conversation—especially one about penetration and penises—but I saw you sitting over here and I wanted to let you know that we're having a party at my place Friday night. You should come." He turns to Jodi. "You should come too."

"Th-that sounds great," Jodi stutters, shaking her head and blinking like she's just waking up. I would roll my eyes, but I think that's the exact same reaction that I had the first time that Cole spoke to me. "I'm Jodi."

"Hi Jodi. I'm Cole."

"Oh, I know who you are." Jodi smiles suggestively.

"Is that a good thing or a bad thing?"

Jodi shrugs. "Well, I haven't heard many complaints…"

"Ugh," I moan. "Please don't feed his ego."

Cole laughs and steeples his fingers. "Now, Jodi, can I trust that you'll get Aimee to the party on Friday night? Because I know that she'll come up with an excuse, but this girl is in definite need of some fun in her life. Don't you agree?"

God. Jodi's nodding her blue-tipped head and batting her eyelashes vigorously—a clear sign that she's fallen victim to a brain fog induced by Cole's quasi-magical green eyes. I understand it. I'm quite familiar with the symptoms myself.

I cough. "Actually, I won't be able to make it to your party," I say, trying to ignore the fact that Cole's leg is touching mine and that every time I catch the scent of him all sorts of crazy, swoony thoughts dance around my head.

"See…" Cole hesitates, shares a knowing look with Jodi. "I told you that she'd have an excuse."

"It's not an excuse," I defend. "An excuse would be telling you that I have to wash my hair, or that my pet goldfish is ill and I need to stay home to take care of him. I happen to have real plans on Friday night."

The corners of Cole's lips fall and his forehead wrinkles as he searches my face. I momentarily wonder if it's possible that he truly is disappointed that I can't make it to his party. Then, almost before I can be sure that I saw something real and solid in his expression, the familiar easy smile is back in place.

"Real plans?"

"Yep," I reply as I finger the lid of my coffee cup. "My parents are coming down to take my sister and me out to dinner on Friday. We're going out for my dad's birthday."

He cocks one eyebrow. "So, your parents are big into the rave scene, yeah?"

The question takes me by surprise. "Wh-what? My parents?"

He nods his head.

"No, they aren't in the rave scene. Carl and Elise Spencer are your run-of-the-mill country club yuppies. I doubt my mother even knows what a rave is."

"Hmmm…" He smiles and leans on his elbow. "Are they wannabe vampires? You know that they have those cults now where people think that they're actually members of the undead and they drink blood and sleep in coffins and do all kinds of weird shit."

"Okay, wait. Are you crazy or something?" Both of my hands are up and I'm on the verge of confused laughter. "No, my parents are not wannabe vampires. They are completely normal. *Painfully* normal actually." This is the truth.

Cole straightens his posture and flashes his dimples. "Then I'm sure that your mom and dad are taking you out to dinner around seven and, even if you have dessert and coffee, you'll be done in plenty of time to still come over to the house. Did I mention that parties at my place tend to go all night?"

"Umm… Did it occur to you that I might not feel like going to your party?" I glance at Jodi for support, but it's no use. I've lost her completely. She's kicked back in her chair watching Cole with an enraptured expression on her face. Traitor.

"Of course it occurred to me, but I don't think that's what's keeping you away." Cole drops his voice and leans in so that only I can hear what he says next. "You have to talk to Daniel sometime, Aimee. And I promise you that it's worse in your head than it will be in real life."

44

Before I can respond or process the incredible way that he smells, he's pushing himself to his feet and picking up his bag from the ground.

"Ladies," he says, making a gesture that's partway between a wave and a dismissal. "I hope to see you there. If not, then I'll catch you around. I've got to go or I'll be late to the field, so please get back to your scintillating discussion about penises." His green eyes slide in amusement between Jodi and me.

"Yeah... um, have fun running or whatever," I mumble.

He bobs his head once and then he leaves us. I can't help but watch him as he pushes past the tables and through the finger-smudged glass door of the Union. His shoulders. His butt. Yeah... um, wow.

I don't know how a person that I hardly know can take up so much space in my head, but there it is. No matter how hard I try, I can't seem to quit the idea of him.

After nearly a full minute, Jodi breaks the heavy silence. "For the love of all that is sacred, *Aimee Spencer!*" She says my name low and fast—sounding more like a parent than a friend. "How in the world have you not told me that you're on a first name basis with Cole Everly?"

Cole

The whistle blows and the reaction is instant. By now it's instinct. When I was first starting out, I imagined that it was like the straps of gravity had been severed with the swift cut of an ax. One. Two. My tensed muscles release, propelling my body forward into space in a single movement.

No thoughts.

No worries.

I am nothing but rhythm and motion.

One. Two. Three. Four. Five. Six. Seven. Breathe.

One. Two. Three. Four. Five. Six. Seven. Breathe.

I pump my arms and push my hips down, squeezing all of the power out each leg extension. My limbs and lungs work in tandem, shredding reality down to this steady pattern of movement and breaths. It's comfortable. It's what I know. I feel it in every pore of my body.

No thoughts.

No worries.

On the track, under the burning summer sun, there is only this moment and the one that follows.

One. Two. Three. Four. Five. Six. Seven. Breathe.

The count pounds in my chest and pulses through me like blood in my veins, driving my muscles harder, faster.

I can sense Nate on one side of me and Brady on the other, getting closer, gaining. I kick my legs out, ignoring the burning sensation starting in my thighs and shooting up my body. Faster.

One. Two. Three. Four. Five. Six. Seven. Breathe.

No worries.

I am ahead again.

One. Two. A final push. Three. Four. And I'm over the line.

I breathe in a sudden rush like I'm coming up for air after being held under water for too long. Everything slows down as my heels dig into the ground and my arms release. I ease to a stop and bend over to brace my hands on my knees. Through the sweat dripping from my forehead, I make out a splash of green. I push my torso up and suck more air into my aching chest. Coach is saying something to me, but my eyes are darting to the digital display board and my hand is running over my face.

I blink. Not bad.

One. Two. Three. Breathe.

No worries.

No thoughts.

Later, with a towel wrapped around my waist and Nate's music thumping against my skull, I lean my bare back against the cool concrete wall and let the words of my teammates seep into my skin. Quentin is talking about some chick he met last Saturday.

"At first I was into the friend because her rack was unbelievable. But then this one hottie, who looked all prim and proper with a pink cardigan on, whispers in my ear that she wants to go down on me right then and there at the bar and…" He spreads his hands and grins. "I'm only human."

The other guys hoot with laughter.

"Speaking of unbelievable racks." Brady turns his gaze on me. "I saw Kate at Ashton's place last night and she was asking me about you."

I knock my head on the wall once and stand, reaching for my shirt and sweats. I don't want to talk about Kate Dutton. "I'm sure she was."

"So… are you still on that?" He inclines his head in my direction. "Because if not then I've got to admit that I'm interested."

Of course he is. Brady is ruled by one thing only: his dick.

"Do you have a problem with me calling her?"

I turn away from him as I slip the thin white cotton shirt over my head and throw off the damp towel. "She's all yours. Just watch out for her because she can get a little bit clingy."

Quentin slaps my shoulder. "Yeah, man, I wouldn't worry too much about that. I think Brady has a few parts that he'd be more than willing to have her to cling to."

I ignore the laughter and the rest of the conversation. I'm not feeling it today. I just want to finish getting dressed, pack my shit up, and get the hell out of here.

Before I can make my escape, Coach comes in and wants to give us a gruff speech about conditioning, getting enough sleep, and laying off alcohol. Yeah, sure thing, Coach…

By the time I make it out of the building, the sky is a purple-black bruise eating up the peach-tinged skin horizon. I check my phone. One missed call and a voicemail from a number that I don't have saved but that I recognize as my mother's cell phone. I delete the message without listening to it.

Here's the thing: I haven't spoken to the woman that gave birth to me since she left us three years ago. Every so often she seems to grow a conscience and she'll call and leave me a message saying a bunch of contrite shit like she misses me and wants to make things right between us. *Make things right?* Come the fuck on.

I let go of a bitter sigh and turn my focus back to the phone. There's a text from Kate asking me whether or not she left her shorts at my place last week and one from my sister, Sophie. I ignore the one from Kate and respond to Sophie. She must be sitting on her phone because she answers right away.

I laugh and start to type back when I hear my name called. I look up and see Daniel jogging toward me with his gym bag and a damp towel in his hand.

"I forgot to ask you about a ride home. My car's on the fritz again and I dropped it off at the shop this morning," he shouts, pushing his wet hair back and draping his towel over his shoulder.

I stuff my phone in my front pocket and point to the truck with my thumb. "Yeah. Climb in."

Three minutes later Daniel's managed to rip my music apart and tell me six times that my truck smells worse than the dirty socks molding on the bottom of his laundry basket.

I turn up the volume on my stereo and flick him off. My truck is a piece of crap but it gets me from one place to the next so who's complaining? I'm on a limited budget and since I can't manage a job in addition to the track team and school, I take what I can get. "Well, you can find yourself a different ride the next time you're stranded after practice, fuckwad."

"Or you could just clean up this junker." He picks up an empty soda can from the floorboard and tosses it in the narrow space behind the seats. "I honestly don't know how you manage to get girls to go home with you in this thing. It's foul."

"Look, I haven't had any problems so far. And this is fair warning: me and my *foul* truck are about to get offended and you need to start asking yourself how you're going to get two kegs to the house in one trip on Friday without my help."

"Fair enough. I'll shut up about it." Daniel laughs and shakes his head. "I guess I forgot that you don't need to bother with impressing girls to get them to sleep with you. At this point, I'm pretty sure that The Great Cole Everly could roll in dog crap and show up on a bicycle in nothing but a pink tutu and fairy wings and Kate Dutton and every other pretty girl within a ten mile radius would still be lining up for a piece of the action."

I involuntarily squeeze the steering wheel and tighten my jaw. I don't know why I'm annoyed, but I am. "Thanks for making me sound like a real douchebag, man. I appreciate that..." I let my voice trail off. "Anyway, I already told you and the other guys that I'm done with Kate. The girl's been texting me and calling me almost every single day like she's... like she's..." I shake my head at a loss for words.

Daniel glances over at me with both of his eyebrows raised. "Oh, you mean that she's been acting like she *likes* you? She's been calling you like she wants a relationship with you after you've been fucking her on and off for the past six months?"

I ignore his mocking tone and roll my shoulders. "I'm just not interested in the girl like that and I think I was pretty up front with her about it. I told her from the beginning that I'm not a relationship kind of guy. So if Kate wants to change the game now, she's going to have to find herself a different player."

"And that has nothing to do with Aimee Spencer?"

My eyes meet his briefly before snapping back to the road. The sound of her name is still ricocheting around my chest like a bullet.

"What are you talking about? What the fuck does Aimee Spencer have to do with anything I just said?"

Daniel shrugs his shoulders. He tilts his head toward the passenger side window and plays with the window controls. "Noelle Melker told me that Aimee's back from wherever she ran off to last year." He coughs twice. "Then I saw you with her at Dirty Ernie's and you two looked cozy. I just thought that something might be happening between you and that's why you're kicking Kate to the curb."

I snort. "Nothing's happening there."

I don't tell him that I invited Aimee and her friend to the party at our house on Friday or that I spent at least an hour on Sunday stalking her online like a psychopath.

I skimmed through a few articles about the accident, but what drew my attention the most were the photos of Aimee from back when she swam competitively. It was strange—like looking at snapshots of a totally different person. Her hair was shorter and her body was thicker with a swimmer's muscles, but that wasn't what got me. In almost every single picture, Aimee was smiling. A real fucking smile. And her smile was just like I imagined it would be—so wide and beautiful that it put the sun to shame. It twisted something down in my gut and kept me transfixed to the point where I had to slam my laptop shut and go on a long run just to be able to think about something else.

I can feel Daniel watching me from the passenger seat. I look over. "Nothing's happening," I repeat.

"I wouldn't mind if there was something there." He takes a deep breath and rolls his tongue over his bottom lip. "I'm not going lie and say that it's not a little strange for me that she's going to school here now. Aimee—" He pauses and somehow the sound of the truck engine rumbling seems louder than it did two seconds ago. "She was… Cole, you wouldn't know anything about this, but she and my sister were like the same person. They shared and traded everything—clothes, guys… everything. I've never known friends like that. They were so close that

50

it was an ongoing joke with my family that Aimee and Jillian were the opposite of Siamese twins—one head controlling two bodies."

Daniel never talks about his little sister. All I know are the scraps of information that I found online about her high school swimming career and the articles about her death. And, of course, I know that he gave up his track and field scholarship at Michigan State to transfer here so that he could be closer to his grieving parents.

He keeps talking. "It's hard to explain the way things went down with her and my mom after the accident. It was bad. My parents were losing their minds and in this unreal pain, so when the police couldn't figure much out, they just... My mom needed something or someone to focus the blame on. Unfortunately, that someone turned out to be Aimee."

My chest constricts. I think of Aimee and how crazy sad and fragile she seems. I don't know why I can't get this girl out of my head, but it's like her face, with that faraway look on it, is pinned to my skull like a nail in hardened concrete. Shit. I need to rein myself in.

I shift on my seat and hook my wrists over the slippery steering wheel. "You should talk to her."

Daniel looks away, his breath fogging up the window glass. "Yeah, I know that I should. I *should* do a lot of things, Cole."

Four

Cole

I don't expect her to come.

She has a hundred reasons to stay away and none to show up, so I don't really think that she'll walk through the door. Still, I find myself checking the time on my phone more often than normal. By eleven, I'm beyond pissed for no solid reason and pretty much everyone at the fucking party has started to ignore me. Quentin was the last person to talk to me and all he did was ask if I was on my period.

Fucking fine. This is my wake up call.

It's the much-needed reminder that I need. This is why I don't date. Flowers and romance and feelings are not my thing for a very good reason. That bullshit always leads to disappointment in the end. Fuck that.

I've seen it happen too many times to one of my dickhead friends. They get some chick that doesn't give a fuck about them stuck in their system and they're gone—can't see straight, can't think right. Why? No one is worth all of that crap. Not when there are plenty of chicks with sweet bodies and low morals ready to step in and fill the void at any time.

Of course, that isn't the line that people want you to feed them. People want to believe in love and monogamous relationships and things that don't exist in real life.

Last year when Nate was losing it for that girl we met at Stubby's, I warned him that he was being fucktastically stupid. He told me that I was heartless and bitter and would wind up sad and alone. A month later when he was crying his eyes out and too fucked in the head to win races, I was banging her best friend and in the middle of the best winning streak of my life. Life lesson: heartless and bitter might not be so bad.

My dad is the ultimate sucker. He romanced my mother for twenty years and the whole time that they were married he actively ignored the fact that she didn't give two shits about him or her own kids. He clung to this idea that we were the perfect American family, complete with the two-story house and white wrap-around fence. He went along, humming and whistling and refusing to acknowledge all of the telltale signs that it was one big fat lie.

He gave my mother his soul, and one day she woke up and decided that she didn't want it anymore so she left. And it wasn't like the movies. There was no note or teary explanation in the pouring rain. The only thing that she left behind was an old bathrobe and a collection of dog-eared paperback romance novels.

That woman raked her own family over the coals and never looked back. And now my dad is just a broken shell. He goes through the motions but he stopped living three years ago. Now he just exists.

That shit is not for me. No fucking way.

I take a sip of stale beer from the red plastic cup in my hand and close my eyes. It's so loud in here. I should probably get up and go outside for some air or put myself out of misery and go to bed. I might even wake up the first time my alarm goes off instead of hitting the snooze button three times. Coach will piss himself if I make it to the field on time on a Saturday morning. Just the idea of it makes me smile.

"What has you looking so happy, Cole?"

I blink my eyes open. There's a cute girl next to me with her arm slung over the back of the couch and one knee tucked up under her butt. She's got pretty soft grey eyes and short blonde hair. I know her from someplace. Shit. I think I hooked up with her last year after a party. Melanie or Melissa or something. I'm pretty sure that she's in Zeta. Or maybe it was Theta.

"Huh?"

Her plastered-on smile wavers a little. "You were smiling and looking happy. I was just curious about it."

I almost laugh at the irony. I feel the direct opposite of happy right now. "Oh, you know…" I stay evasive and take another sip of my beer.

Melanie or Melissa tips her head to the side and sucks in her cheek. "So, do you remember me?"

Damn. This girl is asking for it. I let my eyes fall to her tits and I feel a mild twinge of interest. "Sure I remember you. It's ahhh—"

"Megan," she says coyly, inching closer and reaching for my chin. I don't fight it and this seems to encourage her. She brings her moist lips to my ear and I feel the brush of her nails as her left hand creeps under the bottom of my shirt. "Well, that's very nice to hear because I certainly remember you, Cole."

Aimee

"Is it me, or are you ready to douse yourself in kerosene and light a match?" I ask, waving stiffly as I watch the taillights of my parent's black sedan disappear around the curve in the street.

"Try 'slit my own neck' and you'd be right on target with the way that I feel right now." Mara lets her fake smile drop into a frown. She cups her arms behind her neck and turns toward the front door of our townhouse with a sigh.

I follow her past the small galley kitchen and into the living room. Mara kicks off her black ballet flats and launches herself onto the light green couch. She closes her eyes as she drops her arms against her lap with a slap.

I sink in beside her and reach for the remote resting on the low side table. Powering on the TV, I ask, "Do you want to watch a movie? I think we've got that new one with Ryan Gosling."

Mara's eye pop open. She wipes her brown hair from her forehead. "Aimee, I can't think about Ryan Gosling right now."

"Come on, Mara. You're breathing therefore you can think about Ryan Gosling."

"Can you be serious for a minute? I want to talk about what happened at dinner. I want—" She makes a frustrated sound. "I just can't believe her!"

"Mara, don't..." I blink.

"I'm sorry that she went so far with you. I—" Mara sucks in a jagged breath. "I should have stepped in sooner."

She's referring to our mother. "They just..." I let my voice fall away, not knowing exactly what to say. Handling Carl and Elise Spencer is always a delicate matter. My parents aren't bad people—they just don't like dealing with anything disruptive or complicated. And for over a year, *disruptive and complicated* means *me*.

Mara shimmies closer to me and rests her cheek on the curve of my shoulder. "She just doesn't know when to quit, does she Aimee?"

I grunt.

Mara's head comes up and she looks at me seriously. "I think that Mom's lost her mind this time."

"No, she thinks that I've lost mine." Judging by the sour expression on Mara's face, she doesn't think my joke is even a little bit funny. I roll my eyes and continue talking, "Look, Mara, it's not as bad as it seems with Mom. She's just overly worried about me, and Dad goes along with whatever she wants because he doesn't want to rock the boat with her."

Mara's hands come up to her face. She's annoyed. "But wanting you to drop out of college and spend the entire year at home? That makes absolutely no sense to me."

Mom had called earlier this week and presented the idea of us all having dinner tonight to celebrate Dad's birthday. What she failed to mention was that it was an ambush.

Her voice filters through my brain.

We hear that you haven't made an appointment with that new therapist yet.

You saw Daniel Kearns last week?

Have you tried that make-up I bought you to cover up the scar?

Your new friend has blue hair?

From the way she was going at it, I thought that she was ready to lock me up in some institution to deal with my "emotional instability," so I was almost relieved that all she suggested was that I take the year off and come home. *Maybe college is too much pressure right now,* she'd said. She even tried to entice me with talk of a trip to Europe with her and my dad in the spring.

"You have to give her some leeway. She's convinced herself that I'm going to slit my wrists any day now and I don't really think anything that I say or do at this point will make her believe otherwise. Every little thing sets off some kind of alarm with her. It's like she's decided that if I'm closer to her physically, she'll be able to control the situation and somehow magically turn back time to make me the person that I was... before."

Before.

I don't need to clarify for Mara. It seems like my entire life is broken up into two parts: *before and after.*

Mom preferred before. Before was solid. Happy, healthy, popular Aimee lived there.

After is unfamiliar. It's all scars and therapists and tears. And it doesn't make a difference if I get straight A's or stay out of trouble. To my mom, *after* is an uneven pile of what-ifs.

Mara's hand settles into the crook of my elbow. She makes a big deal of looking me in the eye so that I know that she's serious. "I'm glad that you set Mom straight. And, Aimee, I'm sorry that I've been giving her updates about you. I thought I was helping, but after tonight, I promise that's over."

I swallow. Yeah, it had been hurtful to listen to my mom twist things around that only Mara could have told her, but I already knew that they were talking about me so it's not like I was shocked. And even though my sister and I don't agree on everything, I know that she would never hurt me on purpose. I pat her hand reassuringly. "I know that you didn't mean anything by it so let's just forget that tonight ever happened."

Mara smiles and squeezes me. "Love ya."

"Love ya more."

After that, we fall into a comfortable silence. I don't bring up the Ryan Gosling movie again. Instead there's an old episode of *Law and Order* on TV. We've both seen it more than once so pretty soon we're shouting things at the characters and laughing and eating pretzel M&Ms from the stash that I keep stored next to the couch.

When the show credits roll, Mara turns her head toward me and swirls her finger in the air. "I'm sick of sitting around. It's a Friday night and I think that we should go out."

I pick up my phone and bring the display screen to life so that I can see the clock. "It's almost midnight, Mara."

"And your point is?"

"Where are we going to go? You know that I don't have a fake ID anymore." I got rid of it over a year ago.

Mara snorts. "It's not a problem. I know a guy."

My eyebrows go up. "You know a guy? What are you, like in the mob or something?"

Mara chuckles. "No. It's worse than the mob. I'm in a sorority." She stands and holds out her hand to me. "Come on. I think that after the family dinner from hell, we deserve to have some shots and fun."

Cole's words from the other day flit through my head. Maybe I do need more fun in my life.

Cole

The music at this place sucks. I'm sweating balls. The beer's damn expensive. And I'm pretty sure some chick just went and puked over in the corner near the bathrooms. Classy.

I turn on the stool and prop my forearms against the edge of the lacquered bar top. I still can't believe that I agreed to come out so late. I have practice in the morning and my headache is getting worse by the second but I wasn't ready to call it a night. Maybe a part of me didn't want to sit around that couch one more second waiting to see if Aimee would show. So when Nate and Adam suggested that we move the house party to a dance club, I went along with the idea and encouraged Megan to gather up her friends.

"Want to dance?" Megan asks me for third time since we got here. She's crushing her boobs against my biceps and standing on her tiptoes so that her mouth can reach my ear.

"Nah," I shake my head and raise the bottle of beer I'm holding to let her know that I'm occupied. "I'm good."

I can tell by the look on her face that this is not the answer that she was hoping for. I'm being an asshole and Megan's been taking the brunt of it for almost two hours. She might be an over-zealous flirt, but she's actually not awful. It's not her fault I'm in such a fucked-up mood tonight.

I set my beer bottle down and cup my palm against her lower back. "Why don't you do me a favor and go save my buddy Daniel over there?" I suggest, tipping my chin toward Daniel, who was cornered the minute we walked through the door by a loony chick claiming to be in one of his classes. "My boy looks like he's ready to drown himself in his drink."

Megan's grey eyes follow mine. "You got it." She breaks into a mega-watt smile and runs her manicured fingernails down my arm before stalking away. I will say one thing: the girl has a fine, plump ass on her.

I watch, amused, as Megan bats her eyelashes and works her ample curves to scare off the other girl. In two minutes flat she has her arm hooked around Daniel's waist and is dragging him out with her to the dance floor.

"She's got skills," I mutter and take another sip of my beer.

"Cole, man," Nate yells over the music. He comes up beside me and slams his empty beer bottle down on the bar top. "Ready for another one?"

I move my head sharply to one side. "Naw, I think I'm going to call it. I'll get myself a cab or see if I can catch a ride back to the house with Adam."

"What the fuck? The night's still young!" He chants, throwing back his head and howling toward the ceiling.

"It's almost two in the morning." I take a final swig of my beer and signal to the bartender that I'm ready to close out my tab. "Anyway, I'm just not feeling it anymore, and don't forget that we have an early practice tomorrow."

Nate laughs, his white teeth flashing against his dark skin. "I never thought I'd see the day that you'd be the one reminding me about a morning practice." He jabs his elbow harshly into my ribs. "Before you go, at least tell me where I can find that pretty little number that was wrapped around your leg earlier."

"Ahhh, I'm pretty sure that Daniel's got his hand halfway up her skirt by now but you're certainly welcome to go for his sloppy seconds."

I sign the credit card slip the bartender sends my way and I push off from the bar. That's when I see her. Perched on a chair at a corner table with her long, slender legs crisscrossed beneath her and her head propped up on her upturned palm. She's with another dark-haired girl.

The other girl leans in and whispers something in Aimee's ear and they both smile.

My eyes trace the outline of her body—over the shiny skin of her bare shoulder, down the soft curve of her breasts, all the way to the valley of her waist—and everything inside of me amps into overdrive. My heart starts pumping blood faster, my fucking pores get all tingly, and I feel like the club just got a couple degrees hotter. Damn it. I need to get my dick and my pulse in check or this girl is going to think I'm some kind of deranged creep. It's already becoming apparent that I'm going to need to go home and take the longest cold shower of my life.

Before I can think too much or talk myself out of it, my feet eat the distance separating us and I'm tapping my fingers on the corner of her table, waiting for her to notice me.

Four agonizing seconds later, Aimee's head comes up and it's like watching an entire film reel of reactions play across her features. First her eyelids widen a fraction and her jaw drops open, and then this small, barely-there smile plays on her lips. I have to shove my hands deep in my pockets to keep from reaching out and brushing my thumb along the pink skin that lines her mouth.

I say the first thing that pops in my head. "I thought you said that you had plans with your parents tonight."

With half-mast, unfocused eyes, she studies me for a long moment. Then she tips her face to one side and says, "And I thought that you said that I should have more fun. Maybe I'm just taking your advice."

Aimee

Cole. Everly.

God.

I ignore the ripple of chills moving over my skin and the slosh of the alcohol churning fiercely in my stomach, and I lift the short glass tumbler and take another sip from the thin red straw. Swallowing hard as the vodka burns my throat, I straighten my shoulders and narrow my eyes at Cole. "Are you following me around or something? You keep showing up everywhere that I go like a stalker. I'm starting to wonder if I should be worried."

"Me? A stalker?" He laughs and folds his arms across his chest. I will myself not to stare at the prominent biceps straining against the sleeves of his shirt. *Don't stare. Don't stare.*

"If the shoe fits…"

"I think you might be the one doing the stalking, Aimee. I just happened to be out with my friends and I looked over and here you were. Either you're stalking me or it's a crazy coincidence." He smiles. "The third option is that fate is playing a hand."

I let my head loll back. "I don't believe in fate. It's stupid."

Cole watches me for a long moment while he works out what to say. Mara uses the pause in our conversation to pipe up and flash her sorority-worthy smile. She extends her hand to Cole like they're being introduced at a political mixer instead of under a set of pulsing purplish strobe lights at a loud club. He laughs at something she says and I want to punch him in the face. Or maybe I want to punch my sister in the face. I don't know.

The house music is a strange mixture of synthetic pop and garage rock. It's loud and fast and the beats sizzle down my neck and slice under my skin. My eyes start to turn fuzzy so I close them and duck my head to my bent arm.

I don't want to listen to what Mara is saying to Cole. I don't want to hear about how much they have in common and how they're both fun and alive and everything that I'm not. I don't want to stare at his full mouth or wonder what it would be like to run my fingers through the strands of sunny hair falling into his green eyes. I don't want to think about my parents, or about Jilly, or about school, or that night back in June when it all slipped away from me.

For five minutes, I want to forget this half-life. I just want to push all of the phantoms away and get completely lost in the gaping beats and the burn of vodka moving through my veins.

But when I open my eyes, I'm back in that car with the salty, dark water spilling in all around me.

Do you hear that sound? It's the sound of the world ripping apart.

The water covered my shoes and weighed down my arms. Everything was shifting and dark. How long had we been like this? Minutes? Hours? Only seconds? I coughed, choking on the fear and the bile creeping up my throat. "Help!"

My hands flailed out violently and smacked into something solid and slimy. Jilly...

I was weak. I groaned loudly and tried to move. It hurt to breathe. "Jilly?"

Her limp body was thrown forward over the steering wheel. Her head was angled toward me but her wet, dark hair was splayed across her face so that I couldn't see her eyes—just the tip of her nose and her chin. Her right hand was curled stiffly on the dashboard. One shoulder was bare where her blue shirt was ripped. I could see red but I didn't know if it was her blood or mine.

I gripped the edge of the open window. Glass crunched beneath my fingers.

Oh my God. My brain chugged to life and the fuzziness began to clear. Oh my God.

"Help!" I gasped and pulled frantically against the slippery metal of the seatbelt clasp with numb fingers. "Jilly?"

I waited for her to lift her head. I waited for her fingers to uncurl. The seatbelt buckle gave way and I ignored the fierce crack of pain that ripped up my arm and I scrambled forward through the sloshing, heavy water, reaching and—

Cole's voice pulls me back to the present. His cool fingertips are resting on the hot skin of my neck, just beneath my ear. "Are you alright, Aimee?"

I can tell by the strained look on his face that it's not the first time he's asked the question. I close my eyes again but the lights are too bright. It's like I can feel them through my eyelids.

"Damn it. You're completely wasted. How much have you had to drink tonight?"

I push him away, blinking and muttering under my breath.

Cole picks up my discarded glass and sniffs it. He looks angry and I cringe. "Jesus Christ, Aimee. There's enough vodka in this drink to obliterate me and you weigh about twenty-five pounds. What the fuck were you thinking?"

When I don't respond, he starts asking Mara questions about what we've been drinking and whether or not we're planning to drive home. I dip my head back into the cradle of my arms and breathe in through my nose. The world slows down around me—it goes dark and soft and strangely mushy. With a breathy sigh I close my eyes and feel the table and the chair and the ground beneath my feet fall away.

I am a raft.

I am falling.

I am floating.

"I don't drive."

Did I say the words out loud or in my head?

Hours pass. Or maybe it's seconds. Who knows? Who cares anymore?

There's a flicker of blinding light and I realize that I'm being picked up. Cole shifts my head against his solid chest and quietly directs me to put my feet down on the ground. I teeter to one side, but his powerful arm is wrapped firmly around my waist. He's talking over my head to some guy that I don't recognize. He says something about a car. Then he's smoothing the loose hairs away from my face with his thumb and telling Mara to pick up my purse.

Hmmm… I let my whole body sink into his.

It registers that I should probably be embarrassed that I'm such a disaster, but more than anything, I think about how nice Cole smells. I nuzzle my face deep into his shirt. I make a sound. "You smell really good."

He glances down at me with those star-bright green eyes and I can't help but smile. "Oh yeah? I told you before that I use Ivory soap."

"No, that's not it… It's not soap." I wave my hand and flutter my eyelids. "You smell a little like… chlorine. Did you know that?" I sigh. "I miss it. I love the smell of chlorine."

He laughs and the sound of it moves over my skin like liquid. "I'm training for a triathlon in Gainesville in a few weeks, so I did swim this afternoon. Maybe I didn't take a long enough shower?"

"Hmmm… I like it. A lot." I twist my fingers in the fabric of his shirt. "And you're tall, aren't you? I didn't know that track stars were so tall."

He chuckles some more.

Encouraged, I continue, reaching up to pinch the swell of muscle at his shoulders. "And you've got very nice muscles, Mr. Everly. I kind of want to bite them."

"Miss Spencer, you are extremely drunk right now," he replies, a wide smile busting open on his face. "But you're a nice and very flattering drunk so I'll take it over sullen and mysterious any day."

My hands move higher. I gently brush his lips with my fingertips. "Do you have to use the smile with the dimples? It's too… too *much*."

"What does that mean? Too much of what?"

"Too much of everything." I roll my eyes and sway to the right. "It means that it's distracting. It means that I think about your dimples way more than I should."

Cole closes his eyes and captures my hand in his. He bends his head so that I feel his breath, hot and tingly against my ear. "Then maybe we're even because I think that *everything* about you is too much."

I scrunch my nose, but before I can work out the words to respond, Cole moves his arm and instructs me to duck my head.

Confused, I look around.

Black upholstery. A windshield. This is a car.

Mara is leaning back on the seat next to me with her legs criss-crossed underneath her body. I peer out of the open door. Cole's arms are on the roof of the car and he's looking down at me.

"I'm in a car," I say to him.

Cole chuckles and nods his head slowly. "Yes, you're in my friend Adam's car. We're taking you home now."

"How do you know where I live?" This seems like the question that I'm supposed to ask in this situation.

"I told them," Mara says and lets her eyes fall closed. "I think we should have stayed away from those shots, Aimee."

I vaguely remember the shots of tequila but I'm not sure how many either of us had. "Huh. I'm not usually so... I don't know... *unsafe.*"

Cole slides in next to me and I rest my head on his shoulder. *He feels so nice.*

A car door slams and someone new says my name. I pry my heavy eyelids open and see Daniel Kearns looking at me from the front seat. His hair is darker than Jilly's and his face is rounder, but he's got his sister's caramel eyes and his sister's oversized nose.

"Daniel? Are you? Is that..." My voice is so hoarse. Unhinged thoughts swirl around in my head like a strong wind. "D-did you know that Jillian always wanted to get a nose job?"

Daniel looks perplexed, like he doesn't know whether he should laugh or cry. I think that I feel the same way. *It'll be fine.* Cole's arm wraps around my shoulders. I feel the pressure of his fingers on my bare skin.

"Aimee, are you okay?" Daniel asks me from a million zillion trillion miles away.

Warm tears prick the backs of my eyes as the familiar surge of sadness pulls me under. Suddenly the question is screaming in my head—the one I've wanted someone to answer for over a year. My voice is faint—made of air and hot, steamy breath. "Daniel, do you think that she hates me?"

And maybe I'm dreaming him. Maybe I'll stay asleep so I can hear his voice in my head, like gentle waves lapping at my toes.

No, Aimee. Never. She'll always love you.

Five

Aimee

I moved to Portland because I wanted to live in a world where Jillian Kearns had never existed. I wanted the air in my lungs to be air that had never touched her lips. It sounds cruel, but I wanted to stop remembering. The goal was to get lost so I ran.

Running, it turns out is the easy part.

It's the not getting found where things get complicated.

My grandparents, both older than their actual ages and hard of hearing, let me be by myself for the most part. No one at school bothered me. I spent my senior year as the quiet, slightly off transfer student who ate lunch alone and never looked anyone directly in the eye.

In Portland it's the norm for people to march to their own beat so no one thought it was particularly odd that I didn't go to football games, or join the drama club, or hang out at the Depot after school. No one asked me questions about my past. No one cared enough to try.

By the fifth month of my self-imposed exile from Florida, I was speaking but I wasn't *talking*. There really is a difference.

Even my therapist ran out of letters and words that made sense so we fell into a pattern of obligatory conversation and empty promises handed over on my end. She reported to my parents that I was getting better and I stayed quiet and nodded my head when I was supposed to·

I started to forget. I stopped dreaming about Jillian. I stopped talking to her while I got ready for school. Weeks passed by without incident. Life moved along.

I discovered that normalcy can be like an extra layer of clothing that you put on in the morning. Underwear—check. Pants—check. Sweater—check. Normalness—check. No one worries as long as they can't actually see that you're naked.

And then, all of a sudden, it was a year. A *year* since Jillian Kearns had made a stupid joke. Or called me up just to tell me that I was her bitch. Or twisted her hair into a spiky bun on top of her head. Or laughed. Or brushed her teeth. Or squinted into the sun.

A year since her mother had screamed at me in the hospital. A year since I'd clawed my way out of that car and left my best friend behind to die.

One year.

That's three hundred and sixty five sleeps. Fifty-two weeks. Eight thousand seven hundred sixty-five hours.

I didn't go to school that day. I left the house at my usual time in the morning, but instead of heading to first period Language Arts, I just walked. I walked past my turn and down to the park and then I just kept going. I thought about walking to another city, or to Washington, or maybe Canada, or right into the Pacific Ocean.

I don't remember much of what came after that. I don't remember getting home or looking for the pills or swallowing them or getting into my grandparent's car.

Later, my parents and the doctors wanted me to tell them what happened—they wanted me to purge my thoughts. They wanted a clean slate. I think that they'd decided that it would be easier to build a new person from mishmash spilled on the floor than from me.

I can still see my mother's face—eyebrows perpetually pulled inward, mouth pinched tight.

Did you mean to do it?

Just tell us.

We don't want to lose you.

That's what she kept saying... *We don't want to lose you.*

Didn't she realize that I was already gone?

• • •

The sound starts from far away. Just a buzz on the peripheral of sleep.

Then it gets closer... louder, brassier. The noise makes its way inside my head, pushing me over, sifting through my gauzy dreams and needling at the backs of my eyes.

I open my mouth, but my tongue feels swollen and dry. I lift my arm, but it crashes back to the earth. I try to blink, but it's like my eyelashes have been pasted to my cheeks with rubber cement.

Oh. My. God.

What is wrong with me? My head is throbbing painfully like it's been bashed into my headboard by a giant's fist. My legs feel rubbery like—

"Wake up, Little Miss Sunshine!"

The high-pitched squeal snaps the membrane of grogginess and forces my eyes open. My bedroom is nothing but screaming brightness and sharp noises. Mewling loudly, I roll over and tunnel down deep under the safety of my covers.

"Rise and shine!"

Mara. What is wrong with her?

Mara bounces herself onto my mattress and grabs my arm. Leaning closer, she pushes the knotty hair away from my face and sticks her wet finger in my ear. I swallow and screw my face up. I want to tell her to leave, but nothing is working properly and the sound that comes out of my mouth seem closer to a grunt than an actual word. "Laaahf!"

Mara laughs. "Get up, young lady. Yesterday you told me that you were planning to meet Jodi in an hour."

Dazed, I try to swat her hand away, but my older sister isn't having it. With a loud huff she pulls on my legs until my lower half is dangling off the edge of the bed.

"I'm meeting Jodi at three in the afternoon," I say roughly into the puffy pillow still clutched in my hands.

Mara snorts and slaps me playfully on my butt. "Yeah, Aimee. That's in an hour."

This is what finally gets me to turn over and sit up. The bedroom tilts precariously to one side and the walls swing in, causing my stomach to recoil.

"Ahhhhh!" Dropping my head and rubbing my hands up and down my face, I ask, "Is it really the afternoon already?"

"Yep. Sure is." She stands up. "I would have let you sleep longer but I have to go over to the sorority house to help the girls get ready for the football game. We're hosting Sig Ep after the game tonight. You should come! I could send one of the younger girls to come pick you up…"

I look at my window. I can see slivers of blue through the slats in the blinds. "Oh God. Too much information!" I rub my eyes. "How in the world are you so cheery right now?"

"I have epic hangover recovery powers honed during my two previous years of college." Mara laughs. "And it helps that I wasn't passed out when we got home so I was able to wash down some aspirin with about thirty gallons of water."

Water. Something new flickers in my brain. "Ugh. What the hell happened last night?"

"Let's see…" She pauses like she needs to think about my question. "Tequila, vodka and Cole Everly."

Scrambled bits and pieces of memory start to flicker in my brain, but it's still an incoherent hodgepodge of images. Cole's face comes into focus and then the feel of his arm wrapped around me, and the scent of him, and the car and… I cringe and fall back to my mattress. "Holy crap. Last night was…" I wince. "Mara, it's possible that I told Cole that I wanted to bite him."

Mara snorts.

I groan and look at my sister. "Was Daniel Kearns really in the car with us?"

Mara nods her head slowly. "He and Cole both carried you in and tucked you into your bed. It was actually pretty cute." She takes a few steps backward and gestures to the table next to my bed. "Oh, and Cole left you a note."

I reach out, fumbling over a stack of books and my alarm clock until my fingers find the small slip of paper. Written below a phone number that I assume is his, are just three words: *Lots of water.*

Cole

Six days.

She doesn't call or put up a smoke signal or any of that shit. Not even a text.

Six fucking days.

At first, I'm worried.

When day three rolls around, I'm pissed.

By day four, I'm resigned. What does it matter to me anyway?

I run harder than usual. I push myself on the weights. I tell myself to forget about Aimee and, for the most part, it works.

But at night, I end up staring at the ceiling of my bedroom, watching the fan blades cycle round and round. I think about her face and her wide saltwater blue eyes and that freckle on her cheek. And I think about her mouth.

Fuck. I spend a lot of time thinking about her mouth. I wonder about the secrets that live between her lips and I wonder about the taste of her. After I get that far, it's a short leap to remembering the way that her breath felt against the skin on my neck. Or how my hand sunk into the curve of her waist as I lowered her into her bed.

Damn it.

It's brutal.

On Thursday afternoon I'm walking out of the Union with Daniel and there she is. She's in almost the exact same spot where I first saw her, only this time she's not falling over her feet into my lap.

She's with that blue-haired girl, Jodi, and she's got her legs kicked out and her head tipped back to catch the sun. Her long brown hair is spilling over the skin of her neck and pooling on the grass beneath her. Everything about the moment is so golden and glowy that my heart does an erratic flip and my feet stop moving.

"... that if I can keep my shoulder blade rotated down, I can throw a lot farther." Daniel's voice comes back to me.

"Huh?" What did he say?

He stops and spins around. "Practice. Throwing the discus. Track and field. Earth to Cole." He snaps his fingers sharply in front of my face.

"Uh, yeah. I'm sorry, man." I blink and jerk my head but it's too late. Daniel follows my gaze and spots Aimee.

"You're into her."

I clench my jaw tight.

He laughs. "I mean… You're hardcore into her."

There's no use denying it. I *am* into her.

"What of it?" I ask, my voice low and abrasive.

Daniel's smile turns crooked and his eyes travel back to where Aimee is sprawled out on the grass. "I'm just amazed that you've turned googly-eyed over a girl. It's not your style at all."

74

I bring my hands up and grip the back of my head. I bite the inside of my cheek. "Man, I'm not *googly-eyed*. Who even says that? I'm just..."

"Trust me. You're googly-eyed," Daniel says, cocking his head back and laughing at me. "So why don't you grow a pair and ask her out already?"

"For your information, I did ask her out," I snap.

"And she said no?" He chokes, disbelieving. "Aimee turned you down?"

"Well, not exactly..." I drop my arms and exhale through my nose. "It's complicated."

Daniel flaps his hand like he's not buying any of my shit. "Look, Cole. If you're going to go after a girl like Aimee, things are going to get complicated. She's not going to fall for any of your normal tactics or throw herself at your feet and spread her legs like the sluts that you're used to dealing with. She's different." He takes a visible breath and there's this look on his face like he's carefully editing himself. "And bear in mind that she's been through a lot. She doesn't need to be a part of one of your games."

"I'm not playing a game with her," I say firmly. "I don't know what I'm doing but it's not a game..."

Daniel says something about being late to practice, but I'm barely listening. I'm already halfway over to that sunny patch of grass—to the girl with the long, dark hair and the freckle on her cheek.

When I reach her, Aimee's eyes are closed and I hear her say, "This is a nightmare."

At first I think that she means me and my stomach lurches. But then Jodi answers, barely glancing up from her phone. "No, a nightmare is running from a deranged serial killer who wants to cut your ears off and eat your intestines with a plastic spork. This is just an assignment for class, Aimee."

"What's the assignment?" I ask, casually announcing myself as I plunk down onto the grass beside Aimee.

I can tell that Aimee's surprised to see me. A warm pink blush spills across her skin—probably residual embarrassment that the last time that I saw her, she was crying and drunk and blowing snot all over my shirt.

"Hey," she says breathlessly.

"What's the assignment?" I ask again.

Her clear blue eyes search my face. Puzzlement creases her forehead and drags down the sides of her mouth. "It's nothing. I was just complaining about something for one of my classes. It's not a big deal."

Jodi leans forward. "Aimee's professor informed the class that everyone has to write an article to submit to the student paper. She's freaking out because she has no idea what to write about."

The pink spots on Aimee's cheeks deepen. She shakes her head and sits up. One hand goes across her chest defensively. "I'm not freaking out." She turns to me. "*I'm not.*"

The faint tendrils of an idea are reaching into the corners of my brain. I squint at Aimee, who's fluttering her hands and mouthing something to Jodi—probably something about me. Jodi's got her hands spread out and a what-did-I-do expression on her face.

I clear my throat to get their attention. "What's the article supposed to be about?"

Aimee pauses and sniffs before she answers me. "It can be about anything I want to write about—the price of a cup of coffee in the Union, the fall of communism, how to store tulip bulbs before you plant them... I don't know. He said that it doesn't really matter what the topic is, but preferably it'll be something that the paper wants to print—whatever that means."

"Her professor will weight the grade accordingly if her article actually makes it to press," Jodi adds helpfully.

After another long silence, Aimee sighs and does this adorable little shiver thing with her shoulders. "I've got some time and I'm sure that I'll think of something decent."

"You can always write an article about me. All you'd have to do is ask me nicely."

Aimee looks at me with obvious skepticism. Her nostrils are flared and her jaw is clenched. "And what makes you think that the student newspaper wants an article about *you*? Just because every warm-blooded girl around here seems to want a peek at what's inside your boxer shorts, that doesn't make you a newsworthy topic."

My eyebrows go up. "*Every warm-blooded girl…*" I repeat blithely. "Do you include yourself in that category?"

Aimee sputters. Jodi laughs.

"You don't have to answer that," I continue. "And I don't *think* that the paper is going to want an article about me. I *know* it because they've been hounding me for an interview for at least two weeks."

Aimee sucks her bottom lip between her top and bottom teeth. Her blue eyes darken a shade. "Really?"

I try not to smile at the surprise in her voice. "Really."

"Well…" She scrunches up her nose and twists her hair over her shoulder. "What kind of article do you think they want?"

"Oh you know… the usual fluff piece. You could write about what I'm doing to train during the off-season, and then you could ask me how I think the team is going to do this year, and what makes me tick. That kind of stuff."

Words move beyond her eyes. She's thinking, weighing her options. Finally, she says, "But you want something from me."

Her voice is flat as a board. It's not even a question. I cock my head to the side and lift my eyebrows. "Maybe."

"I already told you that I don't date," she says. Her expression is laced with determination. Strangely, it makes me like her a little bit more.

"I must have missed something." I chuckle. "Did I just ask you out?"

Aimee looks down at her hands, a small smile tugs at her mouth. "No."

"Well, then…"

Her blue eyes swing back to mine. "Spill it already. What do you want from me, Cole?"

"It's simple," I shrug, trying to ignore the way my name sounds coming out of her mouth. "I want answers."

"*Answers?*"

"Yeah." Fuck. She's so close that I can see a tiny bead of sweat dripping down her neck and disappearing under the edge of her grey top. I want to follow it with my tongue. "If you're going to write about me, you're going to have a lot of questions. The deal is that for every one of the questions that I answer, I want you to answer one of mine."

We stare hard. At least a half-minute passes. I catch the uncertainty flicker in her eyes and I almost tell her that I'm joking—that, of course, she can write an article about me and I won't make her tell me anything about herself. But just before I can take the proposition back, Aimee nods her head and tells me that she'll do it.

I rock back.

Shit. There's this feeling inside of me like… I don't know what. It's like a balloon's been inflated behind my ribs. I can't seem to stop smiling at her.

"Wow," Jodi mutters, and I realize that I've forgotten that she's been sitting here with us the whole time. "That was so hot."

Aimee turns to her friend. Tiny lines ripple across her forehead. "What do you mean?"

Jodi makes a movement with her hands. "You and him. Him and you." Her eyes drift between us. "You guys are off the charts, like world-bending, air-pulsing H-O-T."

Aimee looks ready to die. She bends her body inward and dips her head so that her hair shields her face. "Jodi, have I told you that sometimes I want to kill you?"

My laugh is uproarious. "Jodi, have *I* told you that sometimes I want to kiss you?"

Six

Aimee

E arlier today Cole asked me to meet him at seven in the parking lot
adjacent to where the track team practices. I spent most of the
afternoon debating whether or not I should actually follow through.
At six forty-five, I finally broke down and asked Mara for a ride.

"Be careful with him." Mara's voice is loaded with implication.
"He has a reputation. If you could hear a few of the stories that Jenn
has told me…"

Honestly, I've already heard enough "stories" about Cole Everly
from Jodi to keep me mentally occupied for the next fifty years.

"Did Jenn date him or something?" I hate the way my stomach
clenches when I ask the question.

Mara taps her manicured fingernails on the steering wheel. "No,
but she's got the inside scoop on a lot of the athlete gossip because her
cousin plays basketball for the University. And the stuff about Cole is
always entertaining, if you know what I mean."

I click my tongue. "I think I get the gist. Player, womanizer, totally
out of my league."

"Look," she says sedately. "I'm glad that you're putting yourself
out there, Aimee. I really am. And Cole is hot, but…"

Now I'm annoyed. "I already told you that I'm meeting Cole for his help with a class assignment. This is not a date, Mara. It's not even close to a date so you don't need to go all protective-big-sister on me because I've got this covered."

She pauses thoughtfully and I'm not sure if it's skepticism or disappointment, or possibly a little bit of both that I see on her face. I shake my head and step out of the car into the dancing orange and pink lights of evening. As I turn, a soft breeze moves in, tossing my hair around my face and kissing the bare skin of my arms. In front of me, a grey building that houses a ticketing office and locker rooms rises from the black asphalt.

Pulling away, Mara rolls her window down, leans out and adds: "Just don't go thinking that I didn't notice you changed your outfit four times... *and* that you put on mascara and lipstick!"

With a huff, I wipe at my mouth with the back of my hand and watch my sister drive away. When I'm sure that she's out of sight, I sit down on a narrow concrete curb cradled between an overflowing trashcan and a bench and I wait. Cole told me that practice usually gets over just before seven and that he'd grab a quick shower in the locker room and meet me afterward. Trying to stay inconspicuous, I duck my head as the runners slowly trickle out of the east entrance of the building into the parking lot.

I see him before he sees me.

He's wearing a yellow short-sleeved t-shirt and loose black athletic shorts that show the outline of his thighs when he walks. The strap of a dark green gym bag cuts diagonally across his chest, further emphasizing the hardness of those muscles, solidified by hours on the track and in the weight room. In the dwindling evening light, his wet hair looks silvery and he's got it pushed back from his face so that I get the full-effect of his features. Even from this far away I can see the startling green hue of his eyes against his tan skin and the sharp cut of his unshaven jaw.

Maybe Jodi is rubbing off on me but all I can think is: W-O-W. I have to look down at my lap just so that I can get my crazy heartbeat under control.

What the hell is wrong with me?

"Hey!" Cole stops about five feet away and smiles at me. "You came."

I order myself not to stare at his full lips or the way that the fabric of his shorts clings to his damp, just-showered skin. Swallowing down the building moisture in my mouth, I say, "I told you that I would be here."

"Still… I'm surprised." Cole sways back on his heels and looks away—out over a crop of jagged trees silhouetted by the sinking evening sun. "Are you ready to go?"

"I—ahh—where are we going?"

"To a pizza place over on Second Street."

My eyes stretch. "But I thought maybe we could just do the interview here."

"*Here?*" Cole looks around at the fast-emptying parking lot and grimaces. "Aimee, I've just been killing myself in the heat and I'm starving. I vote that we do this interview thing where I can sit in a comfortable booth and shove garlic knots in my mouth. If we don't, I'll have to resort to eating week-old cracker crumbs off the floorboard of my truck."

I don't say anything right away and he continues, "And, if it'll make you feel better, you don't even have to eat pizza with me. You can drink water and suck down a few of those little sugar packets while I sit across from you and enjoy the best deep dish on the planet."

I can't help it—I laugh. Brushing my palms off on my cropped jeans, I stand up. "Well, I don't want you eating moldy crumbs so lead the way."

• • •

Cole asks the waitress to bring out two orders of garlic knots. When he looks up and sees my raised eyebrows, he grins crookedly. "What?"

I shake my head and smile back. "Nothing. I totally respect how determined you are to have bad breath. It's refreshing."

"Well…" Cole squints his green eyes a bit. "Bad breath is definitely the kind of thing that I would be concerned with on an actual date, but since you've made it clear that *this*," he gestures between us, "isn't a date, I thought I'd be safe. However, if you've changed your mind, I'm more than happy to forego the second order of garlic knots. I'm pretty sure that you'd be worth it."

My cheeks go warm and I drop my eyes to the table in the vain hope that Cole won't notice how affected I am. With fumbling fingers, I reach into my oversized purse to find the pen and pad of paper that I tucked in the inside pocket earlier.

"No. The garlic knots are just fine." I try to regain my lost composure by clearing my throat. "So, why don't you start by telling me a little about yourself?"

Cole takes a sip from the icy coke in front of him. He watches me carefully over the rim of the glass and I get a sensation like he can read all of the crazy thoughts sloshing around in my head.

He asks, "What do you want to know first?"

I've never done an interview before so I have no idea how this is supposed to go, but I figure if it has any chance of working out, I should probably start with his track career. That's fairly safe territory.

Internally, I command my voice not to wobble. "Let's talk about your races and titles. Last year, as a sophomore, you dominated the conference in the mid-distance races, but you lost the 400 meter at the Semifinals to Noah Whitman. Have you amped up your training at all this year and what are your predictions for the coming spring?"

Cole leans back and crosses his arms over his chest like he's assessing me. I shift nervously and the corners of his mouth curl up in amusement. His green eyes blaze with excitement. "You looked into me," he says.

I'm not about to admit that I searched him online almost two weeks ago and that in addition to his running and hurdling stats—I know he dressed up as a bare-chested Thor last Halloween and back home his family has a pug named Babs. Instead, I shrug and say, "I did a little bit of prep work. Always be prepared, right?"

"Okay then..." Cole uncrosses his arms. "It's the off-season so right now our scheduled practices only go about three or four days a week, but that doesn't mean that I'm slacking on my workouts and training." He pauses. "I thought a lot over the summer about ways that I could improve after I lost in that last heat to Whitman. I should have won and I know that, so this year I'm making some changes. I'm working out more with the team trainer and I've started prepping for a triathlon that I'm doing with some of the guys in a few weeks."

"Is the triathlon University-sanctioned or just something you're doing for fun?"

"Fun," he says with a shrug. "If you could call running and swimming and biking in the Florida heat fun."

As Cole continues to talk, I watch the way that his mouth moves and how the soft light catches the golden flecks in his eyes. He talks about races and his teammates. He tells me about the playful bets that they have going and the dirty word game that the guys play on the bus on the way to meets.

"It wasn't dirty," I say. "But when I was on the swim team in high school, we'd do this one where you take one letter out of a book title and come up with an entirely new book."

He pushes his thick blond hair back from his forehead. "Like what? Give me an example."

I think about it. "Okay... *To Ill a Mockingbird* is an obvious choice. And *The Sound and the Fur.*" I hold up a finger for every made-up title that I list. *"Rapes of Wrath, Of Mice and Me,* and my personal favorite… *Mob Dick."*

Cole cracks up. "I'm afraid to ask what that one's about."

I'm grinning, pleased with myself. "Now it's your turn."

He clears his throat. "How about… *Rave New World?"*

I nod my head in approval. "Good one."

"Okay, I've got another."

"What is it?"

"The Da Vinci Cod. It's the absorbing tale of a detective who follows the trail of a murder at The Louvre and uncovers a two thousand year old disagreement between the Priory of Scion and the Catholic Church over whether or not Jesus was a pescetarian."

I laugh so hard that I almost spit out my drink. We go back and forth with titles until neither one of us can think of any more. I prop my elbows on the table and lean forward. "So, um, getting back to the interview… Tell me how a Nebraska boy got into running to begin with."

"A Nebraska boy?" He's amused. "I like that. It makes me sound like a wholesome farmhand just trying to get an honest day of work done."

"Wholesome isn't exactly the first word that comes to mind when I think of you."

"Fair enough," Cole smirks. "The way that I got into running is that when I was eleven we had this neighbor who coached a local boy's track team. My mom thought it would be a good idea to get me into an activity. She told me that it would be great for me—build confidence and strength and all that shit." He hesitates, swallowing audibly. "I… I was sort of small back then and kids at school picked on me and she seemed convinced that athletics was the answer to my problems."

I try to picture Cole as a little kid with scrawny arms and a head full of blond floppy hair. "And was it?"

Cole looks down and examines the garlic knot that he's holding between his fingers. "In some ways it was." He pauses and I see his jaw working. "The thing is that when I look back, I realize that my mom was probably just screwing around with the guy—the coach. She didn't want to help or make me better. That woman never gave a flying fuck about me or whether or not I was okay. Even back then she was only interested in one thing. *Herself.*"

I suck in my breath and Cole's eyes flick to mine. "I—I—"

"You don't have to say anything. Please don't tell me how sorry you are. That's the worst thing that people can say." He clears his throat. "I don't really like to talk about my mom because it makes people weird. And I wanted tonight to—" He stops himself and closes his eyes for a moment. "Let's just eat, yeah?"

So that's what I do. I don't let Cole know that the hitch in his voice has turned me inside out. I sit on my side of the booth and obediently eat a few of the garlic knots and way too much pizza. And somehow I wind up telling him about the time that Jillian and I ordered pizza to her car. He looks confused, so I explain. "I was seeing this guy and he was in a band—a very bad one, I might add. Anyway, one night we had to wait for him in a parking lot after a show to give him a ride. It took longer than it should have and eventually Jilly got sick of it so she ordered a pizza to her car."

Cole laughs and shakes his head. "That answers one of my questions."

"What's that?"

"Obviously you used to date," he concludes. "And he was a musician? I didn't take you as the type to fall for a guy with a guitar. It's so cliché."

I feel my skin flush. "Yeah, well… I was a bit different back then." Cole isn't asking but I can see the questions all over his face. I know that I have the words. They're broken, but they're in my head. "You know that Daniel's little sister was my best friend, right?"

He nods.

"After she died, I made promises to myself. That night I—I made a mistake... one that I can't take back. Not ever. And I don't expect people to understand, but it changed me forever. I might not ever be okay again and I don't want to weigh down someone else with all of that baggage." I let out my breath. "I know that makes me sound like a crazy person but it's complicated."

He stares at me for a while. "I don't think that you sound crazy. I think that you sound scared."

"Maybe," I admit. "You know, I agreed to answer questions in return for the interview. Fair is fair. So if you want to ask me about Jillian and that night, just do it. I know that you're curious about it. You have to be."

Cole's quiet for a long time. "That's true, Aimee." His green eyes reach into mine and electrify all of my nerve endings. "I am curious about what happened. But that's not the kind of story I want you to *answer*. It's the kind I want you to *tell*."

Cole

You don't win races by going balls to the wall right off the starting block. You win by running smart—pacing your breaths, relaxing your body into the steps, and powering through the recovery.

I wasn't lying when I told Daniel that I wasn't playing a game with Aimee but that doesn't mean that I'm not working out a strategy.

I like her. Plain and simple. And, yeah, it's fucking with my brain and tying me up in knots, but I'm going to stay smart.

Aimee's skittish. She's like one of those wild animals that you see documentaries about on TV. And I'm the scientist who's got to stay patient and move slow. I've got to leave out a trail of food and gain her trust by getting a centimeter closer each day. I've seen how this shit goes down—if I move too fast, she'll bolt and I'll have to start all of the way back at the beginning.

Tonight it feels like maybe something's changed between us. There have been some moments that have felt, I don't know, like they're somehow *more* than all the others and it's giving me hope. Or maybe I'm just growing a vagina and all of it is a product of my imagination. Either way—Aimee is talking to me about more than the weather so I'll take it.

It's dark when we leave the restaurant. Under the frail silver moonlight, she stops and pulls her phone out of that huge purse that she carries around with her all of the time. I watch her bite her bottom lip and one-handed twist her hair over her shoulder. I realize that it's a nervous habit to try to cover up the scar on her neck. I want to tell her that she doesn't need to bother—that she's fucking gorgeous, but I'm afraid to push her too far. I don't want to rock the uneasy balance that's leveled out between us.

"I'm texting my sister for a ride home," she tells me even though I haven't asked.

My heart amps up but I stay cool. "Don't be ridiculous. I'll take you in my truck."

"Are you sure?"

"Of course I'm sure."

This time, when we walk to my truck, I hold the door for her while she climbs in. Aimee has to brace her weight against the doorframe, and as she does, the fingertips on her hand brush against my forearm, light as smoke. Her eyes meet mine in the half-light and it takes everything in me not to lean in and press my body up against hers. It would be so easy. She'd probably even let me.

Before I can do something stupid, I slam her door and walk to the driver's side. I swallow hard and then we're headed east of campus, and I'm starting to think that offering her a ride was a giant mistake. In the tight confines of the truck cab, I can smell her lotion and her shampoo and I'm intensely aware of every single breath that she drags into her lungs. My body is so jacked up that I can't think of a single thing to talk about and I want to touch her so badly that I'm starting to get jealous of the goddamn truck seat.

She makes a little sound and I glance over. Aimee's got her arms wrapped around her chest and she's almost shivering despite how warm it is tonight. Wordlessly, I adjust the air conditioning and point one of the vents away from her. I catch a quick smile before she turns her face toward the darkened passenger window.

My mind is all over the place. I'm remembering that last run at practice today and how I fucked up and let Brady overtake me at the end. And then I'm silently going through baseball statistics to try to get my mind off how incredible Aimee smells right now. Shit. And I can't believe that I talked about my mom tonight. I *never* talk about my mom and somehow she's managed to slip into my conversations with Aimee twice now. She probably thinks… Fuck. I don't have a clue what she thinks about me.

She's still looking out the window. Her profile is shadowed, but I can see the tiny hairs curling around the delicate skin of her face. I want to push them back behind her ear so that I can see her more clearly. I want to cup my hand on the back of her neck and pull her mouth to mine so that I can open up her lips with my tongue. I want to trace the dips and curves of her body with my fingertips and I want to memorize every single inch of her.

But that's not happening.

Not tonight.

Tonight is about pacing.

Tonight is not about my dick. It's about being smart.

"So," I say as I pull up to the curb in front of her place. She lives smack-dab in the middle of a small row of upscale townhomes a few miles from campus. Each unit is protected from the street by a curved stucco wall. The exterior of the entire complex is painted an obnoxious color that seems to only exist in Florida. I would describe it as the evil offspring of pink and peach. I'm guessing that a girl like Aimee would call it *coral*. "Did you get everything that you need from me for the interview?"

Aimee frowns slightly. "I think so."

I try not to be obvious about the disappointment storming around in my head. I'm about to tell her good night, but then Aimee starts talking. "I think it'll be enough, but I probably should have asked you some more general stuff—you know, for background."

"Like what?" I prompt.

Aimee's shoulders rise up around her neck. She's biting her bottom lip again. "Like your favorite color, and the three movies you would take to a deserted island with you, and what kind of music you listen to when you're getting ready for a race." Her eyes dart to mine. "I guess you can come inside if you want and we can finish up…"

Yes! Yes! Yes!

"No," I say, shaking my head decisively. "I'm actually kind of tired. Can we do the rest of the interview tomorrow?"

Aimee seems a bit surprised, but I'll give her this—she rallies. She opens the passenger door and hops down from the truck. "Do you want to try to meet on campus sometime during the day? It shouldn't take me very long."

"Nah." I let my eyes rest on hers. "I don't have practice tomorrow so that means I'm free at night."

Aimee's face pinches together. She runs a finger through her long hair and bounces the open truck door against her hipbone. "And? What does that mean, Cole?"

"And, *that means* that I'll pick you up at seven." I lift my eyebrows suggestively. "So be ready."

Seven

Aimee

"You're acting like this is a date."

I turn my body away from the full-length mirror to look at Mara. "But it's not a date. Cole and I are friends or at least something sort of like friends. I honestly don't know how to explain it—it's weird."

It *is* weird, whatever it is we're doing. I know that it's just an interview for an assignment, but that's not to say that I didn't enjoy myself last night.

I like Cole. I do. I've discovered that contrary to popular belief, he's not an asshole. And even though I can't go *there* with him, I like the idea of being around him. I just wish that I didn't enjoy looking at him so much.

"Okaaaay..." Mara leans back against my headboard. Her arms are loosely crossed above her head. "But once again, you just seem really concerned about what you're wearing. And let's be clear: the dress that you've got on right now is definitely a date kind of dress."

I glance at the pile of discarded clothes on my bedroom floor and back to my reflection in the mirror. Seeing myself through my sister's eyes is a major reality check. I look like... well, she's right. I look like I'm going on a date. I've got on a white sundress that my mother bought for me last year but that I haven't been brave enough to wear yet. It's strapless with stitching laced across the bust and a scalloped hem that swishes femininely around my knees. I know that even taking into account the scar running down my neck and collarbone, the dress makes my shoulders look dainty. The starch white of the material is nice against my coloring, but it's too much. Way too much.

"Freaking craptastic."

Mara laughs. "I've got to say that aside from the fact that he's slept with half the girls on campus, I think that you could do a lot worse than Cole if you did want to, you know, *try.*"

She's teasing, but her words are edged with a hopefulness that sucks everything in and spits it back out. The truth is that a part of me—the part that decided to put on this dress and apply an extra coat of mascara to my eyelashes—*is* trying. And that's not just unsettling… It's terrifying.

I sigh and trace my fingers along the visible line of my scar.

"Stop it, Aimee," Mara says. "You make too big a deal out of it."

I stare at the mirror. And this strange feeling makes my stomach slip uneasily. It's like nothing about the girl looking back at me makes any sense.

Mara's probably right and I do make too big a deal out of it. *Dramatic* is what our mother calls it. That's what she said to me when I told her that I couldn't go back to my high school for my senior year and that I wanted to go live with my grandparents in Portland.

Don't be so dramatic, Aimee.

My best friend had just died and I had the stitches in my skin to prove that I was there to watch it happen, and she thought I was being dramatic.

I reach for the hem of the dress and pull.

"What are you doing?" Mara asks. She pushes herself forward.

"Changing," I say, bending down to search through the pile of clothes at my feet.

"But…"

I know that she's disappointed. I can tell that she's going to try to get me to keep the dress on but it's too late. I'm already zipping up the baggy jeans I wore to class today.

Cole

"You can't play worth a shit." I stand to the side and watch her throw.

Aimee laughs. "You're right," she shoots back. "I wish I had a real excuse, like, 'I've got a cramp in my arm,' or 'I'm out of practice,' but the truth is that I just suck."

"Yep. You suck." I smile wickedly. "Aimee Spencer, you have a lot to look forward to in this lifetime, but I don't think that a Skee-Ball championship is anywhere in your future."

She laughs again. It's a good sound. A great one actually.

I throw the last of the balls from the side channel and reach down to break off the stream of paper tickets that the machine spews out. I turn to her and ask, "You tapped out yet?"

She casts her head thoughtfully. "Actually, I'm kind of hungry."

"Well, then you're in luck because I've heard that this arcade offers a wide array of culinary masterpieces. There's your standard cheddar and caramel popcorn, a variety of artificially flavored tootsie pops, an exquisite selection of braised corndogs, and the cotton candy…" I pinch my thumb and fingers to my lips and kiss them. "Let's just say that it's supposed to be divine."

"Cotton candy? You pull out all the stops, don't you?"

I like the look on Aimee's face too much for my own good—the easy way that she's watching me and how the arcade lights scatter across her long hair. Without thinking, I reach out and run my fingers over her forearm. "For you—anything goes."

She sucks in a shaky breath and bows her head quickly, but not before I see the ghost of something move across her features.

"Umm…" A flush creeps up her neck. She pulls on her hair and nods at the arcade tickets we've both won over the last hour. "What should we do with those?"

I step back and look around. "Follow me," I say, sliding in between the machines and dodging a couple of waist-high kids.

I know that it's probably strange that I dragged Aimee to an arcade, but I wanted to *do* something with her, and dinner and a movie is played out and reeks of a dating cliché. I was about to break down and ask Daniel, of all people, for advice when it hit me.

My mom left when I was seventeen. I was young, but I was still old enough have my own life—one that was busy and kept me distracted. I was able to lose myself in winning races and getting laid and being pissed off most of the time.

Things were different for my little sister, Sophie. I don't think anyone should have to wake up one day with a mom and go to bed that night without one. Especially not a ten-year-old girl.

She started to do badly in school. She stopped bringing friends home. One night in a bout of frustration because no one was around to help her with her hair, Sophie chopped it off to her ears with a pair of kitchen scissors.

I was a goddamn teenager. I didn't have the first clue how to talk to a messed-up little kid, and it didn't help that our dad was completely checked out. Things were bad—really bad. And then one afternoon, four months after our mother left, I picked Sophie up from school and we got a flat tire on the way home. That's how we wound up at an arcade. It started as a way to waste time while my tire was being patched, but it turned into something more.

For the first time in four months, I saw Sophie laughing. She was lost in the spinning yellow and red lights from the machines and acting like a kid. And it was one good afternoon in the middle of the pile of shit that had become our lives. I started taking Sophie every week. It was a way for her to get out of her own head and have a slice of normalcy—even for just that single hour.

And glancing over at Aimee, I think that's probably why I searched online for the best arcade near campus and drove us here.

We stop near the ticket exchange counter and I point out a scrawny boy with an unfortunate overbite and a bad case of acne. Understanding my intention, Aimee smiles and takes the tickets from me. She walks over to the kid and taps him gently on the shoulder. From where I'm standing, I can't hear the exchange but I see the way his mouth falls open and his eyes widen—first at the tickets and then at the beautiful girl handing them over.

I'm laughing when she returns to me.

"What?" Her blue eyes are amplified.

I shake my head. "You do realize that you just gave that kid a year of wet dreams?"

Two little frown lines pull between her eyebrows making her look unbelievably cute. "What do you mean?"

I don't try to hide the fact that I'm looking at her—all of her. She's got on a pair of loose jeans rolled up to mid-calf and this vintage looking shirt that hangs off her shoulder exposing her collarbone and the thin scar that climbs up her skin like a vine. Her hair is loose and snakes around her arms like it's moving to music. Jesus. Who is this girl?

I smile when our eyes catch. "You don't see yourself clearly at all, do you?"

Aimee

Cole and I end up getting gyros from a food cart that's set up outside the arcade.

He hands the guy money and I want to argue and pay for my own food, but something about his face keeps my lips closed and my hand from going to my purse. Instead of a thank you, I simply take the aluminum-wrapped gyro and follow him over to a nearby wooden bench that's been worn to a dingy grey from the wind and the sun. About fifty feet in front of us the parking lot gives way to sand. Sighing, I lean against the bench and let myself look out at the water.

I've been back in Florida for weeks, but this is the first time I've been anywhere near the beach, and, God, I've missed it. Our townhouse is only fifteen minutes away and I've thought about asking Mara to drive me almost every day since the start of school, but something has kept the words shoved inside my mouth. Now that I'm here, I don't understand why I waited so long.

It's better than I remember. My hair and my lungs are full of salt and the breeze is burning my eyes, but I don't care. I want to absorb all of it.

Cole and I don't talk while we eat. We both stare out at the changing landscape of white beach and blue water as darkness drips steadily down the sky. The juice from the gyro runs over the foil onto my fingers and my legs drift back and forth beneath me like I'm sitting on a porch swing.

The moment is strangely perfect.

I know that it all sounds romantic—the beach, the water, the quiet—but it's not. Not really. It's comfortable and I can't even think of the last time that I felt comfortable.

Once—no—*twice*, I look over and catch Cole watching me. The second time, my eyebrows go up and he drops his face.

"So..." I say, swallowing the last bite of my gyro.

Cole's head comes up. He squints out toward the water. "Blue. *Inception, Caddyshack,* and *Total Recall.* The original one, of course. Mainly rock, but sometimes I mix it up with rap."

I feel like I've been dropped center stage and I've forgotten what my line is. My bottom jaw is bobbing. "Did I miss something? What are you talking about?"

Cole laughs at my expression. "Last night you said that you wanted to know a few things: my favorite color, what my three island movies are, and the type of music I listen to before a race." He shrugs his shoulders. "I just told you the answers."

"Okaaaay…" I scrunch up my face. "I haven't seen *Caddyshack* or *Total Recall.*"

Now it's time for Cole's mouth to hang. "What are you talking about? How is that even possible?"

"I don't think it's that strange. Those movies were made before we were even born, right?"

"Um, yeah, but you were actually *born*, weren't you?"

I roll my eyes. "Obviously."

"Then you should have seen them by now. No excuses," he says in a matter-of-fact tone.

"Fine. I should have seen them and maybe I will eventually. I guess that I'm not really a movie person unless it's got Ryan Gosling or Chris Hemsworth in it."

Cole grins and nods his head. "Ah, so blonds are your type, yeah? Lucky me."

Wow. I stepped right into that one.

I chuckle and flush furiously as I reach to the ground for my bag. "If, um, we're jumping right into the interview questions, let me just get my notebook and a pen so I can keep track. I wanted to ask you if—"

"Not yet," Cole cuts me off. His hand brushes my arm and I can't even pretend that I don't feel the heat from his skin radiating to every part of my body. "I think that it's my turn to do the asking."

"Alright." I sound apprehensive and nervous even to my own ears.

"I only have one question for you, and then I'll let it go."

I balance myself. The fingers on my left hand dig into my jeans and my heart chugs uncertainly. "Okay."

Silence.

"Did you have fun tonight?"

Cole's question is so unexpected that I have to look at him again to make sure that I heard him correctly. He's got a tentative half-smile playing across the lower half of his face like he knows something that I don't.

I nod my head carefully.

Cole's smile deepens. "That's what I thought."

After a minute of quiet, I comment, "You seem awfully pleased with yourself."

Cole leans against the back the bench. He brings one foot up to rest on his knee and crosses his arms over his head. "I am. I feel pretty fucking accomplished right now. It's not every day that I get a girl like you to smile."

I wouldn't be able to keep the grin off my face even if I wanted to. "The arcade got me. I haven't done that in years and I guess that there's something to be said for the sound of a bunch of kids throwing away their quarters with reckless abandon."

Cole looks at me, and I mean he *really* looks at me. For a long, stilted moment I think that he's going to kiss me, and my mind is wringing out all kinds of thoughts and I can't be sure whether or not I want him to close the space between us. But before I work it out in my head, he lifts his hand to wipe the side of my mouth with the pad of his thumb and everything thundering inside of me just *stops*.

"You had something on your face," he says.

I think that I nod in response but I'm not really sure because my nervous system is jammed into overdrive. I can't seem to get enough air into my lungs.

And then Cole is talking again like nothing out of the ordinary just happened and I'm listening and trying to catch my breath. After awhile, we make our way down to the dark beach and I curl my toes in the cool, wet sand and revel in the feel of the salty water licking at my ankles. And for a few minutes, I'm not pretending—I'm just happy.

Cole drives us back in his old truck and when we're in front of my place, he kills the ignition and turns his body toward me. "*The Princess Brie,*" he says.

I need a second to think of one. "*Jurassic Ark.*"

"*War and Pace.*"

"*The Bile.*"

He laughs and then he asks, "Hey, are you going to the football game tomorrow?"

I know that there's a football game because Mara's been talking about it all week and today, in a show of school spirit, at least half of the students on campus were wearing green shirts.

I shake my head. "I wasn't planning on it."

Cole skims his hands across the dashboard. His jaw twitches like he wants to respond in some way, but he simply nods his head and tells me that he'll see me around.

Around?

As his truck pulls away, I hate that I'm watching, and I hate it even more that I already miss him.

Eight

Cole

S omehow I wind up stuck with Kate. She shows up at our house
around noon wearing a green halter-top and a skirt so short that
it should probably be illegal. I don't want to look at her ass and her tits,
but I do because I'm a guy and I have a pulse and a dick and apparently
no self-control.

Kate acts like she belongs here and I don't tell her otherwise when
she helps herself to a beer from the refrigerator and plops down on
the couch next to me. She crosses her legs and bends forward so that
I have a direct line of sight to her boobs.

The girl knows that she looks good and that should be obnoxious
but it's actually sort of a turn-on. Not that I'm going there with her
today or tomorrow or ever again. Kate Dutton's hot and she's conve-
nient but that ship has sailed, so to speak, and I'm over it.

I try not to dwell on the reasons that I'm passing up an easy lay
because when I let my brain go in that direction, it gets all jammed
up with thoughts of blue eyes, the water lapping at my feet, vanilla
cupcakes, and all kinds of crazy-ass shit.

Kate jerks me out of my head by placing her hand flat on my leg.
Fuck me. I twitch uncomfortably. I was hoping that she'd get the hint

that I'm no longer interested when I stopped texting her back and told Brady to give her a call, but I guess I was wrong.

Right on cue, Daniel makes his first appearance of the day. He's got on a team shirt and a backward green baseball hat, and when he sees me on the couch with Kate, his eyes go a fraction wider. He doesn't say anything but I can see it coming and I know that he's thinking about Aimee.

I duck my head and cough into my curled hand. I know that I don't need to worry yet because Daniel's not the type to ask questions right here. He'll wait until he's got me trapped by myself in some corner where he thinks I can't give him one of my bullshit excuses.

There are four of us that live in the house. Nate and Daniel and I are all teammates. Somewhere along the way the three of us picked up Adam and we couldn't quite shake him. It's all good though. Adam keeps things interesting around here. Like right now he's asking my advice on how to sneak weed past the security guards into the football stadium. And I know for a fact that he's already got two little plastic bags of vodka tucked into the inside pocket of his shorts.

"What the fucking hell?" I laugh. "You're already blazed. Are you going to light one up in the stadium?"

Adam gives me a don't-be-crazy look. "Hell no, Everly. I'm not a fuck-tard." He lifts his shoulders. "But I'm not gonna make it home before I go out tonight and I want to be prepared. I just have this feeling that tonight is going to be a shit storm. It's in the air or something. Don't you feel it, man?"

Like I'm some kind of expert on shit storms. Just then, Kate squeezes her fingernails into my thigh and I realize that maybe I am. Maybe I am.

Aimee

Jilly used to do this thing right before a run. She'd huff loudly and pop her arms in the air while she bounced up and down on her toes like a boxer. She did it to make me laugh and it usually worked.

I haven't gone on a run since she died.

That was more than fifteen months ago.

I don't run anymore. I don't swim anymore. I don't go out with guys anymore. And on the bad days I'm not even sure that I exist anymore.

Today is a bad day.

I don't know why. I just wake up with a head full of cloudy grey skies and thoughts that bounce off the ceiling and land heavily in the pit of my stomach. Maybe it has something to do with how I couldn't fall asleep last night after Cole dropped me off. I don't really know and I'm not sure that I want to start analyzing it right now.

My sister is worried. She's been watching me all morning and I can tell that she's wavering about what to do. She disappeared into her room awhile ago, and anyone that knows Mara would tell you that it's a pretty good guess that she's in there making a pros and cons list about whether or not to call Mom. When she finally reappears, I have to sit her down on the couch and assure her at least five times that it's not like it was in June.

I would know.

That's what I say to get her to leave it alone, but the thing is—I'm not sure what it means.

Know what?

What would I know?

Mara is still uncertain. She's going to the game and she begs me to go with her. *Even Jodi's going,* she says. And when that doesn't work, she pulls out the big guns. *Isn't Cole going to be there?* As if being in the same place at the same time as Cole Everly has become the end-all and the be-all of my life at the moment.

I want to be irritated, but I give her some slack because she doesn't get it. Not really. The two of us give our mom a lot of hell for being the person that she is, but in a lot of ways, Mara is the same—she's just less annoying and primitive about it. Deep down, both Mara and our mother think that if I want it bad enough, I can decide to move on. They think that second chances and new beginnings are something you just *do*, but I know the truth. Those are things that you have to earn.

I try to explain to Mara that the thought of being confined in a stadium with thousands of people crushed against me and the noise splintering my head is enough to make my stomach convulse. She doesn't like it, but eventually she gives up and leaves me on the couch staring at the TV.

Hours later I'm still sitting here and I don't even know what I'm watching. It's one of those completely bone-numbing made for TV movies that airs on Saturday afternoons in between infomercial cycles. I can't even explain the plot. All I know is that it has something to with a girl falling in love with a down-on-his-luck prizefighter and that he's doing the signature air-popping warm-up move.

It makes me think of Jillian and our runs Monday and Thursday afternoons and on Saturday mornings when we didn't have a swim meet. We always started at her place and looped around to the north side of the neighborhood because there were fewer cars. Sometimes we'd talk and other times we'd pop in our earbuds and just go. And even if we weren't saying anything to each other and the only thing in our heads was the music, it was still better to be together than alone.

Before I know what I'm doing, I'm on the floor of my closet looking for my running shoes and I'm lacing them up and stretching my legs out on the sidewalk.

Back when I did this kind of thing, I could go far. Maybe even nine or ten miles on a day that wasn't too hot or humid. But that was when my body was strong, and when Jillian was next to me to push me for the last stretch.

Everything is different now. My muscles—the few that I have left—don't do what I want them to do and I'm in pain before I judge that I've gone more than a mile. I try to kick it in—to get my legs to listen to my brain and forget about the way that my heart is bursting behind my ribs, but it's no use. I crack and I'm off on the side of the road, hunched over with my hands bolstered on my knees. Air wheezes in and out of my lungs painfully, and beads of tangy sweat drip into my eyes and my mouth.

A car driving past honks its horn and some jerk leans out and shouts something at me but I'm too focused on not falling down to even care.

Cole

"So what do you want to do?"

Kate's voice pulls me back to the truck. I shake my head and glance over at her. "What did you say?"

She turns to look at me. It's dark in here but I can tell that her eyes are narrowed and her mouth is pursed. "Cole, you've been acting really weird all day. You barely paid attention to the game and you've been ignoring me. What's with you?"

I push a hand into my hair and shake my head.

What's with me?

"Nothing," I say and I want to believe that it's the truth, but it's not and I know it. I'm annoyed that Kate's in my truck in the first place, sitting in the exact spot where Aimee sat last night. And I want to gag because her perfume is so strong that it has me wondering if she's trying to attract bears or some shit. "I'm just tired or whatever. I have a headache."

"Well then…" Kate leans over the console so close that her moist breath pricks my skin. She lifts her hand to my chest and walks her fingers slowly downward until they brush the waistband of my boxers. "Maybe we should skip the party tonight and you know… get you in bed."

I push my back against the seat and briefly squeeze my eyes shut. Despite the overpowering perfume and everything inside my head tonight, Kate's touch on me doesn't feel terrible. Her fingers coast lower and I almost don't stop her. *Almost.*

"Kate," I say her name slowly so that she knows that I'm being serious. "I'm going to take you home now."

Her intake of air is audible and I can tell that she's pissed by the way that she jerks her body away from mine. Not that I'm surprised. Girls generally don't like to be rejected. It makes them irritable.

"You know what?" Kate spits out. Her voice sounds the way that Sour Patch Kids taste. "Take me to Brady's place instead. Last week he mentioned that he was having people over after the game. I wasn't going to go, but I think I've changed my mind."

"Okay," I say, glancing in the rearview mirror and switching lanes. I know that she's trying to make me jealous and a part of me feels bad that she's bothering to make the effort because it's not working very well.

The rest of the ride is awkward. Kate's unasked questions sit like a living, breathing thing lodged into the space between us. I think about explaining myself, but the truth is that I don't even know how to begin. *So, there's this girl...*

Later, I'm home and trying to get some work done for school, but my mind is still elsewhere—a few miles away with a girl that I know isn't thinking of me.

I'm remembering how she looked last night while we were walking on the beach, and the way the moonlight shimmered like moving water in her hair. And her smile—that one is the killer.

I check the clock on my phone. It's close to midnight but I'm not even thinking straight anymore. I'm grabbing my keys and looking for my shirt and the DVD case that I know I spotted last week.

Seven minutes later, I pull up to her place and find an empty street spot to parallel park in. The exterior lights are off and the front windows are dark. I hesitate before knocking, but I've come this far and I decide that I'm not going home without making this last move.

One. Two. Three. Four. Five. Six. Seven. Breathe.

No worries.

No thoughts.

There's a sound like footsteps and a light comes on and then the door is being unlocked. I take a deep breath and start talking before I can see who it is because, somehow, I know that it will be her and not her sister. "I know that it's late but I couldn't sleep knowing that you haven't seen this."

Aimee stands in the doorframe looking back and forth between the *Caddyshack* DVD in my hands and my face.

I try pretending like I don't notice the redness around her eyes or the fact that she's in just a pair of very short shorts and a sports bra and that her hair is pulled up into a messy ponytail and I can see her face like I've never seen it before, but it's no use. I notice all of it and before either of us can stop me, I've got her folded up in my arms and I'm talking low into her hair.

Aimee's arms curl in and her head presses against my chest. I can feel her heartbeat thundering under her bare skin and I wonder if I'm going to be able to keep all of the pieces of her inside.

Aimee

Regret. When it happens, and I mean *really* happens to you, it's like discovering a new sound.

I tried to explain this to my therapist when I first moved to Portland last year. *Aimee, what if,* she asked, *you decided to let go?*

And I wondered if she'd been listening to me at all.

Because all I do is let go.

Nine

Cole

M aybe I'm officially crazy. That's what Adam tells me, and some days I think he's right. Maybe crazy is exactly what it takes to cut off your balls and hand them over to a girl.

Difficult. Damaged. Closed-off. If I were making a list of qualities to avoid in a girl, Aimee would probably match up with every single one of them. But I'm still here, working my ass off for every single smile. And I *want* to be here. I've never wanted anything so much in my whole life.

She tells me everything and nothing all at once and I take what I can get because somewhere along the way that became okay. *Look but don't touch.* That's the deal with us and it doesn't matter if I want more because I'm not going to touch her until she makes it clear that it's what she wants. And that's not a game. It's a promise. No more strategy. No more pushing. No more bullshit.

Just her and me. Me and her.

Her. One word. A simple pronoun that seems like an entire vocabulary.

Aimee

"So, I've been thinking about tattoos."

I look up from my laptop as Jodi falls into the chair on the opposite side of the study carrel. A huge grin has swallowed up her face.

"I'm almost afraid to ask but... what, exactly, are you thinking about tattoos?"

Impossibly, her smile gets wider. "Do you remember that girl Alexis?" Jodi asks. "I think you met her last week. Big boobs," she mimes this with her hands, "and short blonde hair."

I try to think back. For someone who doesn't seem to have many friends, Jodi certainly knows a lot of people. Last Tuesday I think she introduced me to two Kevins and at least four girls that she told me with a sideways glance, were *total skanks*.

"I—um..." I'm pulling a blank.

"It doesn't matter. She's a total skank." Jodi says and one side of my mouth turns up in response. "What matters," she goes on, "is that last night I was grabbing a Frappuccino and I ran into Alexis and the guy that she's currently fucking. We got to talking and he informed me that his cousin works at that tattoo place downtown and that they were going there to take him a coffee. One thing led to another, and somehow I wound up tagging along."

"Somehow?"

Jodi ignores me and continues her story. "So there I was, browsing through the artwork, and I get this feeling. Like I just knew that something was about to happen."

"The sight?"

"Right. So I looked up and there was this drop-your-panties-right-this-minute, gorgeous guy looking at me. I could barely breathe because my mind was trying to wrap itself around his insane body and he walked right up to me in all of his tattooed, raven-haired, sex-on-a-stick glory and asked me out. No pretenses—just told me that he was into me and wanted to take me out sometime. Aimee, I swear that he got my ovaries quaking before I even found out that his name is Kyle."

I feel my forehead crinkle. Two days ago she told me that the ex-boyfriend, Jason, gave her the most earth-shattering orgasm of her life. "Um. What about Jason?"

Her right eyebrow quirks up. "Jason who?"

"You're terrible." I shake my head, trying unsuccessfully to suppress a smile. "For a second when you said that you were thinking about tattoos, I thought you were going to tell me that you wanted to get one."

Jodi's head tilts to one side. A chunk of blue hair falls into her eyes. "Oh, I do. Ever since last night…" She says it like it's been twelve years, not twelve hours. "I've been seeing myself with a really cool design from here to here." She indicates almost her entire upper back from shoulder blade to shoulder blade.

"That's, um, pretty big. Why not start with something smaller and work your way up?"

"Because that's not how I do things. Plus," she taps her forehead, "I've already foreseen my mother's reaction and any future regret that I might have over the ink will be dwarfed by the satisfaction that her shock will provide me."

"Well, that's… really, um… exciting. I can't wait to meet Kyle." I smile tentatively and look back to the keys of my laptop. We're in the eastern corner of the second floor of the library in a quiet nook that I discovered during the third week of school. Jodi knows that she can usually find me here, sitting at a study carrel, between classes.

"Who knows… I might even love him."

This snaps my head up. "Love?" I squeak. "You met him yesterday!"

"I know but…" She laughs, flutters her fingers against her cheek.

I narrow my eyes. "I don't really buy into the insta-love thing. Love isn't an accident or something that just…" I search for the right word. "… happens when you're not looking. Love is a choice, not a chance."

"Okay, maybe *love* was too strong of a word. But I do think that insta-*something* can happen. All it takes is one second, one brush of a finger to feel that... *possibility*. I can't really explain it, but it's like a connection or a sensation that radiates all through your body. Hot and cold. Excited and subdued all at once. And maybe that sounds crazy but I know that it's real. I know it because I've felt it in here." She sighs and points to her chest right above where her heart sits. "Haven't you ever had that happen to you? Isn't that what you felt like when you saw Cole for the first time?"

My breath catches in the back of my throat. *Cole.* I shake my head. "Jodi, that's not—it's not..."

She folds her hands together as if she's about to start praying. "I take it from that look that you're giving me and the general aura of sexual dissatisfaction emanating from you that things with the hot and tasty runner remain the status quo?"

I know exactly what she's asking and I don't think that I'm ready to have this conversation. Again.

"If by 'status quo' you mean 'friends,' then, yes, we're still friends. He's a total movie buff so he comes over some nights and we'll watch something that I haven't seen before and that's about it. It's not... it's not a big deal."

Jodi examines my face. "If you say so." That's all she says, but it's the *way* that she says it that has me feeling off-kilter.

I know how things with Cole look, and I know how they *feel*—I just don't know what to do about it.

For the last couple of weeks we've been hanging out. At least that's what I think I'm supposed to call it if I have to call it anything. Most nights he comes to my place after he's done training and we eat dinner, do our homework, and usually we wind up on my bed listening to music or watching a movie. And, despite what my sister thinks, *watching a movie* is not a euphemism for anything else.

I don't understand it any more than Jodi or Mara, but I don't need to sit around picking apart our relationship to know that I like being around Cole. He's fun. He makes me laugh. It's almost embarrassing how much I've started craving the low grumble of his pick-up truck and the sound of his flip-flopped feet stamping up the walkway in front of the townhouse. After a year of darkness, Cole is like a burning star brightening up my sky.

"Did he like the article?"

The article that I wrote about Cole and submitted for class was published in the student newspaper this past Friday. I can't hide the curl of my lips as I say, "Yeah, he did. He sent a copy of it to his little sister."

"Hmm. Cute. Very cute." Jodi twirls a strand of blue hair over her index finger. "So, the assignment's over, but loverboy is still hanging around? How interesting." She puts on a mocking tone and narrows her gaze.

"He hasn't tried anything with me," I tell Jodi because it's the truth.

She's quiet. It's like she's sifting through the questions in her head, looking for the right one. Finally: "Do you want him to?"

Ah. Do I want Cole Everly to try anything with me?

My thoughts about Cole are so all over the place, it's like everything inside of me is turning off and on all at once. He hasn't asked me out on a date since that night back in August when we were both at Dirty Ernie's. He flirts with me but that seems to be ingrained in his DNA so it's not like I can take him seriously.

Cole hasn't tried to kiss me. He doesn't gawk at my body. God. He barely looks—not even when I'm lying next to him on my bed in nothing but my sleep camisole and a pair of cotton shorts. What we've got going on is a strange kind of friendship, but that's all it's been so far. A *friendship.*

I lift my chin and wince a little. "Does it matter if I do?"

Jodi snorts discordantly. "What is this—1952 and you need to have your Great-Aunt Gertrude chaperone your outings? If you want Cole in your bed then you need to tell him so. Or better yet, *show him* that you want him. Men are better with visuals anyway." She looks a combination of frustrated and amused. "Aimee, it's obvious to everyone on the planet that he's lusting so hard for you that he can barely see straight. Why not put the poor guy out of his misery?"

My mind is whirling and I say the first words that pop in my mouth. "I don't date."

"First of all, I didn't say that you had to *date* him, did I?" Jodi waits for me to acknowledge her question with a shake of my head. "Second, what makes you think that what you're doing with Cole right now is so different from dating him?"

My voice is barely audible. "I don't know."

Cole

"You're joking?" I ask even though I know that she's not.

Aimee gives an exaggerated shrug and squishes up her nose. I love when she does that. "You say that every time."

She's right. I do.

"I say it because I'm horrified every time and I keep hoping that you'll tell me that this has all been some elaborate hoax."

Aimee draws her knees up to her chest and rests her chin on the tops of her kneecaps. She smiles at me thoughtfully and waves her hand around the room. "Hmm. Horrified? *Really*? It seems to me that you're thrilled to be in charge of expanding my cinematic repertoire."

Right again.

I can feel her blue eyes all over me as I mess around with the cable attached to my laptop and the volume of the TV in her bedroom. Monday it was *The Exorcist*. Last night we watched the first of the *Halloween* movies. And tonight I'm cueing up *The Ring*. Starting with

Caddyshack a couple of weeks back, Aimee and I have been systematically working our way through all of my movies. This girl has seen next to nothing and I've made it a personal crusade to change that.

When I turn back to Aimee, she's pulled off her oversized grey hoodie and is leaning against the pillows of her bed with her right hand flat on her stomach. Damn it. She's wearing that pajama top again—the creamy one that barely covers anything. I suck air through my teeth and look away so that I don't stare at the outline of her dark nipples through the fabric.

"I've been meaning to ask you," Aimee starts. "What's with all of the scary movies this week?"

You've got to be kidding me, I think as my mind pushes aside the memory of Aimee grabbing my arm and scooting closer to me during some of the tenser scenes last night. There's no way that I'm going to answer her question honestly and fess up to resorting to pathetic gimmicks, so I mutter something noncommittal under my breath and hope that she'll fucking drop it where she found it.

"Ah, well I kind of like them," she says, watching me carefully. The glow from the TV casts her pale face in a bluish-silver light. "Who would have thought that I'd be into horror movies, right?"

My eyebrows lift. "Just wait until we're an hour into this one tough girl, and then you can tell me if you still think that you like scary movies. I've been taking it easy on you up until now. Let's get started because I have to be out of here a little earlier than usual tonight."

Behind me, Aimee's soft voice cuts through the air. "Why? Do you have a hot date later?"

My head whips around. *Is she fucking serious?* Shit. I can tell by the look on her face that she is completely serious and it's like everything in the room takes a ninety-degree swing.

"No," I grumble, straining to move past the nastiness that's lodged itself in my throat. I haven't even *wanted* to look at another girl in weeks. Fuck. I'm completely pissed off. Aimee and I haven't talked about this kind of thing before and I didn't think that this was how we'd start.

"It would be okay if you did." She looks mildly uncomfortable. Her skin is flushed and she pulls absently on the ends of her hair. "I mean—I don't want to be the one sucking up all of your time. I know that you had a life before you met me and that you..." Now her cheeks go ridiculously red. "Have stuff that you might need to do sometimes."

I'm racking my brain, wondering why she's bringing this shit up now. Is she trying to ease me off because she's met someone? Maybe it's a guy from one of her classes? The thought worms its way inside of me and spreads like acid through my limbs.

"Trust me, Aimee. I still have a life and I can always find time for *stuff*," I say, knowing that I sound like a real dick. That's fine because I *am* a dick. I always have been. "But that's not why I need to get home tonight. I need actual sleep because I've got a fucking early practice in the morning. Plus, I still need to pack because we leave tomorrow around lunch for that race up in Gainesville."

This weekend is the triathlon that Quentin, Brady, Nate and I have been training for. I've been dreading it. Not because of the race—I love the rush and the adrenaline. The truth is that I haven't been looking forward to so many days away from Aimee. And in light of the way that tonight is going, how fucking pathetic is that?

Aimee's face is unflinching. She doesn't wish me luck, or tell me that she'll miss our movie nights. All she says is, "Oh."

That one word—that one gimpy sentiment digs its way under my skin and stays there.

"Yeah, I would have asked you to come because we're going to be going out afterward, but you don't drive, do you?" Fuck. It's like I've just jumped out of a plane without a parachute. I know that she doesn't like to talk about this stuff and that I'm being a total bastard on purpose.

I know some of the *facts* but that doesn't mean that I know the *story*. Daniel won't answer my questions and Aimee sure as hell doesn't want to talk. And up until this point, I haven't forced any of the thousand and one questions going through my head. I've been happy to live in each moment—one after the other—like there's nothing behind us, and nothing in front of us because I've been thinking... I don't even know what I've been thinking.

I keep looking hard and Aimee tugs self-consciously on her hair. Her bottom lip is lost between her teeth. I should let it go, but I can't stop myself. "Why don't you drive, Aimee? Tell me. Is it about the accident last year because I looked up an article online and you weren't even driving, were you?"

We've spent all this time together and I know so many things about her that I could fill up an entire book, but I don't know any of the important stuff. I know that she prefers cherry pie to peach pie, and that her relationship with her mother is crap, and that she's more of a dog person than a cat person, and that British humor makes her laugh, but those aren't all of the pieces to the puzzle. Not by a long shot.

Aimee's eyes are so wide and shiny it's almost like they've taken over the rest of her face. Finally, she whispers so low that I barely hear her, "I don't want to tell you."

I'd been prepared for her to blow me off so it's not like I'm knocked off my feet or anything. "Yeah fine," I say stiffly. This conversation really couldn't have gone worse. I'm tired and now I feel like everything is fucked. "That's what I figured."

"Cole, I—"

I put my hand up to cut her off. "You don't have to explain. Let's just watch the movie, yeah?"

Aimee is sitting up now. She lifts her hand to my shoulder and lets it slip all of the way down my arm until her fingers are wrapped tightly around mine. My breath hitches imperceptibly and it takes everything I have not to squeeze back.

"I don't want to tell you," she's stumbling over the words, "because I'm afraid that when I do, you won't understand and this whole thing will be over."

"What the hell does that mean, Aimee?"

She is still looking at me, holding my hand, and I'm struggling to remember why I got mad in the first place.

"I don't know how to explain, but will you just give me a little more time? I don't want you to go anywhere just yet," she says, her face clouding over.

"What are you talking about?" I sit down on the edge of the bed and pull her hand into my lap. "I'm not going anywhere."

"Don't say that." She closes her eyes and I think it's to keep from crying. "That's what everyone says."

Aimee

It turns out that I am not as tough as I proclaimed earlier and horror movies might not be my thing after all. I feebly tell Cole this and he ends up staying over. He actually seems pleased to be thrown into the role of my protector. Maybe it's an alpha male thing.

It's uncomfortable at first—with him on one side of my queen bed and me on the other, but eventually the weirdness is replaced by sleep. And we do, in fact, sleep.

His phone alarm goes off when my bedroom is still pitched in the slanting amber light of dawn. A high-pitched electronic whine jolts me out of a good dream and it's a few anxious heartbeats before I remember why I'm so warm in my bed and whose skin is pressed up against mine. With a muffled moan and an unwelcome gust of cold air, Cole slips out of the sheets and stands by the bed. I hear him pull on his jeans and search around my desk for his keys and wallet.

Before he leaves, he hovers over my body for a long moment. He's not touching me, but I can feel his heat and his breath on my skin even through the fabric of the sheets. I know that I should roll over to let him know that I'm awake. I should wish him good luck or positive vibes for the race or something. Instead, I let him place a quick kiss on my forehead and disappear without any words exchanged. Maybe it's because I'm infamously bad with mornings. Or maybe it's the good-byes that I can't seem to get right.

• • •

The rain starts out as a light drizzle when Mara is driving us to campus in the morning before class. By noon, it's morphed into a full-on storm with harsh, pelting raindrops and ashy clouds moving quickly across the sky.

This is one of those rare times when I wish that I'd taken my mother's advice and opted to keep that red travel umbrella she gave me last month stowed inside my bag. I'm supposed to meet Jodi and her new boy-toy, Kyle, at a little deli off-campus for lunch in less than five minutes.

Thunder rumbles overhead and a quick flash of lightning lights up the dark sky.

"Crap," I mumble and step back under a curved overhang buffeting the steps of the building. I'll have to wait this out for a bit.

A few like-minded students are huddled against the rough concrete walls—some of them pulling out phones or books to occupy themselves while we wait. I peer out again and sigh. I need to send Jodi a quick text to let her know that I'm going to be late for lunch so I reach into the front pocket of my bag to dig for my phone. I find it but as I maneuver my arm forward, the purple-encased iPhone slips from my fingers and takes a tumble down the steps to land facedown on the concrete walkway below.

"No-no-no-no!" I shout, hunching my shoulders in preparation for a sprint into the rain.

"Hold up." The anorak-clad guy standing closest to me touches my arm before shooting past me into the rain to grab my phone.

A thank you seems inadequate but it's all I've got. "Thank you. I-I—just—thanks—I—" Surprise halts the jumbled words in my throat as he pushes the bright blue hood of his jacket back and shakes out his coppery hair.

"No prob—"

The two of us stare at each other in silence. It's strange how one bit of time and space can pull everything apart and be filled with so much emotion that it chokes you and spits you out. This is what I'm thinking as a dripping wet Daniel Kearns hands over my phone.

"Thank you," I murmur shakily, wiping the screen of the phone with the bottom of my shirt. "It looks like it's probably going to survive." *Survive.* Why would I choose that word? It's like I'm shoving things in Daniel's face that he doesn't need to see.

"Good to hear. I can't stand to see perfectly good iPhones getting chucked into the rain."

I clear my throat awkwardly and pull the ends of my hair over my shoulder. It's a tangled mess from all the moisture in the air and the fact that I barely bothered to brush it this morning. "I thought that you guys left for the triathlon already."

As soon as the words have left my mouth, I want to kick myself. I have no idea what, if anything, Cole has told Daniel about us and I've just admitted that I know what his travel schedule is. Unless Daniel is an idiot, I'm pretty sure he'll be able to put two and two together.

Daniel looks at me and then out at rain-soaked campus. "I'm not doing it. It's just Nate, Quentin, Cole and Brady." He shakes rain from the bottom of his jacket.

"Oh. I just…" I just *what?* I shift on my feet and neither of us speaks for a moment.

Daniel breaks first. "So," he says, and I can tell by his tone what's coming next. "You and Cole?"

I shake my head. "It's not like you're thinking."

Daniel's face smooths out and his warm brown eyes get rounder. "You can tell what I'm thinking, Aimee?"

"No." I shrug, half-embarrassed that I've given anything away. "I'm just assuming because it's what everyone around us has been thinking lately and it's not happening. Honestly. Cole and I are just friends." I wonder how many times I'll have to say that out loud to make it sound true.

"He's asked me about you a couple of times. About... well, you know, but I haven't told him much. I think that the story belongs to you."

"Daniel... I-I..." God. Why can't I speak?

"He likes you," Daniel tells me like it's the most natural thing.

I try not to let him see that my entire world expands and contracts with those three syllables. "I'm pretty confident that he likes a lot of people."

Daniel pauses and I swear that in his silence I can hear the sound of my own heart over the thrum of the rain. There's something different in his voice when he says, "Not like this."

What does that mean?

"Look, Aimee," he continues as he pushes his soggy hair away from his forehead. "I've been wanting to talk to you since I found out that you were enrolled here, and the night that we drove you home I didn't really get the chance..."

"Uh, yeah. I feel like I should tell you that the behavior that you witnessed is really unusual for me. I'm not normally so... um, out of it."

Daniel chuckles. "Out of it, blitzed, wasted, whatever you want to call it."

"It's not my usual thing," I assure him.

Daniel lifts his hand. "You don't have to explain yourself to me."

"Honestly, Daniel, I feel like I do."

Daniel looks at me with his sister's eyes, not saying anything for a long time. I want to turn away but I'm frozen in place. I can see by the set of his shoulders and his jawline that he's trying to censor himself. I should probably save him the effort and tell him that just because he doesn't use Jillian's name, it doesn't keep her out of our conversation.

"No," he says gruffly. "You don't need to explain anything to me." His intake of air is rapid. "What I wanted to tell you was that I don't feel the way my mom did... or does. What happened after the accident wasn't fair to you. If I had been home more maybe... I don't know what I could have done, but *maybe*."

Maybe. It's a word that's full of hope, but it's wasted on me. Mrs. Kearns blames me for her daughter's death and it's not like I disagree. I left my unconscious best friend to die in the driver's seat of *my* car. I should have been driving. I was *supposed* to be driving.

But I wasn't, was I?

There are no take-backs, do-overs, or maybes about it. Every time I realize that, I'm sent back to that car—to that moment of clinging between life and death. And then I drop her hand again and it all becomes new.

"You couldn't have done anything to change what happened, Daniel," I say quietly, my heart aching for everything that we both lost. "And your mother has a right to the way that she feels. I-I don't hold it against her."

"This is probably not the best conversation to have in the middle of all these people, but maybe we can have coffee or something sometime soon." He glances around the covered hallway and back to me. "And anyway, the rain is letting up."

He's right. "Well, if you talk to Cole, tell him..." What do I want him to tell Cole? "Tell him good luck from me."

"Why don't you tell your guy all by yourself?"

"He's not *my* guy." I tuck my phone into my bag and walk into the lightened rain.

Behind me, a voice calls. "Aimee!"

I turn, feeling a little sick to my stomach. Daniel's got the blue hood of his jacket pulled back up around his face.

"Were you being serious?" He asks.

I squint against the wetness. "About what?"

Daniel smiles. "About Jillian wanting to get a nose job?"

I let out a held breath. "Yeah. I was being serious. She told me that she wanted to get a nose job after graduation."

Daniel touches his nose absently. "Huh. She never mentioned it to me." Then he's gone—walking in the opposite direction.

Ten

Aimee

I could say that the girls don't bother me, but that would be a lie. They bother me. A lot.

Every time Mara or someone else mentions Cole's playboy reputation, I cringe. He certainly didn't get it by keeping his hands to himself or his penis stowed safely in his pants.

I know that I have no right to jealousy, but I still don't like being constantly reminded that Cole has many fuck-buddies.

Has or *had*.

I'm still working that part out. I brought it up the other night because all of a sudden, I couldn't *not* bring it up anymore. Maybe that was stupid of me. And maybe he gave me an answer but I'm not really sure.

The emptiness inside my room Friday night is like a sucker punch straight to the gut. I've gotten accustomed to Cole showing up at the townhouse after practice with his cocky smile and his bag slung over his shoulder. The realization of how miserable and lonely my life was before he came into it makes me feel even more ridiculous. It's only been a couple of weeks, but I know that I'm already clinging to moments spent with him—struggling to keep ahold of something that I'm not even sure is mine to begin with.

Without Cole around, everything drags. Jodi wants me to go out with her and Kyle but the only thing worse than being me right now, is being me as a third wheel. I decide to stay home and organize my closet instead. It's scintillating stuff.

By Saturday morning, I'm completely sick of myself. I've been reduced to refreshing the browser on my computer every three minutes so that I can track his Twitter feed. I'm becoming a real-to-life stalker.

Mara comes into my room at ten, takes one look at my face and the screen of my laptop and says, "Let's go."

I don't even ask her where we're going. I just find my sandals and step into them because there comes a point when all that matters is that you're moving.

Cole

I protest, but only half-heartedly when the guys want me to go out with them Saturday night. The race is over and after two days of living inside my head, I need a way out.

"There's this bar on University Avenue," Brady tells us after he's given the cab driver instructions to drop us off in Midtown. I'm in the backseat wedged in between Nate and Quentin. "It's a complete shithole but the drinks are cheap and there will be girls."

Girls. I don't want to, but I automatically check my phone. I sent Aimee a text after my race this morning but she still hasn't responded. A memory of my dad waiting on my mom years ago when she was supposed to meet us at the movies flickers in my brain and it's the fucking slap over the head that I need. Here I've been consumed with the damn idea of Aimee Spencer for days and she can't even bother to text me back. *She doesn't see me the way that I see her.*

The bar is as shitty as Brady promised and by round three, Nate and Quentin are ready to give up and head back to the hotel. Not me. I'm half-lit at this point and there's a girl. She's been hovering around me all night and she's got nice tits and a cute smile. When she asks me back to her place, I find myself following before I can think too hard about it.

Her name is Christine and she's from New Hampshire. According to the pictures in her room, she's a big fan of Nietzsche, and I can't decide if I find that cool or pretentious. Christine has brown eyes and curly hair the color of wet sand. As she's pulling off her shirt and her lacy black bra, I try to keep my gaze focused on her body so that my brain doesn't keep pumping out images of long dark hair and blue eyes so wide and sad that I could swim inside of them.

The sex with Christine is fine but as soon as it's over and I'm lying in her bed staring at a poster filled with Friedrich Nietzsche's words, I feel a pain in my chest like I can't breathe. Being with girls has always been my go-to, but now everything feels... wrong. Christine runs her hands over my abs and asks me to stay for the night. She's hinting at round two, but I'm not into it. I know that I'm defeated in ten million ways but really, only one way that counts. So I tell her that we're heading back early in the morning and I say it like this is something that I've just remembered.

Like a sitcom bimbo, Christine completely buys what I'm selling, which only makes things worse. She even drives me back to the hotel and asks me to wait while she punches her number into my phone and sends herself a text from me.

"So we'll be able to stay in touch," she says.

When she leans in to kiss me goodbye, I can tell that she's still pretending that this might be going somewhere and I hate myself just a little bit more.

As I'm riding the elevator up to the hotel room that the four of us are sharing, my brain is sluggish with alcohol, but I'm clear enough to know that I need to delete Christine's number from my contacts. I pull my phone out of my back pocket and thumb the display screen to life. That's when I see the fucking missed texts from Aimee and my stomach falls about eleven floors.

Sorry. Mara and I went home for the day and I left my phone behind. I'm so proud of you!

And then, a second message sent two minutes after the first.

BTW, I've got one. The Two Owers. The epic story of two hobbits complaining about how their feet hurt the whole way to Mordor. Now you're it.

I don't know if I should laugh or cry. As usual, I'm the asshole who fucked up.

Aimee

For the first time in a long time, *home* wasn't so bad. Dad grilled burgers and we played Scrabble on the back patio and no one talked about anything important, but at least we talked. And when Mara and I got back to the townhouse last night, I had a missed text from Cole. All in all, it wasn't such a terrible Saturday.

"Do you think this thing with him is crazy?" I ask Mara on Sunday morning.

We're both cross-legged on the couch. She's eating a green apple and I've got a bowl of Lucky Charms balanced on my thigh. Unlike my sister, my motto on breakfast foods is that they don't count unless they contain at least twice the recommended daily allotment of sugar.

Mara sets the apple down, crosses her arm across her chest, frowns. "Who are we talking about, Aimee?"

"Cole," I say it like his name has been eating up my tongue for days. "Do you think that it's crazy for me to hang out with him?"

"No. I think you're crazy *about* him. There's a difference." Mara looks me in the eye. "And don't start hyperventilating or anything Aimee, but he's crazy about you too."

"How can you be sure?"

Mara answers my question with a question of her own. "How can *you* be so blind? Cole Everly looks at you like you you're made of rainbows and he's over here almost every single night *not* getting laid. Aimee, what do you think that means? Jeez. The guy's done a complete one-eighty in the past couple of weeks and it's all because of you. I think the only thing left for him to prove himself is to carve your initials into his skin with a penknife."

"I'm not sure that I'm ready for things to change yet," I admit slowly. "I'm not sure if I'm ready, period. I haven't put myself out there in a long time and what Cole and I have is good. If…" I close my eyes and swallow hard.

"If what?"

"I'm just afraid to lose what we've got. I don't know if you've noticed this, but I don't have so many friends that I can just risk them willy-nilly."

"I hate to break this to you Aimee, but you're going to lose him one way or the other because this chasing game that you guys are playing can only go on for so long."

"I'm not sure that it's like that with us."

"It *is* like that. I know it. He knows it. And I think that deep down you know it too," she says. "Let me put it to you this way—it's like the two of you are standing barefoot on an enormous pile of hot coals. A person can only do that for so long. Eventually, you either have to jump off or start moving your feet."

Strangely, the analogy sort of makes sense to me. "Okaaay… there's also the fact that Cole is way out of my league. He's so bright that he burns. He could—" I catch a quick breath. "He could have his pick of any girl that he wants. I just don't understand why me. Why would he want to be with me?"

"Where is this coming from?" She's looking at me like I'm crazy. "Why wouldn't Cole want to be with you?

"Because," I say, feeling exasperated and shaky. "I don't have friends. I don't do anything. I'm home almost every night, like you said, *not* getting laid. I'm weird, Mara."

Mara's mouth straddles a smile and a grimace. "It doesn't have to be like that. Before the accident you were—"

I interrupt her before she can finish whatever she was going to say, because I can't listen to it. "Mara, the way that I was before was all because of Jillian. *She* was the one who was good at parties and guys and all that kind of stuff—not me. I was always meant to be the sideshow act."

Mara doesn't say anything for a minute. "Do you remember Collin what's-his-name? The guy from middle school…"

My forehead crinkles. "Collin *Peskowitz*? And yeah, I remember him. I just can't believe that you do."

Collin Peskowitz. I was eleven, and by my standards back then, Collin was sort of epic. He was amazingly braces-free, had great hair that he spiked up with gel, and in the summer before sixth grade he was learning to play guitar while the other boys in our grade were busy expanding their range of fart sounds and playing touch football.

The look on her face is terribly serious. "That was all you, Aimee. Jillian Kearns had nothing to do with it."

I know that Mara is referring to the fact that I confronted Collin at the Dreffin's annual Fourth of July picnic and told him in front of everyone, including my parents, that I liked him and that he had exactly one hour to decide if he liked me back. That was the night I got my first kiss under a sky full of fireworks.

I shake my head to chase away the memory. "That was a long time ago."

"Somewhere along the way your brain came up with this story that Jillian was the superhero and you were the sidekick, but it's not true." My sister sighs. "I was always in awe of you. You used to be so confident and fearless."

I used to be a lot of things.

Cole

"Let's go out," she tells me and I think I've misheard her.

I hold my phone a little tighter. "Are you saying you want to go *out* out—like to a club or dancing or something, or are you trying to coerce me into giving you a ride to the grocery store?"

Aimee laughs on the other end of the phone and my stomach does this crazy flip. It's Monday afternoon and this is the first time that we've talked on the phone and I'm trying not to make too much of the fact that she actually called me instead of sending me a text.

"Hmmm. Maybe somewhere in between? How do you feel about the arcade and gyros on the beach?"

"I'm a fan." I pause. "There's also a hamburger guy that parks his cart over by the pier if you feel like living dangerously."

She laughs again. I want the conversation to end on a high note and I don't want to give her a chance to change her mind so I quickly tell her that I'll be at her place by seven. We say goodbye and I that's when I start to count because I've got four hours to go until I see her, but somehow it feels like ten.

Eleven

Cole

"**L**ord *of the Lies.*"

"I'm going with *Ride and Prejudice,*" she says. "It's about a modern-day Lizzie Bennet falling for the President of an MC against her better judgment."

"What's an MC?"

"Mother Chapter. You know, like for a motorcycle club."

I chuckle. "How the hell do *you* know anything about motorcycle clubs?"

"You know, Cole, there's a lot about me that might surprise you."

"I don't doubt that."

"So..." She pushes her toes down into the sand. "When is your next race?"

"There's an informal invitational in a few weeks I think."

"Is it here?"

"Well, it's not *here.*" I give a half-shrug with my shoulders indicating the beach that's spread out in front of us. "But, yeah, it's here in town if that's what you mean."

Aimee adjusts her position and dusts sand from the backs of her thighs. Today she's wearing a painfully short white dress that shows off her body in too many ways. When she walked out of her place in it, I was torn between pushing her up against my truck to taste her mouth and asking her to go change into something else.

"Yes, that's what I meant, smart-ass."

If I didn't know better, I'd say that the way that she's looking at me right now qualifies as almost flirty. Her blue eyes are dancing and if they keep landing on my mouth like that, stupid move or not, she's going to get herself kissed.

"So…" I wash down the last of my burger with a gulp of beer and I crinkle up the paper wrapper into a tight ball.

"I think I want to go." She's staring out at the water.

"You want to go home?" I ask, hating the disappointment in my voice. We haven't even made it to the arcade yet. And considering that I haven't seen this girl for more than four days, one hour of her company isn't enough.

"No," she says, turning back to me. The warm breeze is whipping her dark hair around her face and the sun is streaming soft yellow and orange over her skin. I reach over with my left hand and tuck her hair behind her ears. It's so silky. Even though I know I'm not allowed, I can't stop my fingers from drifting farther into the wavy coils that spill over her shoulder and down her back.

Aimee doesn't pull away. She doesn't tell me to stop touching her. She doesn't say anything at all.

Silence.

I'm so afraid to break the moment that I'm not even blinking my eyes. My fingers whisper along the skin of her jaw and my thumb grazes that one freckle on her cheek. She's warm and soft and I want to touch all of her so badly that it's like a physical ache clawing at my body.

Aimee's chest begins to rise and fall heavily. She bites her bottom lip and turns her face out toward the water. Something is different between us tonight. It feels like the rules have all been changed and I don't know what they are anymore. There's this voice inside my head chanting for me to go for it, but I have to be sure that I'm reading this situation right. I *need* to be sure.

Reluctantly, I pull my hand away and let it fall to the sand between us. This is fucking torture. I cough and lean back.

I've been with enough girls to know the signals, but this is the one girl that has me questioning anything and everything. She's had me confusing up and down and left and right and who knows what else since the day that she fell into my lap.

Her eyes cut back to mine and they are darker than I've ever seen them—two swirling seas blinking at me from her pale face.

"I want to go to the meet. To see you race," she says in a whisper and I realize that I've almost forgotten what we were talking about.

Running track. The invitational in a few weeks.

"Do you miss it? Racing?" I'm able to keep my voice flat even though my insides are rioting.

"I miss a lot of things," she says, bowing her head as she works through her thoughts. I love the gentle way her neck curves into her shoulders. I want to touch her there. I want to taste her skin and kiss her eyelashes and drink up everything about her. "I haven't been in the water in more than a year."

I don't think either one of us has moved but somehow our bodies have managed to get closer than they were five seconds ago. Her hip is pressed against my hip and her leg is flush against my leg, and our fingers are brushing the sand between us—almost touching. *Almost.*

"We could go in now," I say gruffly, nodding my chin toward the water.

Her lips curl. She looks from my face to where the waves are breaking over the sand. "I don't have a bathing suit with me."

I think about saying something fucktastically clichéd about not needing a bathing suit, but I can't do that. Not with her. Not tonight. "Ah, well… we'll come again soon, yeah?"

She nods and leans back on her elbows like me so that her hair is dangling in the sand. Each time the air moves around us, I can smell her shampoo and it's sweet, like having a plate of pastries just under my nose.

"Aimee…"

She absently runs the tip of her tongue over her bottom lip and that one small movement stops the earth in place. Just stops it.

I can hear my heartbeat.

I can hear the sound of my brain churning out thoughts and the blood flowing through my body and the air displacing around our bodies and my nerve endings firing off.

I'm aware of every single thing about this moment—the way that the white dress she's wearing clings to her body in all the right places, her toes buried deep in the soft sand, her clear blue eyes reaching far into mine, and the low sound that her body makes each time she exhales.

Right now I really don't want to think about the girl that I had sex with two nights ago, but I do, and I fucking hate myself for it. Technically, it wasn't cheating. But still. I wish that I could take her back. I wish that I could redo most of my shitty life and—

"Cole," she says with her eyes on my lips. My eyes. My lips. My eyes. My lips.

"Be careful," I warn in a voice so scratchy and hoarse that I'm not sure that she can understand me. Fuck. I don't mean that I don't want this to happen with her. I do. But she needs to be sure, because once we go to that place there will be no turning back. Not for me.

Aimee hesitates. Uncertainty is smeared across her face and I think that I've officially blown everything to shit, but then the tips of her fingers breeze up my arm and she seesaws her body, closing the gap between us. I see her eyelids fall shut and mine do the same. How many seconds does it take? One? Only half a second? As soon as her warm, moist breath touches my lips, I'm a goner. Any argument that I may have had with myself leaves my head and the only thing that exists is *now*. This breath. This touch. This moment.

The first kiss is tentative, painfully brief, the same way you take a small bite of food that you're afraid might be too hot. I pull back and look into her blue eyes. Her entire body is bundled tight, held taut and stiff like she's unsure of my next move. Carefully, conscious not to break the moment, I touch her slightly parted mouth with my finger. She gasps and opens her mouth farther and I feel the wetness of her tongue against my skin as she moistens her lips. Man, I already love those pink lips. I already love the way that they feel rubbing up against mine.

"Are you going to kiss me for real or what?"

I laugh and after that, everything happens in a rush. We come together hard and this time my hungry mouth presses firmly into hers and my tongue glides between the crease of her lips and I discover a new taste. *Aimee Spencer*. It's a mixture of salt and fresh air and something that is so *her* that I'm not sure that I'll ever be able to get enough of it.

Pulse throbbing, cock hardening in record time, I skate my hands down her neck and over her shoulders. When I reach her breasts, Aimee makes a little sound that's partway between a sigh and a moan and one of her bare legs wraps around the bend of my knee, drawing me deep into the contours of her body.

"Damn."

She giggles and rains tiny kisses along my jaw, pushing her small hands down my spine until her nails scratch the exposed skin of my lower back, where they linger, digging under the waistband of my boxers.

I am fucking destroyed.

Flayed wide open.

If I've ever kissed another girl in my life like this, I can't think of it. I can't think of anything at all.

My mouth still pressed into hers, I lift both of my hands from her body to clasp her face and graze my thumb over that freckle on her cheek. Aimee whispers incoherently against my lips and her delicious fingers grip my back so tightly that I can feel the sting of her nails.

My mouth dips down to her collarbone—to the pulse that beats steadily against the hollow at the base of her neck—and back up to her soft, welcoming lips. She sucks me inside and teases me with her tongue until it seems like there is so much to feel that I might be drowning. Fuck it. Let the tide take me under. I don't need to breathe oxygen as long as I've got this girl's mouth.

I know that I'm putting everything I am—everything that I have— out there, but I don't think I could pull myself back now even if I wanted to. Aimee has me wrapped up inside this one moment. And if she wanted to, she could reach into my chest and rip my heart out of my body because it already belongs to her.

Aimee

Sometimes a kiss is just a kiss. Other times, a kiss is a revelation.

Part of me wants to attribute this feeling—the one turning me inside out—to the fact that I haven't been touched in more than a year, but deep down I know that's a lie. It's a total cop out. This isn't a rain shower after a dry spell. This is a hurricane. It's both beautiful and devastating.

Cole drops his hands and rests his forehead against mine, his breath drifting into my open mouth in warm puffs. I'm mesmerized by the roughness of his cheek rasping under my palm and how cool he feels against my flushed skin. My lips are sore and tingly from the pressure of his kiss and I wonder if they're bruised or maybe even bleeding. Honestly? I don't think I would mind at all.

"Are you okay?" He asks and I note the slightly nervous edge to his voice.

I look into his eyes, fragmented green and gold under a ledge of dark blond lashes. I slide my hand down the flat lines of his chest until I can feel his heartbeat. It storms up my arm and seems to echo inside my chest.

I force myself to swallow hard. *Okay, breathe. Seriously, Aimee.*

I haven't spoken for about a full minute and Cole must get the wrong idea because he begins to shift his body away from mine.

"No," I hiss, gripping his arm tightly and waiting for him to meet my gaze. I want him to know that I mean what I'm saying even if I'm not sure what exactly it is that I'm going to say. I've spent so much time struggling for control, trying to hold things together that want to fall apart and I'm sick of it. I just want to let it all go. "I'm better than okay. I'm just—I can't..." My fingers drift over the rigid planes of his lean body to the side of his face. His cheeks are rough with the scrape of two-day old stubble and it's just so... sexy. Giving myself a little shake, I trace the sharp ridge of his nose and move my thumb pads along his straight eyebrows. "This is..."

Wow. I'm not making any sense, am I? But maybe that's all right because Cole is nodding his head like he understands what I'm trying to say. He smiles.

I don't know how long we stay like this—the two of us grinning and wound up in each other on the beach. The sun falls to the earth. Stars are drawn on the chalkboard of sky. At some point he kisses me again and from down the beach, a low-pitched whistle floats over us. A little while later, a gravelly voice comments that we should get a room.

Cole drops his head and laughs, soft and low against my neck. "You're going to kill me."

I press my head into the cool sand so that I can see his face. "Is that going to be a problem?"

For a long moment he just looks at me. Then he bursts out laughing.

With the sand at my back and the water at my feet, I relax and let the weight of Cole's strong body pin me to the here and now.

• • •

"The truth is that we barely know each other."

Cole looks over at me from the driver's seat. His face is hidden by shadows, but his eyeballs catch the shine of another car's headlights. "Are you being serious? Is this the part where you let me down gently?"

I laugh and slouch into the seat. "No, I'm not letting you down, but I am being at least quasi-serious."

Cole leans over the console and trails his finger across my bottom lip. I have to fight back a shiver that starts at the top of my head and works its way down my body. How I physically respond to him is both ridiculous and slightly embarrassing.

"I get what you're saying, but maybe that doesn't matter so much," he says quietly, dropping his hand and gripping the steering wheel. He expertly parks his truck in front of my townhouse. "We've been spending all this time together and I know what kind of face cream you put on before bed and what you look like in the morning. It's true that I don't know everything about you, but there's time and…" He shrugs his powerful shoulders. "I know enough about you to realize that I want to know more."

We sit in the dark for a while with the air conditioning running on high and Cole's music playing in the background. On the other side of the tinted windows, the stars fan out limitlessly across the blue-black night sky.

"Does that mean that we'll go on a few dates and see what happens?" God. What an awkward thing to ask. Maybe that's not what he was getting at. I pull my hair over my shoulder and twist the ends around my index finger.

"I hope that we'll do more than go on a few dates, Aimee." Cole furrows his forehead and pushes back his thick hair with a hand. He looks over at me and his entire face seems to narrow a bit. "What I'm trying to say is that I'm totally in this if you are."

I drop my eyes and drum my fingers against the door latch. I know that there are so many things that I should say right now but I don't know how to get the words out. I followed my impulses earlier when I kissed him. I'd been thinking about Cole in so many different ways and when we were sitting on the sand, listening to the rhythmic sound of the water moving over the shore, everything changed. All of my excuses flew away and the only thing that made any sense to me was this idea of wanting him. "I feel like I just walked off a cliff not expecting to land on my feet..." My voice peters out.

"But you did."

I look up and take a deep breath. "I guess I did." He's smiling and I can't help but smile back. "I'm not good at *this*." I point back and forth between us. "And I want to do everything right but I've been avoiding this kind of thing for over a year and now..." I shake my head. "I'm not sure where to start."

"I've been avoiding *this*," he points the way that I did, "for a lot longer than you have so if you're confused then we're completely fucked."

I laugh and give a jerky shrug. "So what does that mean for us?"

He lifts one arm and tugs on my hair tenderly. His look is level. "It means that we start at the beginning."

"I don't know what that is."

"Neither do I, but I think we can figure it out together."

I'm all right with that.

Twelve

Aimee

S ometime during my first class on Tuesday, I begin to freak out
and it's like I can't stop freaking out.

"I don't see what the problem is," Jodi says. We're sitting on a
bench in front of the tattoo shop where Kyle works and we're sharing
a bag of Skittles that Jodi dredged up from one of the interior pockets
of her backpack. She got me here after class by threatening to serenade
me with the first verse of *Teenage Dream* in the middle of the Union.
I've learned that Jodi's big into using intimidation to get her way.

My previous doubts are back with a vengeance. "I told you already.
I just worry that dating Cole is going to mess everything up."

The sun is hiding behind a wall of smoky grey clouds and the air is
thick with the smell of an impending afternoon rainstorm. It's slightly
cooler than it's been for the past few weeks which means that I'm not
sweating. If Florida has a fall, this is it.

"You're overthinking things again. Cole likes you. You like him.
You're going on a date with him tonight because that's what two people do when they like each other. End of story." She shakes out the
colored sugar from the bottom of the bag into her upturned palm.

"I'll admit that kissing Cole was nice," I say slowly. Jodi gives me this are-you-kidding-me look and I amend my statement. "Okay... kissing Cole was sort of mind-blowing. But dating him is a completely different story." I sigh. "I think I should probably just cancel. I don't have anything to wear anyway."

"You are not cancelling." Jodi rolls her eyes. "Because I, for one, am not going to let you talk yourself out of this. I know that there's stuff from before we met that you don't want to tell me about and I'm okay with that, but I've got to be completely honest with you about something."

She's clearly waiting on me so I roll my hands. "What?"

"You're missing out."

I sigh. "Well, that's not exactly news to me. I just..." I glance down at the two Skittles left in my hands. "I don't want to screw with what I've got if it's working just fine."

"Look, Aimee. From everything you've told me so far, going out with Cole is a good thing and you are an idiot if you think otherwise."

"Then maybe I'm an idiot."

"It's going to be okay. Dating is simple because men are very basic. Rule number one is to always keep a guy on his toes. Rule number two is to avoid ordering anything messy like chicken wings or lobster on a first date. Other than that, it's easy. And don't stress out about your clothes because all you have to do is wear something that's either short enough that he can't stop staring at your legs or dips down low enough that he can't stop staring at another one of your assets."

I sneak a peek at my low-profile chest and snort. "Assets?"

Jodi licks the sugar off her hand and keeps going. "Yes, your list of assets is long. In addition to the obvious, I've discovered that you listen to really decent music, you're clever and uninterested in the whole college popularity game, and... well, you know your shit when it comes to Pokémon."

I never should have let it slip that I still have my collection of Pokémon cards. Jodi keeps finding ways to throw it in my face.

"It's true that if we stumble across a battle with another trainer, I'll be ready."

"See."

"Hardy-har-har."

"Aimee, I know that you think I'm just blowing smoke up your ass, but it's the truth. I see all those things and Cole sees them too. Hell, getting him to take you *out* before he takes you *in* is a major coup."

"Umm… thanks?"

Jodi laughs. "You know what I mean… Cole Everly comes across to the rest of the world as your typical arrogant, athletic ass-monkey. It's enlightening to discover that he's not."

We look at each other in silence for a minute and start cracking up. I don't even know why we're both laughing and maybe that's the best part. We just are. And it's… it's new.

I know that I'm not ever going to be able to replace what I had with Jillian, but it feels good to be like this with someone else. And then it dawns on me that even my thoughts are a kind of betrayal. What am I doing? Jillian Kearns isn't going to hear about my upcoming date. She's not going to share a bag of Skittles with me or anyone else. She's gone and she's never coming back. *Ever.* Just thinking about "replacing" her is—

A male voice distracts me from the dangerous path my mind is taking. "What's so funny?"

I turn around and see Kyle standing in the doorway next to the bench that Jodi and I are sitting on. His black hair is spiked up and messy and the sleeves of his t-shirt are ripped, showing off the swirling pattern of colorful tattoos that climb up both of his arms. A long metal chain is attached to the belt loop of his skinny black jeans. To say that this guy intimidates me would be putting it mildly.

"You're done!" Jodi jumps up, brushes past me so quickly that I can practically smell her lust, and sinks into Kyle's chest. He stumbles back and laughs.

"I would hug you back, but…" He holds up two cans of diet coke. Jodi leans away from him and her forehead buckles. "What's this?"

"Earlier you said that you were thirsty and—"

"But why *diet*? Are you implying that I'm fat and need to be on a diet or something?" She steps backward. "Oh my God, Kyle. Are you saying that Aimee is fat too? "

Kyle's expression changes—his dark eyes go wide and his lips tighten. He looks horrified. "No. I didn't mean anything by it. I thought that's what was in your fridge at home so that's what I got from the machine. Shit. I swear that I think you're perfect."

After a handful of tense seconds Jodi breaks into loud laughter. She takes both of the cans away from Kyle and hands one to me. "I'm just fucking with you, babe. This is great. Thanks."

Shaking his head and grumbling under his breath, Kyle grabs her and pulls her back into his body. He loops his long arms around her neck and ducks his face low so that he can whisper something in her ear. Jodi's so tiny that I can barely see her when she's all wrapped up like this, but I can hear her laughter and for the first time in a long time, I want *it*. I want all of it.

"See," she says, freeing her head from Kyle's grasp and glancing over at me. "Always keep them on their toes."

Cole

"So…" I scratch the back of my neck.

She sets down her fork and glances up at me. Her hair is pulled into a loose braid that drips over her right shoulder. She's wearing a light blue dress. She's got on silver earrings that dangle against her jaw when she moves her head. If she tilts just right, I can see the silky strap of her bra peeking out from under the dress. It's pink and for the past hour I've been wondering if she's one of those girls who does the whole matching bra and underwear thing.

"So…" she parrots back.

Maybe I shouldn't have worn a suit. It's so fucking uncomfortable and hot. If there's a hell, I'm guessing that the fucktards that end up there have to wear suits.

I clear my throat and wipe my mouth with the starch white linen napkin from my lap. "Uh—how's your food?"

Aimee looks at me for a long time. Her lips twitch and my stomach clenches tight. She moves her eyes over to where our waiter is stationed against the wall. When she speaks, her voice comes out as a low whisper that only I can hear. "Is it me, or is this really awkward?"

I think about the question.

Shifting in my straight back chair, I look around the ridiculously fancy waterfront restaurant with the white tablecloths and the crystal water glasses and the extra forks that I have no idea what to do with. There's a gaudy chandelier dropping from the ceiling above us and the walls are draped in heavy fabric the color of dried-up blood. The sound that's filtering in through hidden speakers can only be described as a hybrid between elevator music and a funeral dirge.

I'm trying too hard. I squint and feel my mouth creeping up. "Maybe a little?"

Aimee lets out a held breath and half-smiles. It's one of my favorite smiles. "Okay," she says like she's deciding something. "I thought it was just me and I was starting to get a little panicked. Cole, I seriously think that we're the youngest people here by at least fifteen years."

She's probably right. The guy at the table next to me has been messing with his dentures since the hostess walked us over here. "It's Florida. Everyone is old."

Aimee's eyes widen. "Not like *this*. This is geriatric."

Shit. I feel sweat beading at my hairline and I push my hands back through my hair, pulling on the ends. It's not like it should come as a surprise that she's having a terrible time. I haven't taken a girl on a date in… well… ever. It was almost a given that I was going to fuck it up colossally. "I thought that this is the kind of thing that all girls want.

You know—the nice restaurant near the water and the debonair guy in the suit," I gesture to my tie.

"The debonair guy—yes. The other stuff?"

I don't reply right away and Aimee's brow creases. Her fingers wrap around the edge of the table. "I'm sorry," she says quickly. "Was it bad for me to say something? I just wanted you to know that you didn't have to go all out. I would have been fine with Skee-Ball and a corndog."

I cock my head to the side. "You can't play Skee-Ball worth a shit. Remember?"

"I don't think you're allowed to say 'shit' in a place like this, Cole. The waiter is in a tux."

"You're probably right," I agree, easing back into my seat. "So the restaurant was a stupid choice. Does this mean that you're having an awful time? I'm hoping that dates are like everything else and they get better with practice."

"I'm not having an awful time." Her voice is soft but strong and it unglues me instantly. She gnaws on her bottom lip. "I didn't mean what I said in the way that you're thinking. I just don't want us to pretend to be something that we're not, you know? I faked my way through all of last year. It's not... it's not good and I'm trying to be done with all of the fake crap because I know that eventually it catches up to you."

Her expression is fractured and I get the sense that her words are hinting at something else. She's allowing me a rare peek inside, but I don't want it right now. Not in this stuffy-ass restaurant.

"Got it," I say lightly, rubbing my finger over the bump in my nose. "No fakeness and you're not into the flowers and romance stuff."

"Well, I don't remember saying that I wasn't into flowers..."

I chuckle and let my body relax. "Okay. I can work with this. Flowers you like. Corndogs and donuts you like."

"All true. Did I tell you that there's this famous donut place out in Portland called Voodoo that makes a maple syrup donut topped with bacon?"

"That sounds disgusting."

"Don't knock it until you try it."

"Fair enough." I arch my shoulders. "In addition to flowers and bacon-flavored donuts, I've peeked at your kindle so I know that you like books and *Harry Potter* in particular. Even though I've never read the books or seen any of the movies, I think—"

Aimee interrupts me. "You're kidding me, right? *You*, of all people, haven't seen the *Harry Potter* movies?"

I shake my head, enjoying the look on her face. "I know the basic plot and it didn't really seem like my thing."

"Didn't seem like your thing? It's *Harry Potter*! Did you grow up under a rock or something?"

I chuckle. "Turnaround is fair play so maybe we can watch them sometime."

"Well, I think you should read the books first, but that's just my humble opinion. Though I should warn you about something." She places her elbows on the table and that pink bra strap winks at me. I can feel blood drumming in my ears, sliding down through my body. Maybe this date isn't fucked after all. "I have this theory that the world is broken up into two kinds of people."

"Yeah?"

"Yep. On the one side are the people who love the *Harry Potter* books and wish that they could attend Hogwarts and have Ron and Hermione for best friends and vanquish Death Eaters and He-Who-Must-Not-Be-Named."

She's smiling at me, and she's just so fucking cute. I have to ask: "And the other side?"

Aimee shrugs. "Douchebags."

I pretend to be shocked. Then I toss her own words back at her with a smirk. "I don't think you can say the word 'douchebag' in here. I'm not sure if you noticed this or not, but the waiter over there is wearing a tux."

"Oh really?" She scrunches up her nose and I get the sudden, nearly irresistible urge to reach across the table and yank her onto my lap.

"Yes, really." I take a deep breath and pick up the crystal water glass in front of me. "So, what the hell is a Death Eater?"

Aimee's eyebrows pull inward. "A supporter of Lord Voldemort. Basically, that means someone who is intent upon purifying the wizarding world of all muggles."

"What's a mu—You know what? Never mind." I circle the rim of my water glass with my thumb. "So far, we've established that you're a fan of donuts, flowers, corndogs, *Harry Potter*. And I know that you're into artsy—fartsy music…"

"Hey! I listen to good music," she defends.

I smile so that she knows that I'm teasing her. Even though I've never heard of most of the obscure indie bands that Aimee plays, I've reluctantly accepted that they aren't terrible. "Okaaaay… You listen to good music and enjoy singing along in the shower."

Aimee frowns warily. "How in the world do you know that I sing in the shower?"

My chest rumbles in amusement. "I didn't. It was just a random guess, but thanks so much for confirming it."

"Oh." Her cheeks flush pink.

"What else?"

She thinks. "Scrabble."

"You like playing Scrabble?" I mentally record the information for a later date.

"I do."

"Okay. Scrabble, donuts, flowers, corndogs, pre-pubescent British wizards, and indie music. Am I missing anything important?"

She's still blushing and it's like the heat in her face is trapping all the words inside of her. "What is it?" I ask, an involuntary grin tugging on my mouth. I love it when she blushes like this.

Aimee sighs, looks up toward the chandelier. "You, Cole. I like you."

Shit. Shit. Shit. I think my mouth actually drops open.

I'm fucking sunk.

Aimee

Cole's gaze is locked onto mine and his jaw is hanging loose. I think what he's doing is commonly called *gaping*.

It's obvious that he can't believe my bluntness. Well, I guess he can join the club because I can't believe it either.

"I'm sorry. That was insanely cheesy," I say, trying to cover my red face with my hands.

Right now would be the perfect time to slink out of my seat to the floor so that I can hide my embarrassment under the corners of the stiff white tablecloth. Saliva builds on the roof of my mouth and I swallow it down. God. Cole's eyes are so raw with emotion that I'm starting to feel lightheaded. I trace the woven sections of my braid with two of my fingers. "So... do you want to, um, get dessert or something?" I ask haltingly.

Cole doesn't answer me. With fire flashing in his green eyes, he stands up from his chair and reaches for my arm, dragging his hand along my skin from the elbow to the base of my palm. Instinctively, I grip his fingers and let him pull me past the mess of elegant tables and diners. We don't pause at the hostess station or in the waiting area.

A warm rush of humid air breaks over my skin as Cole pushes through the main door of the restaurant. I follow—tripping over my feet, my out of control heart thudding loudly in my ears—as we move past a wall covered in a thick curtain of dark creeping jasmine, to a secluded nook. To one side of us, there's a small koi pond the color of the coppery pennies that line the bottom of it. On the other, I make out a Mediterranean style archway that leads down to the boat docks. Breathing harshly through his nose, mouth set in a grim line, Cole pulls me to an abrupt stop just under the rise of the arch. He lifts his solid arms, effectively caging me between himself and the cool stucco pier at my back.

"What are you doing?" I ask delicately, a nervous energy swirling in the pit of my stomach.

The trickling light catches on the surface of his eyes as he leans in and brushes his lips just under my jawline. My eyelids fall involuntarily and the breath is expelled from my lungs all at once. Still gingerly exploring my throat with his mouth, Cole's strong hands find my waist and he anchors his thumbs just below my navel, fanning his fingers out across the small of my back. I grip his forearms and push back, flattening my shoulders to the solid surface of the pier as I absorb the sensations ripping through my body. Slowly, like it hurts to push the sound off of his tongue, he whispers into the crook of my neck, "Aimee..."

Seconds tumble away from me. They slip from my fingers like rain on clean glass and I am falling with the drops—no definite direction. Cole squeezes my hips and crushes his body closer to mine so that I can feel the hard lines of him through the thin fabric of my dress.

"Cole," I manage in between gasps. "What are we doing out here? My purse is still back at the table."

"Fuck!" He moans ruefully, tearing himself away and pressing the heels of his palms into his eyes. "I can't control myself around you."

Not knowing how to respond, I drop my eyes to my silver sandals and spread my palms on the wall for balance.

"We'll go back inside for your purse and we can get dessert or we can leave if you want to, but first I needed to get you out of there because..." his voice is gruff. "I couldn't stand to not touch you. Please look at me, Aimee."

Too overwhelmed, I shake my head and keep my eyes trained on my toes. "I can't..."

"Please." His hands return to my waist.

Neither one of us speaks or dares to breathe. I know without looking that beyond the archway, the moon is coming out—spilling its reflected light across the dusky sky, lingering on the silhouettes of palm trees and the outline of the single-story buildings across the street. I know that Cole is watching me, waiting with heady intensity for me to do something, anything. The wind changes direction, brushing the tiny hairs on my arms, fluttering the hem of my blue cotton dress around my legs.

I swallow and set my jaw. I think that I'm shaking a little. As soon as my eyes flick up to meet his, a current of energy buzzes from my breasts down to my thighs. Cole's fingers knot together, digging into my back as he bends his head to kiss me. It's a kiss so deep and hungry that it drenches me—soaking every pore of my body, weighing me down, making me go soft in the knees.

He doesn't stop there. He separates my lips and traces the roof of my mouth with his warm, slick tongue and glides the tip across the back of my teeth. He tastes me like this—greedily sliding into me and drawing my body nearer—until my legs are tucked between his hips and I can't tell which one of us is holding the other up.

I slip my hands inside the lapel of his jacket and run my fingers up over the taut muscles of his chest, feeling for his heartbeat through his shirt. When I find it, I flatten my palm over the spot as if I can hold the beats inside of him with just my hand. For a few tangled moments, I am nothing but heat and taste and smell and touch.

"I know," he murmurs into my mouth like he's responding to something I've said. Then he dips his lips to my bare arm and I have to squeeze my eyes shut and arc my back to keep myself from letting go of an embarrassing moan. Secluded or not, this is not the place to come apart.

Seeming to understand, Cole wrenches his mouth away from me. He cups my face between his firm fingers and finds my eyes with his.

"I need to be honest about something," he tells me, maintaining eye contact as he rests his forehead against mine and sweetly kisses the end of my nose. The pads of his thumbs stroke my cheek. "I like you too."

I'm not sure if I feel like laughing or crying or what, but I'll admit that it's nice to just be... *feeling*. I smooth my hands over his hips and lay my cheek on the scratchy fabric of his jacket. One of the discoveries of this night is that Cole Everly can seriously rock a suit and tie.

We stay like this for a long time—me two steps off the stone walkway with my back pressed up against stucco and Cole pressed up against me. No one is around. We might be the only two people left of the planet.

Finally, my thumping heart settles and my legs steady beneath me. I manage a shaky smile. "They do say that honesty is the best policy."

He touches his lips to my temple and muses: "They do say that, don't they?"

Cole

"I have an idea." I reluctantly peel my body from hers. Damn, she feels nice.

Aimee's cheeks are flushed pink, her mouth is pursed in an oval. "What is it?"

"An idea," I say elusively as I trail my knuckles down her biceps and watch in fascination as the tiny hairs on her arm spring up in the wake of my touch. "I'm going to pay our bill so they don't call the cops on us. And you should go inside to get your purse and meet me back here in a few minutes."

She narrows her eyes and makes a sharp clucking sound from the back of her throat. "We're going to leave the restaurant in the middle of dinner?" I nod once. "Where are we going?"

"Not far." I chuckle, enjoying her confusion. "You're going to have to trust me on this. Remember when I told you that a million things could happen?"

The crooked valley on her forehead deepens so I explain myself. "That first day when you tripped over me, I said that if you told me your name a million things could happen…"

Her eyes crinkle at the memory. "Uh-huh. I'm following."

"Well, Aimee Spencer, this is one of those things." I kiss her nose and pinch her butt playfully. "Now go get your purse or we're going to miss it."

"Miss it?"

I make a shooing motion toward the front door of the restaurant. "Go!"

"Okay, okay…" She laughs and skips up the stone walkway toward the door.

I glance over to the moored boat that caught my eye a few minutes ago. People are milling about the upper deck. I can hear the faint tinkle of music and voices.

I inhale and adjust my tie so that it falls straight. I have about two minutes to make this happen. It's a good thing that I'm fast.

Aimee

I lean my chest into the cool metal railing and tip my chin up so that I can see his face. "I can't believe that you expect me to lie. I'm a terrible liar."

Cole's right arm is wrapped around my waist and his left hand is resting on my shoulder. He bends his mouth close to my ear. "I don't expect you to *lie*. I just want you to act happy for…" he surreptitiously checks the enlarged photograph hanging above the appetizer table. Two names are emblazoned in a silvery metallic font across the bottom. "Eric and Bailey. And, honestly, who wouldn't be happy for them? They're damn adorable."

I can't help it. Cole's dimpled grin is contagious. Ten minutes ago he grabbed my hand and tugged me down to the docks and we boarded the *Island Lady*, a chartered dinner yacht complete with a small band and twinkling white lights affixed overhead. At first, I was all coiled nerves and pinched breathing, but so far no one has questioned our presence and I have to admit that it is a beautiful night for a cruise.

"The hostess at the restaurant told me that this is an engagement party," Cole continues, his hot breath lingering in my hair. "And the beauty of crashing a wedding or an engagement party—especially when you happen to be dressed for it—is that everyone on Eric's side thinks that we're with Bailey's side and everyone on Bailey's side—"

"Thinks we're with Eric's side," I finish his sentence. "I've got it, I just..." I run my hands over the smooth deck rail and leave my spread fingers there. "I'm new to the whole crashing scene and I'm slightly nervous."

"But you've seen *Wedding Crashers* before, right?" I open my mouth but Cole puts his hands over my lips and shakes his head. "Never mind. Don't answer that because I already know what you're going to say." He squints one eye and pushes my braid over my shoulder so that it falls down the center of my back. "We'll put it on our to-watch list, but for now I think that I can talk you through the basics."

"Which are?"

"Most importantly, we're going to need fake names. I'll be Axel."

I almost choke. "Axel?"

"Yeah." He laughs. "It's metal as fuck and I think I can pull it off. You can be..." He looks at me like he's thinking hard.

"I can't just be Aimee?"

"Nah, that's no fun. How about Poppy?"

"Poppy?"

Cole nods.

"Okay," I say, rolling my eyes. "Poppy it is. What else do I need to know?"

Cole takes my hand and leads me over to the bar area. The boat engine rumbles somewhere beneath our feet, but overhead the violet-edged sky beckons smoothly. A light, salty wind dances in from the water and lifts the skirt of my dress.

"Well, Poppy… You should have fun, act like you belong and no one will think twice about why they don't know you because half of the people here are unfamiliar." He grabs two water bottles from a tub full of ice and holds one out to me. "And, if possible, avoid Eric and Bailey as much as possible. Just to, you know, be on the safe side."

I take the water bottle from him and scan the upper deck of the boat. The music has picked up a notch and people are starting to dance under the fanning white lights strung up on the deck. Through the crowd, I can make out the soon-to-be-newlyweds through the tinted windows to the interior cabin. Near the appetizer table there's a little girl—maybe five years old—swaying her torso back and forth, cycling her arms like a windmill. "And what's the rule on dancing?"

"Dancing?" Cole takes a sip of water and considers this for a second. "If I'm remembering the rules correctly, dancing is highly encouraged."

"It is?"

Cole nods and looks down the deck. "It helps you blend in."

"Well," I say wistfully, not really believing that I'm about to do this. "Maybe we should."

Cole rubs the back of his neck and smiles crookedly. "Dance?"

"Yeah." I shrug. "Just to blend."

"It would probably be a good idea," he says, seeking out my eyes.

And then we do. Dance. Right there in the middle of a party that we weren't invited to and it's great. It's better than great. It's like the rest of the world falls away and it's just Cole's hands on the small of my back, my cheek pressed into his shoulder and the evening wind kicking up my hair and the bottom of my dress.

Thirteen

Cole

"Stop it," I tell her. "They're going to love you."

Aimee looks over at me. "It's not about that," she says, stuffing a tube of reddish lip gloss into the bag on her lap and flipping the lighted mirror back to the roof of the truck. "I don't care what people think."

She shrugs to emphasize this but I know that she's lying. It's obvious. She cares what my friends think of her and it's stupid and ridiculous and goddamn adorable.

I get it. I've been feeding myself the same pile of lies. I said it out loud even. That it didn't matter what her sister and anyone else in her life thought about me because I'm with her, not them. Then I found myself searching the grocery store for organic roasted garlic hummus because she mentioned her sister liked it, and I wound up at a fucking punk show in the backroom of some sketchy club last Saturday because her friend's sorta-boyfriend wanted to go.

"I'm calling bullshit."

She laughs. "Whatever. You know that you like my bullshit."

"I do."

Silence.

"Hmmm… then why don't you ever stay the night?" Occasionally Aimee does this—surprises me by doing or saying something really forward. It's just another contradiction. She's shy but she's not shy. She's sad but she laughs at my jokes. She's quiet and reserved, but sometimes she starts talking and she doesn't stop. Maybe one of these days I'll figure her out.

"Aimee…" I stress her name slowly like a warning. "I told you—"

"I know what you told me, but—" She bites off her own words and turns to face the window.

"But what?" I wish that I could see her face right now.

"It just feels like… I don't know. For you, there have been all these girls… but with me… maybe you don't want—"

"I do want," I correct.

Aimee sighs. "Never mind. I'm being stupid and insecure, right?"

I grip the steering wheel tight. I want to tell her that I would trade every single touch for one single taste of her… that she's *everything* I didn't know I wanted, but I don't want to freak her out. "Reputations are usually greatly exaggerated but, yeah, I know that there have been 'all these girls.' Shit, Aimee… I hate that you know it too. And those girls? They don't matter to me. I—" I suck in a long breath. "I probably don't deserve it but I'm begging you for the chance to show you that you're different—that I want you for more than… that."

I hear the breath catch. "Okay…" She turns and smiles at me and right on cue, my dick twitches.

"And it hasn't been easy," I admit sheepishly.

"Good, because it's not easy for me either," Aimee says and laughs when my eyebrows go up. "Can we agree that you're staying over tonight?"

"Fuck," I growl, glancing in the rearview mirror. I need to maneuver my truck into a street spot between two cars, but I'm not going to be able to manage this shit if I can't get my head straight. "Let's just talk about it later."

Her mouth goes sideways. "Fine. Right now is about me going with you to a party and meeting your friends."

"Yes. And you have nothing to worry about. I honestly don't give a rat's ass what they think because they're bastards for the most part. But I do like that you care. It's the same for me. Why do you think I let you drag me to that bar on Saturday? You know, the place with the black and red lacquered walls where dreams go to die."

"Are you saying that death-punk or whatever that was called isn't your scene and you went just for Jodi and Kyle?" She teases.

I kill the ignition and turn so that I can look at her. My right hand automatically goes the side of her face. Fuck. Her skin is so soft and warm. Now that I know that I'm allowed, I'm always touching her. I can't seem to stop myself.

She closes her eyes, bends her cheek into my palm, and my greedy dick starts to harden even more. I lean forward—close enough that her breath tickles my mouth and nose. "No," I say quietly. "I did it for you."

Aimee

The party feels like a test. *How well can you pull off this whole normal thing, Aimee?*

Cole says that it doesn't matter how tonight goes and maybe he's telling the truth. Maybe it really doesn't matter to him.

The truth is that it matters to me.

As soon as we walk in, we're assaulted with the loud, brassy thump of music and voices that are even louder. The house is full to the brim with people pressing into the high-ceilinged living room from all sides. The furniture has been pushed to one wall to form a makeshift dance floor in the center of the room and there's a group—mostly girls—grinding and sweating with their bright red plastic cups held high in the air. The bitter smell of weed filters out of a narrow hallway to my nose.

Everything about the scene reeks of familiarity. House parties used to be the norm for me. *This* used to be the norm. Smiling, laughing, flirting, dancing, drinking, getting stoned.

The last party I went to was on the night that Jillian died. Standing here just inside the front door, I can't help but think of her with her hair down around her shoulders and that blue shirt on. She was laughing. She was *always* laughing.

"Give them to me," she said as she took my keys out of my hand and stuffed them in the front pocket of her shorts. "You're toasted my dear."

I pursed my lips and cocked one eyebrow. "And you're not?"

She smiled cockily, pushed her bangs out of her face. "I'm fine."

But I knew better.

I knew it. *Didn't I?*

"You okay?" Cole shouts above the noise.

I nod stiffly and swallow.

"Let's go outside. "He links his fingers with mine and pulls me closer to his body. "I'm guessing that's where the guys are."

I follow him, squeezing through the bodies and trying to ignore some of the looks that I'm getting. A blonde girl with impossibly long legs and in-your-face breasts is openly scowling at me from the other side of the room. She has one of those faces that you remember and I place her as the girl that Cole was with on the day that I met him. *Kate,* he'd said her name was. Kate and her friends are whispering about something and I can't help but think that the *something* is me.

Cole looks back once and smiles reassuringly but a nasty sensation has already slithered down my throat.

I wish Jilly were here, I think suddenly. She'd push a finger into my side and say something generically reassuring like *just go with it,* or *show 'em what you're made of,* and I'd roll my eyes and tell her that she was being silly and clichéd, but secretly I'd feel better.

Still holding my hand, Cole leads me down a set of wide wooden steps to an exterior porch spanning the length of the house. Floodlights angle down from opposite corners, spilling circles of yellowish light over the space. A badly made tiki bar surrounded by mismatched stools is leaning against one wall. Just beyond the porch railing, there's a long rectangular table where some guys are playing beer pong.

We're met with a chorus of greetings. "Everly!"

Everyone here seems to know Cole and the attention brings him to life. He makes an effort to introduce me to a few of the guys from the track team but I think it's clear that I'm not part of this world—*his* world. There's a lot of backslapping, talk of races, and inside jokes that I don't understand.

Cole gets roped into a game of beer pong and I hang back, preferring to be where thoughts can needle around my head without anyone noticing. After each throw he looks over his shoulder and winks at me, sending a rush of chills to my toes. A couple of nearby girls make a partial attempt to include me in their conversation, but I'm distracted and eventually they give up and leave me to myself.

Right after Cole sinks his last shot, his phone beeps with an incoming text. I glance down to where he left it on the top of the tiki bar. The sender is someone named Christine.

Are you coming back to Gainesville soon? My bed is lonely.

Instantly, I know that he must have seen this girl when he went to Gainesville to race in the triathlon a couple weeks ago and my heart seizes frantically. I can hardly breathe over the sensation of betrayal swimming in my belly. That was the same weekend that I was thinking about him obsessively.

"Hey." Cole is at my shoulder. He slips one arm around my waist and slides his palm across my lower back to my hip. When I feel his lips against my ear, a surge of heat burns its way down my spine.

"Hey." I jerk my head away, pretending to be distracted by my phone.

Cole steps around me so that he can see my face. He pulls on the ends of his blond hair and frowns. "Is everything okay?"

The lump in my throat expands, threatening to suffocate me. I attempt to smile but I'm pretty sure that it comes off closer to a grimace. "Yeah, of course. Why wouldn't it be okay?"

"You seem…" He twists his fingers farther into his hair. "I don't know… You seem like you're irritated or something."

"Maybe you just don't know me very well," I spit out a lot harder than I intend.

His head moves back in surprise. He clenches his jaw and narrows his eyes like he's wondering what the hell my problem is. Well, good for him because I'm wondering the same thing.

I take a shallow breath and turn to watch the progress of the current beer pong matchup. After a few minutes of silence I hear Cole reach around me for his phone.

"Aimee?" His tone is cautious.

I release a breath that I didn't realize that I'd been holding, but I keep my eyes on the game.

"Aimee." This time his voice is stronger, demanding my attention.

I keep my face relaxed and neutral despite the torrent of emotions swirling inside of me. "What?"

"Something is obviously bothering you." Cole holds up his phone, his gaze direct under the straight line of his eyebrows. "Is this text the problem?"

"No." I lie stubbornly.

A flash of green tells me that he's not buying it. "It's not?"

"No." I close my eyes and sigh. My heart is throbbing with nervous energy, sending blood to my cheeks. "I mean, yes, it's bothering me. But...but... you don't have to explain." Maybe I'm overreacting. Cole has made no secret of his history with other girls. I knew the score the day that I met him. It's old news. "She was from before, right? It's in the past and none of my business and even if..." I quickly amend my words. "And even now, it's not like—well, we don't owe each other anything yet. What's happening between us doesn't have to be official or... whatever."

"Or whatever?" Cole pauses, scrapes his hands over his mouth. When he speaks again, his words come out slow and I feel every crack in his voice like a prick against my skin. "I don't even know what to say to you right now. If I claim that when I was with that girl, I was pissed and hurting over you, I sound like even more of a jerk. If I could just..." He squeezes his eyes closed. "You have every right to be mad and I wouldn't blame you if you hate me right now, but... I..."

"God. I don't hate you. I-I don't know what I'm feeling but it's not hate." I look up at the night sky to keep tears from rolling down my face. "We weren't together then and I-I think more than anything I want us to start from now. From *this* moment. I don't want my past to drag us down and I don't want yours to either."

Cole cups my face and wipes his thumb over a tear. "Do you mean that? Because I swear that you're it for me. I'm all in this thing if you are."

I shiver, remembering the first time that Cole told me that. I want to trust him. I do.

"I wish I could take it all back," he continues softly. "I wish... damn it... I wish that I could change it all and start all over but I can't. I'm trying to prove that it's not like that with us, but I keep fucking everything up, don't I?" His shoulders seem to deflate a bit.

I swallow down the lump in my throat and shake my head. "You're not fucking everything up, Cole."

He raises his brow and slides his thumb down to my chin. "I'm not?"

"No." I bite my lip, the burn from his fingertips beginning to liquefy my body. "I can't pretend to be completely okay but you're right that you can't go back. None of us can. And, honestly, your life isn't my business."

"Not your business?"

"You know what I mean."

"Aimee, come here," he says gruffly, eating the remaining space between us and hooking his arm around the dip in my lower back. He lowers his face to my hair and inhales deeply. After a minute, he whispers, "I want to be your business."

"Was she anything to you?" I ask into his chest.

Cole thinks about my question for a long time. His arm tightens and his hand comes up to cup the back of my head. "No, Aimee. Don't you get it? No one has ever been anything to me until you."

• • •

We leave the party early and Cole drives us back to my place.

"Come inside." I'm awkward but determined.

Cole's quiet. He moves his hand over that small bump in his nose and makes a funny sound. "I can't seem to make myself tell you no, can I?"

"Is that going to be a problem?"

He laughs and follows me up the walk to the townhouse. As I search for the keys, I can feel his breath moving over the back of my neck and the delicate pressure of his fingers at my waist. A force moves inside of me, rocking me back into the channel formed by his arm and body. His warm hand comes around me and slides down my ribs to graze the sensitive skin under my shirt.

"Focus," he chuckles soft and low, plucking the keys out of my open purse and placing them in my quivering fingers.

By the time I manage to get the door open, my lungs are pumping rapidly and I'm a bundle of hemmed in tension. I move through the hall quickly and stop at the threshold of my dark bedroom. Cole is behind me, breathing as hard as I am, using his right thumb to make a jagged path up my arm.

"I love the way that you taste," he says as he pushes my hair aside and kisses my neck.

In one fluid movement, I turn my body, slip my hands under the bottom of his shirt, and press my hungry mouth to his. The floor shifts beneath my feet as Cole walks us through the doorway into my room. We stumble in the dark and collide with the edge of my dresser.

"Oomph."

"This way," I rasp out.

Not breaking our contact, my entire body burning with want, I urge him toward the bed and pull his weight down on top of me. Cole flattens his palms on either side of my waist and pushes his knee between my legs. My fingers brush across the soft line of hair that disappears under his waistband and travel up to explore the smooth skin of his chest. When I graze his hardened nipples, he makes a low sound from the back of his throat and flexes his arms. His face dips to my neck and I feel his tongue move across my collarbone and over the raised skin of my scar.

Too hollowed out to fight my impulse or be embarrassed, I let my thighs fall open and push my hips up in a request. "Please?"

"If I don't stop soon, I won't be able to," he warns in a croaky voice as he rubs his thumb over the button of my jeans.

My pulse is jumping up and down. I tangle my fingers in his hair and pull his head against my tingling breasts. "I—I don't want you to stop."

Silence. A draft of cool air sneaks in over my skin.

Finally: "Are you sure?"

I'm sure that I want Cole Everly's hands on me—on *all* of me. I can just make out his eyes shining and the outline of his face in the shadowed room. I trace a line down the center of his body, over his neck and sternum and the rigid contours of his chest, until my fingertips are resting below the waistband of his pants. I can feel the soft, silky fabric of his boxers and the crest of springy hairs.

"I'm sure." I lean in and nip at his earlobe.

"Fuck." Cole moans and automatically grinds his pelvis in a circular motion against me.

"I remember telling you that I wanted you to stay over tonight."

"That was before the party. I didn't want to assume that the offer still stood," he grits out, his control clearly as frayed as mine.

"Trust me. The offer still stands."

Cole pushes my hair away from my face, tucks it behind my ears, and bends until I can feel his breath tickle the sensitive skin just below my earlobe. When his tongue flicks out, I shiver and arch my back off the bed.

Suddenly, there is too much fabric between us. I want to feel his hot skin against mine. I tug the bottom of his shirt and he seems to understand my silent signal because like me, he sits up in the dark and pulls his shirt above his head. Then he's back, kissing my lips and rubbing his hands over the scratchy fabric of my jeans. He moves to my breasts, paying careful attention to them with his mouth and I grip his solid muscles, gasping for air like I can't get enough oxygen. He picks up my hair from my neck and lets it fall forward over my shoulder.

Murmuring things that I can't understand, Cole moves above me. He holds his weight on his arms and he looks at me like... well, like he's not sure that I'm real. And, honestly, inside this moment I'm not sure that I *am* real. Slowly, he lifts my open palm to his mouth and kisses it. I smile, shiver, and wrap my arm around his shoulder to draw him down to me.

"You don't just taste good... You smell good too. Like sunlight," he whispers huskily against my neck, his free hand running over the swell of my hip to my thigh.

I groan, weave my fingers into the strands of his hair, and press my head back into the pillow. "I didn't know sunlight had a smell," I manage.

He laughs and my stomach tightens at the sound. "Neither did I. But that was before I met you."

"Ahhh," I murmur as skilled fingers graze up my leg to cup the inside of my thigh.

"Perfect," he says. And then he's at my feet, pulling my shoes off, sliding my jeans off my legs, trailing a line of soft kisses across my waist.

One finger. Two fingers. When his whole hand slips under my panties, I can't help the needy sound that escapes from my mouth. My hands rake down the length of his muscular back to the rise of his butt. Then I'm fumbling with his pants, earnestly pushing them down over his hips with the soles of my feet, grabbing at his bare skin.

God. He's unbelievable. Clothes don't do his body justice and I wish that I could see him clearly right now, but then I think of the scar on my body and my pale skin and I'm glad for the dark.

"Aimee." He clasps my face between his fingers and pulls me to his mouth. His tongue is hot, sliding into the crease of my lips. He skims my stomach with his hand and gently tugs my right nipple between his thumb and his finger.

"Oh my God." I roll my head to the side and bite down my bottom lip.

Cole's hand moves to my other breast and I think I might combust before we get to the main event. His mouth roams down my throat and the rough stubble around his jaw burns my skin but I don't want him to stop. Ever.

"Don't stop," I say out loud.

Cole chuckles, pushes away and reaches to the floor beside the bed for his pants. I hear the tear of the condom wrapper and I close my eyes in anticipation.

"Aimee… you're shaking," he says quietly, his mouth back at my ear.

"Not in a bad way," I whisper, guiding his hips so that our bodies are aligned. I *am* trembling, but it's not from fear. It's the opposite.

"Damn," he moans into my neck. "You already feel so good. I…"

The weight of him is pressing into every part of me and I am so stirred and lightheaded that I think if it were possible to levitate, that's what I would be doing right now.

I reach down with my hands. Cole sucks in a sharp breath and then he's entering me, filling me from the inside out. I close my eyes and grip the bed sheets. There's just so much to feel that I can't—

"Aimee." Cole's soft voice snaps me out of my head. In the dark, he kisses my eyelids one at a time, then he pulls back and his eyes search mine. "Are you with me?"

I can barely lift my voice to a whisper. "I'm with you."

Cole

I've never been a cuddler.

I'm a love 'em and leave 'em kind of guy and as soon as the condom's off, I'm usually out the door. I know that makes me sound like a jackass but it's the truth. Cuddling after sex is messy and hot and fucking uncomfortable. Who needs to put up with that shit? Not me.

Until now.

Apparently I'm becoming a cuddler because here I am, wrapped up in an Aimee Spencer blanket, and I swear that it will take a fucking natural disaster to get me out of this bed. Shit. Even then I'll need some serious persuading.

I love this girl's body. She's slim with narrow hips and limbs that just keep going. Her tits are only a handful but that's okay because I don't need any more than that. Everything about her is warm and tight and even with her here—right underneath me—I can't seem to stop fantasizing about her in every different position. I've just left her and it's like I can't wait to go back. That's never happened to me before.

I exhale through my teeth and give myself a shake.

My fingers are making patterns down her back and I bend to nuzzle her long, silky hair. Our bare bodies are meshed together skin-to-skin and it's perfect. Fucking perfect. She's got one knee crooked over my hip so that my cock is nestled in between her warm thighs and I have no words to describe how good it feels.

"What did you think of me when you first saw me?" She asks quietly and I almost laugh because it's such a girl thing to ask.

"Aside from the fact that you were gorgeous?" I feel her smile against my chest and I want to high-five myself like an asshole because she likes my answer. "I wanted to know more about you. I wanted to know your thoughts on teacher shortages and mandatory drug sentencing laws. I wanted to ask you how you got this scar," I lightly trace the thin pink line down her neck and she gasps. "I wanted to climb inside your bright blue eyes and never come out of them."

I sound like a complete pussy and I don't fucking care.

Aimee needles one finger into my side. She's laughing. Apparently she likes me acting like a pussy. "Flattery will get you nowhere."

"Flattery?" I rotate my leg and push up with my hips, flipping her over onto her back in one smooth motion. "That's not flattery, Aimee. It's the truth. And I'd get used to it if I were you because I plan to show you a lot of truths."

She reaches up and touches my face with the tips of her fingers. There's so much that I want to ask her. So much that I want to know. I grip her shoulders and bury my face in her neck.

"Cole," she whispers my name like a prayer. My heart accelerates. I kiss her deeply. Then I draw her earlobe into my mouth and suck it between my teeth. She moans and her knees fall to the sides inviting me in, and I feel like a god. A Titan. An immortal. This is better than winning races. This is better than just about anything.

I capture her hands and bring them up over our heads. It's new but I think it's safe to say that I love this—her pinned beneath me, our bodies slowly rocking in unison. My tongue glides across the ridge of her collarbone. Down. I take one of her soft pink nipples into my mouth.

"Oh God!" She rolls her chest and pulls up against my hands. I squeeze her wrists and push them farther into the mattress to let her know that I'm not going to make this easy on her.

"Tell me," I say in a conversational tone as my mouth skims the bumps of her ribs and moves farther down her body. "What did you think of me when you first saw me?"

Aimee pants and her body tenses beneath mine. "You mean aside from the part where I thought you were gorgeous?"

I chuckle against her warm skin. "Yeah. Aside from the obvious." My wet tongue dips into her bellybutton and I hear her suck in a sharp breath. I lift my head and rest my chin on her stomach. "What else, Aimee?"

"I—I thought…" Fuck. Her breathing is crazy hard and it's such a turn on. I'm not sure that I'll make it through my little game. "I don't know. I g-guess that I was a little scared."

I stiffen. That's not the answer that I was looking for. "Why would you be scared of me?"

Aimee tilts her head and her eyes meet mine. They are desperate—nailing me in place. "Because I knew that you could change everything."

Fourteen

Cole

On Sunday afternoon I tell Aimee to get her bathing suit on because I'm taking her to the beach.

The truck windows are down and the air is rushing in all around us. She leans her head toward the open window and her loose hair whirls in over her face. Once, when she comes closer, I get whipped in the eye by a long dark tendril but I don't ask her to put it up because I like it. I like *her*. I like her this way—smiling and all sunlit and relaxed like she's something other than sad.

I follow her through a canopy of palm trees to an open stretch of white sand. She drops her bag and kicks off her flip-flops and shorts and I stand back and appreciate the sight. She's so incredibly hot in a dark green bikini and I can tell that she doesn't even know it.

After opening up both towels, she braids her hair to one side and asks me if I want lotion. I don't really give a shit about getting burned but I like the idea of her hands on my body so I say yes. And when she's rubbing circles in my skin, her slender fingers sliding over my shoulders and down my arms, I start wishing that we were alone. I close my eyes and lean my back against her front so that I can feel the perky mounds of her breasts. She stills. In those few quiet seconds the

173

world blurs and comes back into focus. Then Aimee sighs and wraps her arms across my chest and she kisses my neck. I feel her eyelashes flutter against my jawline. Fuck me.

We lie out on our towels and pass our phones back and forth to take turns choosing songs. I get her an ice cream cone because she saw some kid with one and started drooling. Two scoops. One chocolate and one strawberry. She lets me have a few licks and when I run my tongue from the cone to her wrist, she laughs and flicks ice cream at me. I lick all of the way to her elbow. She's sweet and sticky and I'm getting caught up in all of it—all of *this*.

After awhile, the blue water starts calling out to me. I tilt my head and make a sound and it's like she can tell what I'm thinking because she squeals and makes a go for it but I'm a lot faster. I run track for Christ's sake. It would be pretty fucking disappointing if I couldn't catch up to my girl.

Under a breezy sun-filled sky, I scoop her up by the waist and make a big show of throwing her into the surf. She sputters, splashes, swims out past me and resurfaces. If she was beautiful before, she's unbelievable in the water. I go to her, lower my head to her skin. Her shoulders are salty and tipped with sun. Today she tastes the way that the air feels.

Later, when we're back on the sand, our bodies warm and raw with dried saltwater, I thread my fingers with hers and I think about telling her how I feel. I turn to her, take her chin in my hands and kiss her deeply. That's when I hear the scream.

There's a lady at the shoreline yelling her head off and people are jumping up from their towels going apeshit. I quickly figure out that it's because some little kid went under and didn't come back up. Within seconds, I'm moving into the rolling water along with a bunch of others, my heart pumping furiously and my eyes scanning in every direction. And that's when the fucking kid comes up and he's waving and smiling and it's clear that it was all a game to him.

"Holy shit." I look at this guy who is standing to my right and we both sort of laugh nervously. When I get back to Aimee, I'm still shaky with adrenaline.

"He was pretending to be a dolphin," I say in a can-you-believe-this-shit voice. That's when I see her face.

She's so white that she looks transparent and her eyes are wide and blank. I know in an instant what she's thinking of and I can't stand it. I pull her into my chest and I cup her head with my palm. I tell her it will be okay but I'm not sure if that's what she wants to hear.

• • •

"I drove after Jillian died," she says simply.

I look over at her and I wonder if I heard her right. We're back in my truck and this is first thing that she's said since we left the beach. I shift in my seat but I don't make a sound.

Aimee continues to stare out the window so that all I can make out is the back of her head in the dying daylight. Her legs are curled up on the truck bench beneath her. "People just assume that I don't drive because of the accident and I get that, you know? It makes sense because she died in my car." She stops, catches her breath. "Did you know that it wasn't the impact of the crash that killed her? Everyone thought so at first... but it was actually the water. That was what the coroner told us in the hospital."

"Aimee..."

She twists her body around but her head is still bent to the door. I think about pulling the truck over so that I can look at her and see into her eyes. This feels important.

"I don't drive because I can't drive. I have a suspended license."

My head is spinning in too many directions. But she wasn't even driving the car that night. How would she have a suspended license?

Aimee sees the thoughts spilling out of me and answers them. "Last June," she whispers. "I took a bunch of pills and crashed my car into the side of my grandparent's house." She pauses. "I tried to kill myself, Cole."

Aimee

I'm not sure what to expect after my revelation. Curiosity? Disgust? Pity? All week I steel myself for the inevitable reaction and the questions but they never come.

Cole is just... well... he's the same.

And that's weird. *Very weird.*

"Pamela, you've met my daughters, haven't you? Mara and," my mother's eyes dart to mine, "Aimee. They're both in college now."

We're on the patio of the country club eating a late lunch. Dad is finishing up a round of golf with Mr. Frank, whom my mom revels in describing as "influential."

I lean back, shading my eyes from the sun with my forearm. Green crowds my vision and sweat drips down my forehead over my nose. I feel like I'm in hell.

"Of course I remember Mara and Aimee," Pamela says with a polite nod, her eyes lingering on me for a second too long. She's a few years older than my mom and she's so thin that I can see the bones of her shoulder joints through her pastel tennis shirt. I'm trying to place her in my parent's catalog of completely boring, waspish friends and I'm pretty sure that her husband is some kind of attorney. "It's lovely to see you both. What are you girls majoring in at school?"

Mara goes first. She taps her fingernails on the outside of her iced tea glass and smiles like the pro that she is. "Finance."

"Just like her father. She's also social chair of her sorority and she just joined up with the school's competitive debate team," our mom adds proudly.

Pamela turns to me. "And you, Aimee? What's your major?"

"Undecided," I say with as much fake cheer as I can muster. "But I'm leaning toward Library Sciences."

Pamela's smile wobbles. "And what is that, dear?"

"Oh, you know…" I take a bite of my salad and make everyone wait while I chew and swallow. "I would be working in a library."

Her brow furrows. "Like a librarian?"

I point my fork in Pamela's direction. "Exactly."

"Oh."

Oh.

Mom looks uncomfortable. She clears her throat and says, "Aimee is just in her freshman year so she's still got plenty of time to explore her options."

Thanks for the vote of support. I dig at my salad and chew vigorously, too annoyed to pay attention to the rest of the conversation. I despise coming to the club because it always ends up with me wading through a swamp of awkwardness.

I look up and catch Mara's eyes on me. She smiles sympathetically before going back to her sandwich. After Pamela walks away, my sister steers talk in the direction of our mom's favorite topic: her social calendar.

Mom clasps her hands in front of her chest. "Let's see," she says. "This Wednesday is the annual mixer we put on to benefit that animal shelter east of Regent's Harbor. It's a no-kill shelter and I'll tell you, that costs money. Vet bills, food expense… the building maintenance. It's a nightmare." She pauses, signals to the waiter that she needs a refill. "Oh, and then Saturday night we're going to The Roberson's for a gala. I think that one has something to do with some kind of cancer, or maybe it's Alzheimer's." She waves her hand and smiles. "Whatever it is, I'm sure that it's dreadful."

Elise Spencer is nothing if not charitable.

"Mara," she goes on, eyes narrowing at my sister. "I actually thought that you might want to drive down next month because we're having a little event at the house for your father's firm. It would be the perfect opportunity to introduce you to that Langley boy that I was telling you about. I'm sure that he'll be there with his parents."

"I don't know, Mom. What about Aimee? Maybe she wants—"

Mara makes a sound and abruptly drops her gaze to the table.

"What is it?" I ask.

Mom's face stiffens. Then she shakes her head and fidgets with her silverware. "Not to change the subject, but Mara, didn't you have a big test last week?"

"What is with you both?" I blow out an exasperated breath and turn in my chair to scan the patio. When my eyes land on them, all of the air is forced out of my lungs.

"Aimee..." Mom's face is deeply flushed. "I swear that I haven't see the Kearns here in ages. Nancy told me that they'd given up their membership. I—oh my..." She touches her forehead and squeezes her eyes shut. "I never would have asked you to come today if I thought there was a possibility that they'd be here."

"Don't worry. I'm not going to embarrass you," I hiss.

My mother flinches like I've just slapped her. She coughs, clears her throat. "That's not what I... Aimee, how could you think that?" She tentatively reaches forward and pushes my hair off my shoulder. "Just remember to take deep breaths. Dr. Galindo said that would help with a panic attack."

"I'm not having a panic attack." *Am I?* I glance back to where Jillian's parents are talking with another couple. Her dad is wearing khaki pants and a crisp white button down and he's leaning one hip up against the metal bannister. Mrs. Kearns is beside him in a floral dress with a small collar. Her hair is shorter, greyer than I remember and I realize that she doesn't look happy or sad. She just looks tired.

"Do you want to go?" Mara asks me gently.

I pick up my glass just so that I have a second to think. "I—I'm fine. Let's..." As if she can sense me, Mrs. Kearns shifts her head to the right slightly and, just like that, we're looking at each other. I want to go to her and hug her or fall on my knees, but she just goes on staring at me and, my head spinning wildly, I stare back.

This is a woman who made me pancakes shaped like Mickey Mouse on Sunday mornings and helped me get gum out of my hair in the fourth grade. Armed with a needle and thread, she fixed the strap of my first cotillion dress when it broke right before the dance. This is also a woman who barred me from her daughter's funeral and told me that she never wanted to see my face again and wished that it had been me stuck in that car.

My mouth silently forms the words before I realize what I'm doing. *I'm sorry.*

Dry-mouthed, white fingers clenching my thighs, I wait for her reaction. One. Two. Three. I take a deep breath and count again. It's like I'm bleeding out onto the club's patio and waiting for Mrs. Kearns to notice.

One. Two. Three. Deep breath. One. Two. Three. Before I can take another breath, Jillian's mother flutters her eyes, wraps her arms around her body and walks away.

Fifteen

Cole

I blink against the bright sunlight to make sure that I'm not seeing things. I'm stretching out with the team on the grassy lawn in the center of the track. Today we're hosting an informal invitational—just a chance for the division teams to showcase what they're capable of. I sure as shit hadn't planned to push myself, but then Aimee surprises me by actually showing up.

"Isn't that your girlfriend?" Quentin elbows me just below my ribs.

With hungry eyes, I swallow and watch her make her way up the stands. She's wearing a pair of shorts and a plain white top that molds to her chest like a second skin. The air is heavy with humidity so she's piled all that hair of hers on the top of her head in a messy bun and a few strands have fallen down to play with her neck. When she sees me, she smiles a wide, toothy grin and waves.

Quentin shakes his head. "She's got a killer body, man. Be sure to give her my number when she finally figures out what a shithead you are."

I don't know if I'm pissed because he's looking at her or if it's because I'm not really allowed to call her my girlfriend since that's a label that has yet to be approved. "She's not my girlfriend. And don't fucking stare at her. It's rude."

"Not your girlfriend?" Quentin cocks his head to the side. "But she is your girl, right?"

I pull on the back of my neck and frown at him. "Yeah, I guess…"

"Then chill, man." He hooks his arm around my shoulders. "The rest is just semantics."

Maybe he's right. I want to believe it.

I'm up in the third heat. Kicking out my legs and rotating my ankles, I settle in at the start. I can feel the tingle of Aimee's eyes on me and my heart pounds harder than ever. When the high-pitch signal sounds, I push off and I swear that my feet sprout fucking wings.

As I cross the finish line going full out, my body completely jacked-up, I know without seeing the digits on the clock that not only have I easily trounced the pack, I've just run my fastest time. It's mayhem. The guys are on me all at once, yelling and slapping me on the back, hooting in my ears. Pushing back, I lift my eyes to the stands and find her. She's jumping up and down and clapping like everyone else and this crazy, awesome feeling zips through me and it's all I can do not to hop the barrier to the bleachers and go to her.

Much later, after I win in the finals and we celebrate with a large pizza and a bottle of warm champagne that I stole from Adam, I watch her while she sleeps. She's cocooned between my arms and the pillow with the soft light from the TV playing across her features. Using one finger, I trace the faint jagged line of her scar. I kiss each of her eyelids. Her sooty lashes flutter and she mumbles but she doesn't wake up. I smile and kiss her again, just craving her skin and everything that is inside of this moment.

I wish that she could stay like this—peaceful, no trace of the fear or sadness that she wears around during the day. I hate what she told me last week about the pills and the fucking car. I keep thinking of her voice and how small she had seemed curled up on the seat of my truck.

Suicide. It's goddamn terrifying. I can't wrap my head around the fact that this beautiful, brilliant girl ever considered ending her life.

"Hey you," she murmurs, blinking her eyes open. She lifts her arm and runs her finger from the top of my forehead down the center of my face. "What are you thinking about? You look so sad."

I grip her wrist. I am sad but I don't want to tell her that. "Didn't you have anyone else after Jillian died?"

Her eyelids fall closed and she's quiet for so long that I start to think she's fallen back into sleep. Then, she swallows purposefully and I know that she's still awake.

"No," she says finally. "I didn't need anyone else until Jillian died."

I'm quiet, thinking. Aimee's arm relaxes over my chest and she wraps her leg over mine. When her breathing has evened out and I know that she's gone back to sleep, I pull her body closer and breathe in the scent of her hair. "Now you have me."

Aimee

insecurity [in-si-kyoo r-it-ee]
noun, plural in-se-cu-ri-ties.
1. lack of confidence; self-doubt
2. the state of being insecure

"It's Aimee, right?"

I pop an earbud out and I look up and see bright purple fingernails tapping the barrier that surrounds my study carrel.

"I'm Kate Dutton." She drops into the seat next to mine and leans back. Her light blonde hair is wound into a loose knot below her left ear. She's wearing fitted shorts and a lime green tank top. Her earrings are tiny golden starbursts. "Alpha Chi in case you were curious.

I actually know your sister from a couple of Greek events. Oh, and obviously I know Cole."

I don't say hello or tell her that I already know her name. I don't ask her what she wants. I just sit there with one white earbud dangling and a blank expression on my face.

"You're really pretty," she says, surprising me. Kate Dutton is honestly one of the prettiest girls that I've ever seen. I don't want it to be true but she's better up close than she was from far away. She's got straight teeth and perfect golden skin—the kind you see on models in magazines post-Photoshop. Sitting here next to her makes me feel dark and pocked and small. "Not that I'm surprised about that. It's par for the course, right?" When I still don't talk, Kate shrugs, makes a funny face. "I just saw you and I figured that I should introduce myself. Considering…"

I swallow. "Considering what?"

She smiles brazenly. "Considering that soon you'll be like me and all of the other disposable pretty girls. Passed over for fresh blood."

Cole

"Wait a second!" Her hand darts out to the side table. "What is that ringtone?"

"It's nothing." I climb on top of her and grab the phone from her hand. She starts laughing and poking me in the stomach just below my belly button.

"Umm, that's not nothing." Her nose twitches. "Cole, is that… *Rihanna?*"

I silence my phone and settle my head back into the bed pillow. "For your information, Rihanna is my little sister's favorite."

"That was Sophie calling?"

I nod warily.

She crosses her arms over her chest. "Why didn't you answer it?"

"Because I know that she'll want to FaceTime and I'm…" I look around her bedroom and down at her bare, creamy breasts, and I smirk. "I'm *here* in your bedroom, and you're pretty close to being buck naked. That's not exactly the message I want to send to a thirteen year old girl."

"Excuse me? Are you trying to call me a slut?" She pushes herself out of the bed and finds her shirt on the floor.

My hands are over my head, showing that I'm defenseless. "I would never call you a slut. In fact," I laugh, "I think that I like you slutty. I simply m—"

She cuts me off, slipping the wrinkled shirt over her head. "Forget it, Everly. Call your sister back."

"Now?" I ask, kind of enjoying this bossy side of her.

Aimee is digging around her desk drawer for something. She looks over her shoulder and smiles impishly. "Yes. Now."

"But…"

"No buts, Cole." She finds a rubber band and starts winding her dark hair into a knot. I love watching her do mundane things like this. "I'm dressed now and I want to see what she looks like."

"You've seen photos." It's true. I showed her some pictures of Sophie the other day.

"I want to see her with *you*." Her voice is subdued and it instantly unhinges me. The mattress dips as she rejoins me on the bed and bends her legs under her butt.

"Yeah?" I trail my finger down the slope of her nose.

"Yes, so put your shirt on too. We don't want your sister to get the wrong idea about us."

Feeling a bit of a rush, I laugh from deep in my chest. "Okaaaay, bossy lady."

Aimee props herself up a bit straighter and waits. The phone rings twice before Sophie answers. I can tell right away that she's in the backyard of our house. Her long blonde hair is speckled in sunlight and the ridiculous dog is wheezing and slobbering all over her.

I launch right into it. "Sophie, I got that dog to keep you company, not turn you into a slimy ball of drool."

"Awww, be nice. You know that Babs can't help it. She's just excited to talk to you. I told her it was you calling and she ran over here as fast as her little legs would carry her."

"I should have gotten you a lab or some kind of real dog. That thing looks like she's missing half her face."

"Hey! She's a pug and that's how she's supposed to look," Sophie defends. Then her eyes zero in on the screen and I can almost hear the squeal before it even begins. "Who's that? Is it *Aimee*?"

Aimee looks at me with surprised eyes. Did she think she was a secret or something?

"Yes," I say turning the phone. "Sophie, this is Aimee. Aimee, this is my bratty little sister, Sophie."

"Ohmigosh, it's so nice to meet or, um, talk to you finally. I thought you might be a fake person or like a figment of his imagination because Cole *never* has a girlfriend, but here you are. You're real and you're so pretty."

Aimee flushes pink. I wonder what she thinks of the "girlfriend" comment. She takes the phone out of my hand so that she can see my sister better. "Not as pretty as you. And your dog there is adorable. Don't listen to what your brother says about her. I've always loved pugs and when I was your age, I begged my parents for a dog but my sister is allergic. I thought we should get a dog anyway and get rid of her."

Sophie laughs and they talk some more about the dog. Then my sister changes the direction of the conversation. "So, Aimee... my brother has told me *so* much about you."

Aimee's eyebrows go to the top of her head. Her gaze slides over to me. "He has? All good stuff I hope."

Sophie giggles. "Of course it's good. Actually, it's better than *good*. For the past few weeks, every time your name comes up he starts gush—"

"That's enough!" I interject. It's okay for Aimee to know that I've mentioned her to my little sister. She does not need the detailed play by play. Taking the phone back, I lean on my side. "So, how is he?"

Sophie knows that I mean our dad. She shrugs. "I guess he's fine. We had dinner together Tuesday night. I made us tacos."

"That's progress at least. And what about everything else? Have you heard from her?" I wonder if Aimee understands that I'm asking my little sister about our mom.

My sister drops her head, shielding her eyes. "Yeah, she called the house last week and left a message."

"She tried me a few weeks ago."

Sophie looks directly at the camera. "Did you talk to her?"

I frown. "No."

Sophie is quick to answer. "Me neither."

"Sophie," I say, brushing my hair out of my face. "You know that if you want to talk to her, you can."

My little sister's mouth is set in a grim line. She swallows hard. "If you're not going to talk to her then neither am I."

Shit. This conversation is getting a little intense considering the fact that Aimee is right next to me. I'll deal with it later. "Fine. I want to hear how school is going."

"Oh, it's the usual. Aaron Miller is coming over in a little while so that we can finish up a project for our science lab."

"The Miller kid, huh? Is he still giving you a hard time?"

I make it a point to be on top of my little sister's social life. She's got no mother around and a dad that's basically checked out. I'm more than halfway across the country, but the least that I can do is play the big brother role when I can.

"Well…" Sophie pauses, looks up at the sky. She's got straight blonde hair and a narrow nose like me, but that's where the similarities end. Sophie inherited our mom's dark brown eyes and olive complexion as well as her petite build. "Sort of."

Something in her tone makes me sit up in the bed and bring the phone closer to my face. "What do you mean?"

"I mean…" Sophie is playing with the ends of her hair. "Remember that I told you he was being completely obnoxious to me at school?"

"Uh-huh."

"We, um, got paired for this group project thingy, and yesterday he apologized for acting like a dickhead and he…"

"And he what?" My teeth are clamped together.

Sophie lets out a big sigh that blows the bangs from her face. "And he gave me a flower and asked me to be his date to the school dance next week."

"Oh." My insides twist. "What did you say?"

"I said yes." Sophie's forehead rumples. "And don't start with the 'you're too young' crap." She alters her voice. "Because I don't want to hear it, Cole. Not a single word."

That was exactly what I was going to say but I'm not going to tell her that now. I scoot up so that my back is pressed into Aimee's headboard and I clear my throat. "That's not what I was going to say."

"Sure…" Sophie smiles knowingly. "Look, Cole, I actually have to go get ready for Aaron so I'll call you tomorrow, okay?"

"Uh, okay."

Aimee leans in, her chin pressing into my arm. "It was nice to meet you, Sophie. I can't wait to hear about what you're going to wear to the dance."

Sophie's smile is so wide that it takes up the whole screen. "You too, Aimee. I think I'm going to go shopping with my friend Kylie later this week."

"Get a turtleneck! Long, thick wool pants," I beg.

"Whatever." Sophie rolls her eyes. "I love you, big bro. Stay fast." She blows a kiss to the screen.

I pretend to catch the kiss. "Love you, little sis. Stay slow."

We hang up and a moment later, Aimee says, "The protective big brother look is a nice one on you."

I turn to her and laugh. "It is?"

She nods her head and crawls on top of me—long legs straddling my waist, arms on either side of my head like a cage. Her hair dangles down to gently tease my chest. She lifts one hand and tenderly rubs her thumb over my nose and down to my lips. "How did you get this?"

"How did I get what?"

She touches the bump in my nose with her mouth.

I spread my hands under her shirt to the little dimples above her ass. "I broke it in the fourth grade."

"I figured that you broke it, but how?"

"A bird."

She looks skeptical. "A bird attacked you?"

"Not quite." I give a chagrined sigh. "A bird shit in my eye."

She half-laughs. "Ew. Is that even possible?"

"Well, apparently it is. We were playing kickball and I just looked up at the exact moment that the fucker must have been overhead. It freaked me out so much that I tripped and fell over a bench and… Well, I think it was a one in a million chance."

Aimee breaks into silent laughter. Her shoulders are shaking, tears are building in her eyes, and she's clutching her ribcage. I raise my eyebrows and make a sound of disapproval, but I'm smiling. "So you think that's funny? It was horrible—hot and wet bird shit right in my eye. Not to mention that my nose hurt like a bitch and I got made fun of for the rest of the year."

She sucks air into her lungs and wipes at her eyes. "I-I'm sorry, but…" She laughs some more.

"It was awful."

She gets herself under control and touches my face. "I'm sorry that I laughed, but…"

"But what?" I run my finger along the neckline of her shirt, pulling it down so that I can kiss the hollow of her neck.

Aimee gasps and a surge of sudden heat washes over me. "You just keep surprising me."

I grip the backs of her knees and run my hands up her smooth thighs. She shivers and closes her eyes, tempting our bodies closer together as my fingers continue their journey towards her tender flesh. "I could say the same for you." Holy shit. My voice is strained, needy.

She parts her lips and makes a low sound. I pull myself up so that I can kiss her mouth. Fuck. I can't not kiss her.

"You know that in real life, you're not anything like the cocky bastard that I first met." Aimee murmurs against my lips as she rocks her hips into my groin.

I roll our bodies so that I'm over her, pinning her down with my weight. "I'm still a cocky bastard. You just bring out the best in me."

"Mmmm…" She runs her fingers through my hair. It feels amazing.

"Hey, I've got to get something. I'll be right back."

Aimee lifts her head from the pillow and looks at me like I've lost my mind. "What? Where are you going?"

Before she can work it out, I kiss my way down her neck and pull her panties down her bare legs.

"Oh," she says in a very small voice and it is so fucking hot.

I laugh and spread my left hand on the inside of her thigh. "Oh."

Each touch, each whisper urges me deeper inside her flesh and when I find the right spot, she grips my hair with shaking hands and swears under her breath and I laugh again.

I love this. The way that she sounds when she's heaving for air. The way that she smells. The way that she's moving her hips up to meet me.

Sixteen

Aimee

E very couple of days I have to remind myself that I'm really okay. And it's not the pretend kind of okay. It's the kind that you feel from the inside out. It's the kind of okay that has me thinking about outfits and coffee first thing in the morning, and homework that's due later this week, and that I need to call Jodi back, and what Cole's abs look like when he flexes. It's the kind of okay that makes life a zillion times more bearable and also has me waiting for the other shoe to drop.

I lie in my bed staring at the slowly circling fan and the thin crack in the ceiling that runs from the center of the room all the way to the door. He left over an hour ago to make it to an early morning practice but I can still catch his scent on my sheets and it's awesome. I roll over and bury my face in the pillow and just... breathe. I'm full of this incredible feeling. It's like laughter caught in my chest.

"Ugh. You are pathetic. You know that, right?"

Exhaling, I turn my head, push the hair from my face, and see my sister leaning against the doorway. She's holding a bottle of nail polish remover and some cotton balls in her hands.

"What are you talking about?"

Mara rolls her eyes. "Don't try to hide it, Aimee. I saw you sniffing that pillow like a lovesick fool."

"I'm not—"

"Pathetic? Lovesick?" Mara finishes for me. She's smiling now but she also looks a bit worried. "You are a pathetic, lovesick fool. Really and truly. It's the worst case that I've ever seen, but I think it's alright."

"Enlighten me. How is it alright if I'm pathetic?"

"Because…" She shakes her head a millimeter. "I think that he might be just as pathetic as you are."

• • •

I balance the brush on the edge of the paint can and stretch out my fingers. They're coated in purple latex paint. When I rub my skin together, the dried paint pulls into little balls and scatters to the drop cloth like candied confetti.

"Yuck!" I exclaim. "My fingers are so stiff that I think they might fall off."

Jodi turns to me, a slow smile spreading until her whole face is lit up. She's got purple paint flecked through her hair and her shirt and jeans are ruined. "Have I said thank you?"

"Only about fifteen times in the last hour." I roll my shoulders and pick up the brush. I'm on trim detail which means that I'm going around the edges of Jodi's bedroom with a thin, angled brush. Jodi and Kyle are following behind with two rollers coated in the purple paint.

Somehow I let Jodi talk me into painting her apartment. Actually, that's a lie. I know exactly how I ended up here. It was self-preservation.

Cole's gone this weekend. He's at some kind of clinic that's supposed to make him faster, better, stronger. I knew that if I didn't get a project going, I'd get sucked onto the couch for a *Law and Order* marathon and I wouldn't get up for two days. On Friday afternoon I could almost hear my mother's voice blaring in my head. *Not healthy, Aimee!*

Jodi mentioned over a text message that she was going insane looking at the boring masking tape colored walls of her place and the light in my head started to strobe.

We started in the kitchen with a tangerine backsplash. After a taco run, we painted an avocado green accent wall behind the couch. Two vinyl albums later—because she insists that everything sounds better on vinyl—we moved to the bedroom. The shade that Jodi chose for this room is close to a ripe eggplant. Basically, it looks like a produce stand exploded in her apartment. Jodi loves it. And though I have my doubts, she swears that her landlord will love it too.

When we're finished with the bedroom, the three of us stand back to admire our work. I'm disgusting—sweaty, speckled in paint, high on the fumes—but at least I feel accomplished.

Jodi claps and does a little bouncing on her toes. She's all about vivid displays of enthusiasm. "So... what do you guys think?"

"It's different," I say and then I worry that my comment isn't positive enough. "And fun."

Jodi nods, looks at Kyle.

He sets the roller down on the tray and rubs his palms on his jeans. "It's bright."

"Of course it's bright." She stands on her tiptoes, kisses his chin and hooks her fingers onto his elbow. "Don't worry. It'll grow on you."

Kyle grins and tells her, "It doesn't need to grow on me. I like it, babe. I love... color."

I can tell by the way that he's fingering the blue chunks of her hair that he's referring to something more than the color of paint on the walls and I suddenly feel like I need to get going. "Hey! I'm going to text Mara and ask her to come get me."

"No way," Kyle says, cracking his knuckles against his palm. "After you just wasted your weekend painting this place, I'll give you a ride."

I try to argue but it's useless. Jodi walks us toward the door where she hugs me tightly and says, "Aimee, you'll have to think up a way for me to pay you back." She points a thumb in Kyle's direction. "I'm rewarding him with sexual favors later but I don't think that'll work for you."

Kyle whips his head around. "Jodi!"

For someone who works in a tattoo shop and exudes edginess, Kyle is surprisingly reserved about this kind of thing. Last week he overheard Jodi telling me the details of their sexcapades and he looked ready to pass out. His face was redder than a tomato.

Confusion loosens Jodi's features. "What? It's the truth."

Kyle groans and slaps his forehead. "That's private. You're not supposed to tell people about our sex life."

Undeterred, Jodi shrugs. "Kyle, what are you talking about? Aimee isn't 'people,' she's my best friend. Private isn't part of the equation."

Two words.

Best friend.

In the early days of my therapy, Dr. Galindo was always asking: *How does that make you feel?*

The moment that I think of the answer to that question, I feel myself flush. Because I feel fine. I feel better than fine… I'm freaking *happy.* And I shouldn't be happy, right? I shouldn't be thinking happy thoughts and painting apartments to music and falling for a guy and making new best friends. Not when Jilly is decaying under the ground all by herself.

Cole

The transition from *I* to *we* isn't a conscious decision. It slips in out of nowhere like a freak storm that springs up in the middle of a nice afternoon. One minute you're thinking: *that movie that I want to see is coming out on Friday.* And the next minute you're telling yourself: *we should get pizza tonight,* or *I wonder what we're doing for Flag Day two years from now.*

Maybe you get to a point where you're so invested and wound up in another person that your brain really has no other option other than to consider them.

For me, the realization happens on one of those postcard-worthy Florida days that makes you want to fall back and close your eyes and catch the clean air on your tongue. There's a blue sky that stretches for miles above a thin roof of palm trees. Everything is perfect. To steal one from Goldilocks: *It's not too hot. It's not too cold. It's just right.*

Aimee and I both have a break between our classes and she wants to use the time to catch up on a reading assignment. I want to use the time to catch up on her.

We've both been busy over the past week. Her classes are getting tougher and I had to be at an out of town clinic last weekend so it seems like we've barely had any time together. We don't have classes this Friday and I plan to surprise her with another beach trip. I want to erase the bad memories from her head and make new ones. Maybe I'll pack a blanket and we'll stay past dark, lying in the back of the truck staring up at the stars.

Smiling to myself, I drop my eyes. Right now her head is resting in my lap and I've got my fingers threaded through the dark strands of her hair.

My phone buzzes and I grudgingly pull my hand away. It's a text from Nate asking me if I'm down with poker Thursday night.

Without thinking much about it, I ask her, "Hey. What are we doing this Thursday?"

Aimee breaks her concentration to glance up at me. "No plans. Why?"

"I think I'll play poker with the guys."

"Hmm." She's already back to reading. I watch her finger make a vertical path down the page.

What are we doing Thursday?

The thought had been as natural to me as taking my next breath. For the briefest instant, I struggle, wondering if this is how things went down with my dad and the rest of the schmucks who've had their hearts plucked out of their chests and eaten by a woman.

Is that what's happening to me?

The spinning in my head ceases when Aimee shifts her attention to me. "You're making me nervous," she says, lightly touching my jaw.

I grin slowly, hypnotized by the blue of her eyes through the screen of dark lashes. *I am not my dad.* "How am I making you nervous?"

Her mouth twitches. "You're staring at me. It's getting weird."

I touch the gleaming freckle on her cheek and lean closer. "I can't help it that you're so fucking nice to look at."

"Watch you language." She laughs, turns her head to the side and presses her lips against the inside of my thigh. The movement is so intimate that a jolt of awareness stabs between my shoulder blades. I brush my thumb over the jagged ridge of her scar.

"Will you tell me about it?"

Aimee knows what I'm asking. She places the book facedown on the slope of her stomach and looks up. Her bottom lip is caught in her teeth. "Anything that I tell you will be sad and depressing. You don't want that in your head, Cole."

"How do you know what I want in my head? I want *you* in my head…" My breath snags in my chest. This conversation suddenly feels too serious for the sunny day and the bright blue sky. "And that scar and the story behind it is all a part of you."

Aimee sits up and turns from me so that I can't see her face. She folds her right arm across her chest protectively. Her left hand holds the book in place against her body. "It's not a part of me that matters."

"It matters," I say decidedly. My hand grasps her shoulder and I pull her close so that her head falls to the center of my chest, just beside my heart.

• • •

I've thought of everything. There's a cooler in the back, a large blanket that I stole from Daniel's closet and a bottle of decent wine tucked underneath it. I even brought along a Scrabble set that I jacked from Nate because I remembered that she said she liked to play. The best part is that Aimee thinks I've got some bullshit all-day practice session so she's not expecting me. I ran the idea by Mara earlier this week and she said that she'd make sure that Aimee would be home and not doing anything this afternoon.

I knock. I know the grin on my face is so wide that it's ridiculous but I don't give a rat's ass. I've been looking forward to this too much to hold back now. Earlier, Aimee told me that her plans for the day include boredom, maybe a pizza for lunch, and some more boredom just to round things out.

Just as my hand is descending to knock again, a middle-aged woman answers the door. She takes in my crazy-ass smile, black board shorts, worn flip-flops, and frowns. "Can I help you with something?"

We haven't met but I know instantly that this is Aimee's mother. Take away the crisply ironed shirt she's wearing and the pearls around her neck, and they look so much alike that it's a little disconcerting. I take a step back. "Uh, I'm Cole."

It's obvious that my name means nothing to her and that almost knocks the wind out of me. I know that Aimee has issues and it's not like I expected her to tattoo my name on her fucking skin or anything like that, but I at least thought that I had earned a mention to her parents. For fuck's sake, her mom calls her at least once a day.

"Well… Cole, did you say?" She smiles warmly and extends her hand. "I'm Elise Spencer. Is there something that I can do for you? Are you here to see Mara, because I'm afraid that we're just about to take the girls out for a late lunch."

I shake my head to stall. "I… I'm…"

197

"Oh good." Mara appears in the doorway and grabs ahold of my arm. "You're here. I wasn't sure that you'd make it in time."

I'm confused, but I let Mara pull me through the front door. Aimee is in the living room standing next to a man that must be her dad. She's wearing the same light blue dress that she wore on our first official date and I can't help but think of that kiss we shared outside the restaurant. When she sees me, she wrinkles her nose and squints her eyes like she's not sure that I'm really standing there.

"This is Cole," Mara announces to the room.

Aimee's dad steps forward and gives me a long appraising glance before shaking my hand. "Carl Spencer."

"Cole Everly," I mirror his tone and dart my eyes to Aimee in inquiry. She's twisting her hair around her finger and staring at her shoes.

Behind me, Mrs. Spencer clears her throat. Now that I look closer, I see that this woman's hair is streaked with amber highlights, and her eyes aren't nearly as vibrant a blue as Aimee's. Her right hand is at the base of her throat where her necklace hits her skin. "Cole, would you like to join us for lunch? It's always nice for Mr. Spencer and I to get to know one of Mara's friends."

"Mom," Mara says with a surge of impatience. "Cole isn't with me. He's Aimee's boyfriend and I wanted you both to meet him."

Aimee

If looks could kill, my sister would have been toast twenty minutes ago. She and I have been waging one of our sisters-only staring contests since we sat down at the restaurant a half an hour ago.

I have to give a figurative round of applause to my parents. Despite the frostiness between Mara and me and the fact that Cole is wearing his bathing suit at a restaurant that employs a sommelier, they're trying. My dad has asked all of the standard parental exploratory questions and Mom's been nodding along enthusiastically to everything that Cole says. Her head is bobbing so fast that if I weren't so irritated, I'd probably laugh.

"Cole, it seems that Aimee doesn't tell me much of anything and I can't help but be curious... How long have you and my daughter been dating?" My mom asks, casually refolding the napkin in her lap.

My daughter.

Cole's eyes flick to mine. So far he hasn't given me much indication how he feels about all of this. He coughs, catches a hand in his hair and runs it down the side of his face. He didn't shave this morning and there's a light smattering of fair hair along his square jawline.

"Since August," he says.

September would be more accurate but I'm guessing that he doesn't want to get into all of that right now.

"August?" The hurt in her voice hits me squarely in the chest. "That's quite awhile. I wish..." she sighs and looks at me. "I wish that you felt like you could talk to me."

I squeeze my eyes and take a deep breath. "Mom..." This has to be the most awkward lunch in the history of ever.

"Aimee? Mara?"

Scratch that. It just got a lot more awkward.

I turn and see Brian St. John standing just behind my chair where the aisle opens up to the main dining room of the restaurant. His raven hair is longer than it was the last time I saw him and curls just around the edges of his ears. He's got on a soft blue button down and dark grey pants. I'm so surprised and he looks so good that it takes me a moment to register that there's a girl standing next to him.

"Brian!" My dad bellows. "Nice to see you, son."

Son. My God. Both of my parents are standing up to shake Brian's hand. Big smiles on their faces, they start in on him with the questions. *Yes,* he's in school. *Yes,* his parents are doing well. *Yes,* his dad still plays golf at the club twice a week. *No,* he can't believe that I'm back and didn't call him. Brian looks at me then. I mean, really looks at me with his large brown eyes and it's obvious that he's crestfallen and hopeful all at once.

"Forgive my manners. I'm Elise Spencer," my mom says politely, her eyes trained on the girl standing beside Brian.

Brian falters. "Oh, sorry. Sara, let me introduce the Spencers. Carl, Elise, Aimee and Mara." He nods at each of us in turn. "This is my friend, Sara."

Sara's eyes swing to Brian's face and I get the impression that she doesn't like the way he just threw around the word *friend*, but she recovers quickly and shakes everyone's hands. She's tall—taller than me for sure, with cropped brown hair and warm hazel eyes.

"So..." Brian glances at Cole and takes note of the thin t-shirt, bathing suit and stiff shoulders. "Who's this?"

Cole

I don't do the jealousy thing. I never have. I've always told my friends that there's no chick out there worth getting your panties in such a tight wad. And until today, I believed myself.

When this Brian prick walks up, at first I don't recognize the chill that zips down from my scalp to my groin. What the hell? Then it hits me like a rock on the head. *Jealousy.* Fuck me.

Brian St. John has dark hair that's flipped and messy in a way that girls dig. And here he is prancing around our table in an ironed button down shirt and slacks while I'm wearing a goddamn t-shirt and board shorts because I had no idea that this was meet-the-parents day.

While everyone else is chitchatting, I clench my jaw and move my hands to my lap. It's crystal fucking clear that Aimee and this Brian guy have a history. He *knows* her. He knows her parents and they know him. Shit. They seem to love him. And it doesn't matter that he has some cute chick on his arm because I can tell that he's got a thing for Aimee.

Aimee

I can see that Cole is annoyed. It takes every scrap of my will not to climb into his lap right in front of my parents and tell him that Brian St. John is not even a blip on my radar.

"We have to get going." Brian coughs, shakes his head slowly. "It was... Aimee, it was really good to see you." His fingers wrap over my shoulder and he leans in to kiss my cheek, his mouth lingering on my flushed skin too long.

"Ahh, you too," I say, blinking heavily as I jerk my head away.

Brian smiles. "Call me sometime so we can catch up. My number is the same."

I'm not sure how to respond so I just nod my head and watch Brian and his date walk away. When I turn my attention back to the table, Cole is staring at me with guarded eyes like he doesn't want me to see what's moving behind them, and his mouth is compressed in a hard, unyielding line.

Despite the best efforts of my parents, the climate during the rest of lunch is frigid. No one says much on the ride home and when my dad reverses into a spot on the street in front of the townhouse, Mara jumps out of the car before it's come to a full stop. She waves to our parents over her shoulder and dashes up the walkway in a sad attempt to put off the inevitable confrontation with me for as long as possible.

Cole won't look at me directly, but he continues to talk to my parents and even agrees to come out to the house for my dad's company party next week. When all of the niceties are over and we're standing on the sidewalk watching them go, I shake my head and blow a strand of hair out of my face. "I guess my sister really threw us under the bus."

He stabs his gaze at me but only mumbles something that I can't make out.

I shake myself and push forward. "So, um, thanks for coming to eat with my family. It was… interesting."

"Yep," Cole says blandly, fishing his keys out.

"And you don't have to come to that party that my mom mentioned. I'm sure that it's going to be awful. All of their country club friends and my dad's clients in one place… Talk about a nightmare."

"I'll think about it," he says, shifting his weight to one hip.

"Do you want to come inside?" I press, swallowing down my nervous energy.

"Nah." With shadowed eyes, Cole dangles the keys in front of himself like some kind of explanation. "I'm going to head home. I've got some stuff to do."

Stuff to do? Is he really this irritated about Brian?

My feet are nailed in place. I can't put it into words—the feeling like I'm trying to hold water but it's slipping through my fingers. Cole makes his way round the hood of the truck and unlocks the door before I've worked up the nerve to speak. "Cole?"

He straightens his spine and takes his hand off the door handle. "Yeah?"

I open my mouth, falter, take a breath and try again. "Why did you come over today? I thought you had practice all day."

"I lied about that. I had a whole thing planned for us. I wanted to take you to the beach."

"Oh," I say, summoning a smile that feels all wrong on my face. "That would have been nice…" *Nice?* What a boring adjective. A flush creeps over my features. "Will I see you later?"

He inclines his chin and gives a non-committal shrug, effectively sidestepping my question. "We'll see."

Seventeen

Aimee

I splash my face with water and stare at my reflection. I want to hit something. I want to toss myself onto my bed and scream bloody murder into my pillow. I saw Brian St. John today. My mom is going to want to have one of her "talks" with me. My sister and I are in a fight. Cole would hardly look at me.

I don't think about what I'm doing. I pull my hair into a high ponytail and use an exfoliating sponge to scrub my make-up off. My face is blotchy red and there are still dark smudges under my eyes from the rubbed off mascara but I don't mind. I feel bad so I might as well look bad, right? Bending my arm awkwardly behind my back, I grip the zipper and slip out of the dress I wore on that first date with Cole. I leave it rumpled on the floor by the bathroom and go look for a sports bra and a pair of cotton workout shorts. My running shoes are over by the window.

Today I don't stretch. I don't take it easy. I run full out and I don't stop even when I start to feel sick to my stomach and everything blurs like I'm trying to look through water. I push myself harder, pounding the pavement like I've got a point to prove to my legs.

I don't think about where I'm headed until I'm standing at the door, my hands steadied on my hips for support, wheezing like an asthmatic. Sweat gathers in heavy droplets on the end of my nose and steadily drips down my neck.

Wiping my face with the bottom of my shirt, I look up and see that Cole's silver truck is in the driveway so I know that he's home. I take a deep breath and lift my hand. I'm not a hundred percent that I'm going to go through with it until my finger actually depresses the doorbell.

I hear some minor shuffling beyond the door and muffled voices. Someone laughs. Daniel Kearns swings the door wide. He's shirtless, carrying a bowl of popcorn under one arm.

"Hey there," Daniel says, rearing his head back. He's surprised to see me but not in a bad way.

"H-hey," I say, still catching my breath and rubbing my sweaty cheek against my shoulder.

He steps back from the doorway to let me inside. "If you're looking for Cole, he's back in his room."

I step over a pile of discarded gym bags. The hall opens up into one large room with a slanted ceiling and wide bay windows. Right now, the back blinds are drawn shut, casting the room in inky shadows. The entire place reeks of stale pizza and the cheaply made coffee table is littered with empty amber beer bottles. Adam's prized bong collection is lined up on a shelf above the TV. Typical.

Nate is sitting on the couch—legs spread wide, arms braced on his knees—playing a video game. He glances up and smirks at me. "Hi-ya girl. So tell us… What the hell crawled up Cole's ass and made a new home there?"

My eyebrows go up toward my hairline. "What do you mean?"

"He stomped in here a while ago, tripped over Adam's sneakers, threw some shit around and then disappeared into his room and cranked his music up to ear-splitting."

I can hear the music crashing through the walls. I grimace. "It's—we had lunch with my parents and... I don't know. It went okay, but then it didn't." I shake my head to clear it. "I'll go talk to him."

"Here," Daniel says as he comes out of the kitchen holding a bottle of water. "Take this with you. And don't let him give you any of his shit."

"Thanks." I smile warily and roll the cold bottle of water across my hot forehead.

The feral music gets louder as I walk down the hall. I give two warning knocks against the door before pushing it open. It's go-time.

"What the fu—" Cole stops yelling when he sees that it's me standing there. He's stripped down to just his bathing suit, hunched over on the edge of his bed with his head resting in his hands. He looks like shit and a small part of me wonders if it was a bad idea to come here.

Sucking in one more breath for courage, I shut the door behind myself and walk over to his computer to mute the music.

The room prickles with the sudden and charged quiet. "We need to talk."

Cole crosses an arm over his bare chest defensively. "So, talk."

I take four deliberate steps to stand in front of him. Resting my fingers under his jaw, I pull his head up so that his face is level with my navel.

"Look," I begin carefully. "I'm sorry about today. I really am. I know that meeting my parents should never have happened the way that it did. And I know that lying to you about my plans this afternoon was incredibly stupid."

Cole lifts his eyebrows slightly. "How come you never mentioned me to your parents? Are you embarrassed to be with me?"

"No, I—" I'm momentarily thrown. How could he ever think that I would be embarrassed? Cole is amazing. I've witnessed firsthand the blinding effect that he has on people, especially girls. They can't even think clearly around him. *He's athletic and gorgeous and smart and fun and...*

My thoughts fade out and I sigh. "Cole, I'm not embarrassed. Not even close. You're everything that I'm not and I can barely get my head wrapped around the fact that you looked at me twice. I-I've spent so much energy trying to gain some kind of... control over my life, and when I'm around you that just flies away. It scares me."

He doesn't speak so I continue. "I didn't tell my parents because... I don't know. I just didn't. And I understand that you're mad and maybe annoyed or whatever, but I have to ask you a question. Have you ever said anything to your dad about me?"

He tightens his jaw and flicks his eyes to mine. "That's not fair. I've told So—"

"Have you told your dad about me?" I repeat my question.

"No. But I don't talk to my dad about shit, Aimee. He's far away, and aside from his work, he lives his entire life like he's in a fucking coma. It's amazing that he knows my sister's name let alone my girl-friend's name. So don't ask me about my mom or my dad like that can buy you some kind of currency. It's not the same thing because we don't have what you have with your parents."

"Wake up, Cole. How can you not see that what I currently have with my parents is just as dysfunctional as what you've got with yours? My dad and I used to be close. He came to every single one of my meets and cheered me on. He loved taking me to his club and showing me off. Now? I'm an embarrassment! Everyone knows what a big, fat failure of a human being I am and my dad doesn't know how to handle that. Since Jillian died, he barely speaks to me. And my mom? She only says things *at* me. It's like both of them think that I'm going to kill myself at any moment or come up with some new way to ruin my life. Do you know what that feels like? To have every person in your life staring at you, just waiting for you to fall apart?" I take a shaky breath. "And I'm sorry that I hurt your feelings but... I-I just wasn't ready to tell them about us. They'd have questions and I wasn't ready to answer them because I... I don't know..."

I watch him think about this. "And what about Brian?"

"What *about* Brian?"

His golden hair tumbles low over his forehead as he rolls his shoulders forward and shakes his head. "It's obvious that something was going on there."

"Are you being serious, Cole? Do you really want to play the ex game with me?" I choke on a laugh. "Because I assure that I'll win. Should I describe in detail all of the nasty looks that I get just for standing next to you? Or the smug smiles from the random girls that you've screwed? Do you know how that burns? How it twists my guts and makes me feel like I'm deluding myself to think I'll be enough for you? Every day, I wonder when you'll wake up and get sick of me."

"I'm not..." He shakes his head. "You don't understand. Those girls? They meant nothing. I barely remember their names."

"Is that supposed to make me feel better? All that does is make me think that one day you'll forget my name." I force myself to keep going against the wave of emotion trying to pull me under. "I want to trust you but I'm scared."

He cranes his neck so that his gaze is locked onto mine. "I'm scared too." A long pause. When he finally speaks, his voice is low and soft and I can tell that the earlier anger is gone. "Sometimes I feel like I'm just going to wake up one morning and you won't be in bed with me. You'll be gone for good."

"Why would you think that?" I croak.

He lowers his face and rubs his stubbly cheeks between his hands.

Dropping to my knees and placing the water bottle on the edge of the bed, I rake my fingers through his hair and bend his face to mine. The skin of his scalp is smooth and cool beneath my nails. Butterfly wings beat in my chest, sending a ripple of vibrations through my limbs. "Cole, why would you think that?"

His intense green eyes squeeze me. He spreads his hands open in a gesture of frustration. "Because you won't tell me anything. Because you keep so much inside of you that I'm not sure that I'm imagining that what we have is real or if it's all in my head."

As I slide my hand to the back of his neck, the thrum of my heart goes up my throat and falls down to the bottom of my stomach.

Words crowd behind my lips. I'm afraid to speak. Afraid that once the seal is cracked, everything will come pouring out.

I take his right hand in my left one and turn it over so that his palm is facing up. Slowly, so that he knows that I mean it, I trace the words on his skin that I can't make myself say. He watches me, eyelids lowered in concentration as he follows the outline of each letter. His knee brushes my shoulder and his breath tickles my sweaty skin and sends a wave of goose bumps over my bare arms.

Three simple words.

This is real.

Cole

I end up taking her to the beach after all. It's dark, so instead of trudging our stuff down to the sand, I park on the side of the road in an empty lot that hugs the coast. I go first and Aimee follows me around to the back of the truck. I shift the cooler out the way and we each take one side of the blanket and lay it out under the watchful night sky.

Scooting until my back is against the cab, I loop my arm under her waist and pull her to me so that I can feel her heart thumping through her skin. I twist her ponytail out of the way and bend down to kiss that space between her neck and her shoulder.

"Don't," she says seriously, jerking her chin back. "I'm gross."

She's still in just a sports bra and shorts from her run earlier and she's tangy and warm like the ocean. Grinning mischievously, I kiss her neck again and this time I run my tongue up her neck to her jaw. She swats at my head but she's laughing.

"I told you that I'm gross!"

"You're wrong," I tell her, laughter lifting my chest. "You're perfect and I want all of you. Even the sweaty parts."

Aimee

It's nice like this—lying with Cole in the back of his truck with the sound of waves licking the shore feather-soft in my ears. The moon is a white fingernail clipping at the top of the dark sky. Splinters of pale starlight push their way through a veil of low ash-colored clouds.

I'm not sure how much to tell him and how much to hold back, but I know that I need to let him inside of me and this is the only way that I know how. I'm sick of trying to hold so many pieces together with just my bare hands.

I suck one cheek into my mouth, suddenly worried that the back of Cole's truck isn't big enough to contain all that I have to say. "I always think that one day I'll wake up and I just won't remember her anymore."

"Is that what you want?" He asks me.

"No. Maybe. I don't know." I shake my head sharply. Forgetting feels like a lie. "If I think about having her and losing her or not having her at all, I'd still want to have her."

When I close my eyes, the blood in my body rushes up to the surface of my skin.

Cold water poured in over my flailing arms onto my lap and flowed down the path of my legs. The coppery taste of blood coated my tongue. I sputtered, blinked against the terrible, burbling darkness and the tears. "J-Jilly?" A flash of pain sliced through me from my neck to my shoulder and I screamed—almost choking on the sound of my own fear.

"I promised her that I wouldn't leave and then I left anyway," I say gingerly. "I've asked myself so many times if I knew... Well, whether or not I knew that she was still breathing. I've tried to think back. Did I see her chest moving? If I had known, would I have still left her there? I don't—Was I just trying to save myself?"

"Maybe you only *could* save yourself."

The temperature plunges as memories of the accident—fighting to breathe against the pressure pinning my chest to the seat, the harsh jolt of the impact, the creeping inky water—batter me painfully and swirl behind my eyelids like a galaxy of hazy stars. I squeeze my hands into fists, clear my throat and try to think back. Back to before the grinding of metal on metal, and the faint, metallic smell of blood and salt.

My ear was pressed against the rough fabric of the seat. I burned hot and cold all at once. My legs felt heavy, like they had been weighted down with cement blocks at my ankles. I tried to turn my head but my hair was caught on something. It took me a second to realize that it was the seatbelt. Fumbling, I reached down and dug around for the metal clasp. My stiff fingers clawed at the button, working desperately until one of my nails caught, pulled away from the skin and snapped in one motion.

Jilly? My head swam. I tasted blood in my mouth.

Where was I?

The car.

The water.

The angry groan of metal compressing assaulted my ears. I wrenched my neck forward and pushed through a blinding heat that stabbed at my head when a clump of hair ripped from my scalp.

I needed to take stock. The water was already at the bottom of my ribcage. Sucking in a fast breath, I brought my hands to my face to clear my eyes and I twisted to my left. "Jilly?"

The air moves around me as I struggle to sift through the images. "Just relax," Cole whispers from beside me. "I'm right here."

The whirring in my head slows down and I relax my fingers. The images sink in around me, taking me to a place where I want to be.

Now, I can see Jillian smiling like it would go on forever. I remember her diving into the pool in the middle of a rainstorm—all knees and elbows and freckles. Sitting with me under the slide—rough dirt sticking

to our thighs while she showed me how I should take a drag off a cigarette. Dancing around her bedroom sophomore year in her favorite purple bra and underwear set. Rolling her eyes at one of Katie McLaughlin's
stupid cheerleading stories. Laughing. She was always laughing.

Blues and blacks shift behind my eyelids and a picture of her the
way that she was on that final night rises. Her coppery hair was down
around her face and she was wearing ripped jean shorts and worn-in
sneakers with no socks.

"We almost didn't go to the party," I say tightly. "That afternoon
Jillian heard from one of our friends that this guy that she used to see
might make an appearance at the party. She didn't want to deal with
him because he'd started to get pushy. He was leaving voicemails, driving by her house at random times... stuff like that. Jillian didn't want
to encourage him."

*"Come on, Aimee! Pretty please..." Jillian stuck out her bottom lip. "We'll
watch a cheesy movie and eat ice cream straight out of the container."*

*I wrinkled my nose. "How many times do you think you can fool me with
that pout?"*

I pause to get my bearings. "I couldn't even tell you why I wanted
to go out so badly, but I did, and I convinced her to go with me." As
the words move off my tongue, the band wound snuggly around my
chest loosens. It feels good to speak out loud. "I think it was the first
time that I ever had to talk Jillian into going out. It was always the other
way around with us."

Cole is still holding me. I can feel the steady rise and fall of his
chest against my back.

"To be honest, I don't remember much about the actual party. I
know that you don't want to hear this part, but I was on and off with
Brian at the time." I feel Cole's body harden, but he stays quiet and lets
me continue. He knows that this is my story to tell. "We were never
serious or anything like that, but we were in one of our 'on' phases so
I stuck with him and I just... I lost track of Jillian. How shitty is that?"

A long silence stretches out. I think of Jillian the first time that I saw her—pigtails and round cheeks and huge golden brown eyes like pools of maple syrup. She told me that she liked my lunchbox and asked if I knew anything about roly polies. I didn't.

I gather air in my lungs and push it out through my nose. "It got late and everyone started passing out or heading home. Brian wanted me to leave my car and let him drive us home. I was stupid drunk at that point so I blew him off."

"Give them to me," she said as she took my keys out of my hand and stuffed them in the front pocket of her shorts. "You're toasted my dear."

I pursed my lips and cocked one eyebrow. "And you're not?"

She smiled, pushed her bangs out of her face. "I'm fine."

"I let her take the keys away from me and I didn't even think." I shake my head and feel tears roll down my cheeks to my hair. Cole touches my arm. He gently folds our fingers together and pulls our hands over his heart. "Actually, it's worse than that. I did think. I just didn't stop it."

How can I explain the rest?

How can I describe that it seemed impossible that anything bad could ever happen to Jillian Kearns? If people were colors, the rest of us were greys and greens while she was electric orange. She was a *force*. A world of promise captured inside of one body. I never— not for a second—considered the possibility of that promise being broken.

She leaned her head back against the headrest and flexed her fingers over the steering wheel. I felt hot. Too hot. Groaning, I propped my leg on the dashboard for balance and opened my window. Moonlight and humid night air rushed in and streamed through my brown hair. My ears were charged and my vision was blurry. I gulped at the oxygen like I couldn't get enough.

"Are you okay?" She asked, craning her neck to me.

I grunted. A sick feeling churned deep in my gut. "I feel like I've been stuffed full of cotton balls."

Jillian laughed, blinked a few times. "I have no idea what that means but it sounds bad."

"It is."

"If you have to puke, just say the word."

"Will do." I adjusted the volume on the stereo so that the sound of David Guetta lifted over the uneven howl of the wind. "Hey, did you see that Tam got highlights?"

"Yeah, they looked good with her skin tone." She glanced over at me. "You should consider it. You could pull a lighter color off."

"What about you? You've been talking about dyeing your hair for years."

She picked up a lock of hair and scrunched it between her fingers. "I don't know..."

"I will if you will." It was our battle cry.

Jillian laughed.

"Let's do it at the end of the season," I continued, thinking suddenly of the pool. "That way we don't have to worry about the chlorine killing the color."

"Speaking of swimming..." Jillian's voice dropped and she rubbed at her cheeks. "If I oversleep tomorrow and have to do laps at practice because we're late then I'm blaming you."

I closed my eyes against the intense pounding in my head and let myself fall into darkness. "Bring it on," I whispered.

The despair of the memory spills over me—harsh and unsteady and terrible.

"One minute we were on the road talking about swim practice, and the next... we were..." Piercing sounds and turbulent images surge through me.

Tires fighting with asphalt, the impossible crunch of glass, and the rush of salty water coming in through the open window. Jilly slumped unnaturally over the steering wheel—her hair tangled and dark with water and blood, her wrist braced on the dashboard.

I pulled on her shoulder. I tried to get her to move but her body was weighted down with water. I screamed. My neck burned. Blood dripped down my arm.

"Wake up! Please!" I begged. "I'm not going anywhere. I just..." I looked to my right through the dark to where the water was getting higher. "I just need to get help. I promise I'm not leaving you."

Like static on a TV screen, my mind pushes through the images. What if this is all that I am? Chaos and shadows. Confused memories desperately seeking out the light. What if all the bits of me that meant something good are still trapped in that mangled car? What if I was able to crawl through that window, but I never really got out?

"It took the ambulance seven minutes to reach the site of the accident," I say. "And by that time it didn't matter anymore because Jilly was already gone."

Cole's voice is earnest, determined to find me over the void stretching underneath my skin. "But you weren't gone."

It feels cold, floating inside my own body like this. I turn to him and tell him the truth. "Maybe I was."

Eighteen

Cole

I hold her against me while she tells me what she knows for sure: Jillian Paige Kearns drove a 2009 blue Honda Civic off of Beatty Pass at 1:29 AM. The time can be nailed down precisely because a woman—a forty-one year old grocery store cashier named Angela Sharpe—was on her way home from the night shift and witnessed the entire thing. By the time that Angela reached the scene of the accident, the Honda was almost completely submerged in water. Later, she told police that she helped Aimee—barely conscious and bleeding—climb up the steep bank out of the water but had no idea that there was a second girl trapped in the car.

In a small, steady voice, Aimee strings together a series of memories so painful for her that I can hardly bear to listen. She tells me about the panicked moments after the car slammed through barrier and went off the side of the pass. Then she describes the intensity of the impact and the water and the thick flashes of pain and the blood that burned through her vision.

"I still don't know exactly why the car swerved off the road that night," she says. "The police asked me about the details of the accident a hundred different ways but I couldn't tell them anything that made a difference because I didn't know. All I could say for certain was that we were listening to music, talking about our hair… I closed my eyes for a fraction of a second and then—like I'd blinked myself into a nightmare—the car was skidding off the bridge into the water."

"The thing is that it doesn't really matter if Jillian missed the curve and overcompensated, or if she thought she saw something in the middle of road, because she never should have been driving my car in the first place. If I had kept my keys or let Brian take us home… Every single thing would be different. Jillian would be alive. She'd be at college now and she'd fall in love and she'd travel and she'd get married and have babies. I took that from her. And if I could just do it all over again… I—" Her words break off, collapsing into her mouth.

"You can't…"

Aimee moves. Her hand comes up to cup my cheek. "She was my best friend, Cole. They did tests after the accident and determined that she'd taken a bunch of pills—Vicodin, Valium—I don't…" Aimee's voice teeters and she shakes her head. "I don't know how she got the pills or why she took them. I had no idea. They told me that after… after the accident they found a stash in her room. She never said anything to me about it and I still can't understand that. I thought that I knew *everything* and it turns out that I knew *nothing*! I-I feel like if I could… I don't know… If I could understand why she was taking the pills then maybe things would make more sense."

She keeps going. "You know that they told us that she probably could have lived. I mean, they didn't say it like that. They just said that the official cause of death was drowning. *Drowning.* I know what that means. It means that she was alive after the car crashed and I—I left her there, Cole. I saved myself and left her." She shudders. "Jillian was the best swimmer that I knew and she drowned in the dark all by herself. Every day…" The last word cracks as it leaves her mouth. "Every single day of the rest of my life I have to think about that and wonder if she woke up and knew what was happening to her. I have to wonder if she called my name or cried or tried to save herself, and I…"

"That's not fair. You can't blame yourself." I hesitate. Aimee's guilt is tangible. It pulses beneath her pale skin and seeps out through every pore on her beautiful body.

"I don't even remember the lady that found me. The doctors told me that she saved my life and that I was incredibly *lucky*." She laughs, but it's humorless. "Lucky was their word, not mine. They said that if Angela Sharpe hadn't called for an ambulance then I probably wouldn't have made it. I was in shock—losing blood from here," her finger touches her scar, "and my spleen was ruptured. After I was discharged from the hospital, my mom wanted me to meet Angela in person. When I said no, she tried to get me to at least send her a note. I agreed to it but every time I tried to write the words, I couldn't finish… Do you know why?"

"No." I squeeze her, not sure that I want to hear the answer.

"Because I didn't feel lucky at all, Cole. I didn't want to thank the woman who saved my life because secretly I hated her. I hated her for saving me because I wished that she had just let me die along with Jillian."

"Is that what happened last summer when you… when you—"

She finishes for me. "When I tried to kill myself?"

I nod into the darkness.

"I don't know really. I'm not sure that I meant it." Aimee sucks in her breath and holds her hands up in front of her face. "Th-there was this guy at school that I knew would have pills… I got them but I wasn't sure exactly what I planned to do with them. And for a long time, I just kept them sort of like a backup plan that I promised myself I would never use. It's not like I—it's not like I planned it out really. It was a moment." She pauses, holds her breath uncertainly. "Just a single moment when everything slipped away from me. And even though I knew, somewhere in the back of my head that it wasn't okay—that my parents and my grandparents and my sister all loved me and were counting on me to be okay—I… it was just like none of that stuff mattered enough."

"What about now?" I'm not sure how to ask this question but I need to know. "Do you still feel that way?"

She's doesn't hesitate. "No."

Aimee

Once my story is purged, I feel so raw that I can hardly breathe. Cole is staring up through the muted darkness toward the sliver of clear, bright moon. His face is faintly creased with concentration.

He glances at me. "It wasn't your fault that Jillian died," he says. We are so close that even in the dark, I can see the detail of color in his luminous eyes. A thousand shades of green. "It wasn't."

"Maybe," I say, letting my heart float just outside my body. "Maybe not. We were both stupid. She was too out of it to be driving and I should have known it. But I… I can't think like that anymore. I can't go back and change it. All I can do is go forward, right?"

Cole is quiet for a long time. When he finally fills the silence, his voice is low and steady. "The day before my mom left us, we had a fight. I called her a selfish bitch right to her face. Sometimes I think that our fight was the last straw—the thing that pushed her out the door. I wonder if she decided that if her own kid thought about her that way, what did she have to lose?"

I crawl over him, no longer worried about the fact that my skin is salty with dried sweat from my earlier run, and I gather his hands between our bodies. Gently, I press my lips to his and slide my tongue into his parted mouth. His stubble scratches my skin as I absorb the taste of him—faintly charged and electric like the air right before a storm.

Cole tips his head and feathers his lips right above my temple where my hair meets skin. "You're so amazing," he whispers as his hands skim my waist and grab at my hips. "You know that, yeah?"

Maybe it's strange after all that has just passed between us, but desire, fresh and hot, pumps through every nerve ending in my body. Cole's mouth is on mine, his tongue winding me senseless until my entire world is reduced to the sensation of his hard, strong body pressed into mine.

Cole groans approval. He wheels his hands greedily up my bare back over the fabric of my sports bra to rest on my shoulders. He fingers the tiny hairs at the nape of my neck and rotates his thumbs along my jaw, drawing me closer, his lips clinging, sucking, sending a spiral of heat down my back.

The salty breeze pushes in from the water, coaxing me, rousing a ripple of tiny pinpricks over my exposed flesh. Cole rocks me against him and slips his mouth to the side to brush that tender spot just below my ear with the edge of his teeth.

"Aimee... Can I? Do you?" His hot breath teases my skin.

I'm quivering, caught up in the storm surging beyond his eyes. My breath is fast and hard, keeping time with my heart. "I...I... yes, I want to."

Cole sits up quickly, bringing me with him so that my knees straddle his hips and his arms twine around my thighs. He shifts his back against the rigid metal of the truck and maneuvers the thin blanket so that it's carefully bunched around my lower half. Watching my eyes closely, he reaches up and frees my hair from its ponytail. I drop my head to one side, feeling my loose hair fall damp and cool against my flushed skin.

With the moon and stars as our only spectators, Cole clasps my face within his strong hands and drives our mouths together. As his tongue sweeps over mine rhythmically, I realize how much I want to remember this moment. I want to write it down in black ink on a sliver of plain white paper and keep it in my pocket forever. I'll write about the sound of our kiss, the coarseness of his face rubbing against my cheek, and the sensation of his hands mapping my body, memorizing every curve and depression of bone and skin.

"Aimee." My name is a moan and a plea. He pushes his tongue inside my mouth and glides his fingers underneath the elastic waistband of my athletic shorts to where my upper thighs meet my torso.

"Ahh!" I close my eyes and tip my chin down toward my breast.

Considering that this is a public place, I should be more worried about what could happen if someone were to find us, but I'm too distracted by what Cole's fingers are doing to me and how his hot tongue feels moving against my neck.

Panting, I shift so that my ankles are hooked in the middle of his back and we kiss like that until we're both out of our minds with wanting. Cole breaks away, digs a condom out of his wallet and looks back at me with an intensity that has my body practically begging.

I draw in a breath and skim my hand under his shirt across the expanse of his muscled chest. I wonder if he feels it too—this huge sensation like the sky opening up and swallowing us both.

He grins sheepishly. "I wish I could give you more than the back of my truck."

"I'm pretty happy with the back of your truck if that's where you are."

Cole's smile deepens until I can see the shadow of his dimples. He kisses my shoulder and runs his fingers down to the small of my back and around my waist. As he removes my shorts, his blunt nails scrape across my bellybutton creating a delicious friction.

Holding his eyes with mine, I tighten my legs around him and pull him inside of me. Cole goes very still then he kisses me hard and presses his palms deep into my skin.

It's hard to say how it happens. How all of the bits of me—even the broken ones—start to tumble. I think it's my toes that go first. Next—my legs and the hollow spaces behind my ribs. And then my arms all the way down through my wrist bones to the tips of my fingers. My lips part and I realize that this is what it feels like to *fall*.

We move with the low rumble of the waves as our soundtrack and I live again and again. His fingers trace letters on my flesh. He's handing me back my own words.

This is real.

Cole

I never used to think about things like death and life and all the hundreds of thousands of seconds that get stuck in between. Back then I didn't know the way that a person can crawl so far inside of you that your organs voluntarily shift to the side to make room for the shape of them.

Her smell is all around me. I clutch her head, my knuckles brushing the smooth line of her jaw, and I tilt her chin back so that I can see her eyes better. Clear blue pools swimming beneath a flutter of dark lashes. She makes a faint sound as her body gets closer and then she cries out and buries her face in the skin of my neck.

Damn. I close my eyes and give in to the feeling swelling hard and fast under my flesh. It intensifies with each ragged beat of my heart until I think I might explode. She's everywhere—grabbing at my skin, pulling my hair through her fingers, clenching her muscles tightly around me. I bite back the primal sound scratching at the back of my throat, and all at once I'm erupting, breaking free, coming apart from the inside out.

That was…

The damp heat of her breath exchanges with mine as she fits her mouth over my lips and collapses her weight against my chest. I wish I could describe this. This moment. If only I could fuck. For the first time in my life I want to tell someone how I feel and I don't even know how to find the words—solid and honest—to do it. Isn't it considered a chump move to tell a girl all the ways that she rocks your world right after sex?

I stroke her long hair and pull her into my side.

"Don't let me go," she says so quietly that I have to replay her words in my head to make sure that I heard them right.

I run my thumbs over the bumps of her spine. "Don't worry," I reply. "I won't."

Nineteen

Cole

"It's way too hot for this shit. Where is autumn? It's almost November and I'm still sweating my balls off over here." I drop to the grass.

Daniel laughs, takes a rasping breath, and bends over to reach for the blue plastic water bottle that he tucked beside the base of a scraggly pine before we took off on our run. "It's going to be like this until a storm breaks. A patch of warm air is pushing its way inland. Don't you ever check the weather?"

"Do I look like someone who checks the weather?"

Daniel ignores the question. "I think that you've lived in Florida long enough to know that changing seasons are a myth anywhere south of Tallahassee."

"Then no more afternoon runs."

"Hey, you're the one who couldn't go later on—not me. If we had waited to run until seven then it wouldn't have been so bad," Daniel says as he lowers himself to the ground. We've just endured a brutal eleven miles and now it is time to sprawl on the lawn in front of the track and field offices and let our muscles cool down.

"I told you already… I have plans later."

"It's Friday and we don't have practice tomorrow. What kind of plans do you have that are so important? It wasn't too long ago that the only planning that you did revolved around getting drunk and getting laid."

"Things change." I don't tell him that my plans happen to be showering, putting on presentable clothes, and picking Aimee up to go to some swanky party at her parent's house. Just the thought of managing small talk and eating off a tiny cocktail plate has me cringing, but when Mrs. Spencer invited me, I couldn't exactly say no.

"So you're really in this, huh?"

I glance over at Daniel. "What do you mean? In what?"

He pushes damp hair away from his forehead and takes a large gulp of water out of the bottle in his hand.

"You and Aimee," he clarifies, stretching one arm over his head and bending his knees so that they crest above his chest. "I don't know. It seems sort of serious."

How the fuck am I supposed to respond to that?

The corners of my mouth twitch. "I don't know that serious is the right word, but yeah, things are good with us."

Things *are* good. Shit. They're better than good. Ever since that night at the beach—the one that I keep on a steady repeating pattern in my head—things are more settled between us. When I close my eyes, I can almost feel her small, tight body against mine. It was unbelievable and if I let my brain drift too much longer I'm not going to be able to keep my hard-on at bay.

"I've got a ton of shit to do. We should—" The roar of an engine drowns out my voice. I pick my head up off the grass in time to see Adam's car screech to a stop near the curb. "What the hell?"

"Cole!" Adam calls out the open driver's side window. "Get over here, man. Your sister has been trying to call you for the last hour but you forgot to take your fucking phone with you."

A nasty sensation shoots down the column of my neck and settles deep in my stomach. I stand up and cross the distance to Adam's car. This can't be good. Not a fucking chance.

Aimee

"Door!" Mara shouts over the noise of her hairdryer.

Grappling with the bottom of my dress, I dart a quick look at myself in the mirror and decide that the lipstick that my sister suggested is too much. It's a shade that belongs on the sorority and pageant circuit. I wipe at my mouth with my thumb as I scramble down the hall to answer the knock.

The door swings wide, pulling in a puff of sticky air. "We're almost r..." The sentence shrivels up and dies in my mouth. I drop my pink-smudged hand to the doorjamb and crease my forehead.

Cole is standing on the paved walkway in his sneakers and sweat-stained gym clothes. He tilts his head up and I see that his skin is pulled taut and pale over his cheekbones and his eyes are a starker green than I've ever seen them.

"What's wrong?" I ask immediately, bile creeping up the back of my throat.

"It's going to rain," Cole says absently.

"Um..." I can smell the impending storm in the air and feel it like an electrical charge crawling over my skin. A strange, sudden breeze rushes over us and the light shifts. I watch shadows slide into place over Cole's face. "What's wrong with you?"

He narrows his eyes, trails his fingertips over the uneven bridge of his nose and shifts his weight to one foot like he's uncomfortable. He coughs. "You look nice."

My eyes fall to the dark grey sheath dress that I borrowed from my sister and swing back to him. "Cole, what the hell is wrong?" I repeat my question for the third time.

Cole looks away, nudges the rock-lined path with the side of his foot. "I was going to call you and just tell you over the phone but I... I..." His voice is gruff, filled with an emotion that I don't understand. He shoves his fingers back into his light hair and shakes his head once, then twice. "I can't go to the party with you tonight."

Feeling shaky, like the ground beneath me is moving as fast as the gathering clouds, I take a tentative step forward. "I-I'm getting that from your clothes, but that still doesn't answer my question. What's wrong?"

"I know that it was important to you that I make a good impression on everyone and—"

"I don't care about my dad's thing," I say firmly, laying my palms on either side of his biceps. His muscles stiffen and he moves back out of my reach.

He brings his hands in front of his body like a shield. "Aimee, I can't right now. I just..."

My indrawn breaths are shallow. I feel a stabbing, cramping sensation starting low in my belly. *This is wrong. All wrong.* "Cole," I whisper, my body shifting back and forth. "What happened to you?"

I don't understand the carved-out look in his eyes. I talked to him earlier and everything was fine. We made plans for him to come over at seven so that he could ride with Mara and me. He was laughing, joking about getting dressed up for my parents.

Cole turns so that I'm looking at his back. The grumble of distant thunder punctuates the quiet. His head falls back and he lifts his shoulders as he drags air into his lungs. "I can't talk to you about it right now. Maybe later, but... I just wanted to let you know about tonight. Tell your parents that I'm sorry. Tell them that something really important came up and I couldn't get there, yeah?"

"No." My throat is closing in on itself. I'm only inches away from Cole's body but I know that he doesn't want me to touch him and that feels a bit like dying. I squeeze my eyes tight and bite down on the inside of my cheek. "No, I won't tell my parents that you're sorry because I don't understand any of this. Cole, I-I want to know what happened and why you're acting like this and looking the way that you look right now. You're scaring me. Ha-have I done something?"

"Fuck," he moans loudly. "Fuck!"

I blink my eyes open in surprise and see him pacing the walkway, murmuring and seething air between his teeth. He stops and rests his clenched hands on his hips.

"You haven't done anything," he says tightly. "It's…it doesn't have anything to do with us. I got a call from Sophie and she told me that my mom showed up there today."

Another gust of wind moves over us. I take an involuntary step forward. "Cole…"

"She's dying, Aimee." His voice catches and his eyes reach into mine. "She's got a terminal fucking brain tumor. She has six months—maybe a year—and she's at my house with my little sister and my dad and they want me to fly out there and pretend that we're all of a sudden a normal family again or some shit." He curses and hits the wall next to the door with the flat of his hand.

My insides are twisted and tight like a thorny vine is growing straight up my middle. I don't know what to say. Cole and I have come so far and I want to hold him and brush the pads of my thumbs across his lips and kiss a circle around his red eyelids but I know that's not right. My voice is thin, barely above a whisper. "Did you speak to her?"

He moves his head sharply. "No. She tried to get on the phone to talk to me but I-I just couldn't. Not yet."

"Cole, you have to talk to your mother and hear what she has to say. I know it's hard, but if she's—"

"But nothing," he cuts me off. "And where do you get off telling me that I should talk to my mom? When do you talk to your mom about anything important? When have you faced anything?"

His words scorch my skin. I'm shaking. "Cole…"

He closes his eyes. "Look, I know that you're trying to help but you don't know what you're talking about. And I really can't do this right now." He gestures to me and backs away before I can protest. "I'm fucking sorry, but everything is messed up and I need some time to think."

"Please?" I don't even know what I'm asking him for. I just know that I don't want him to leave. Not like this.

He waves over his shoulder without even looking at me. "I'll call you."

My head spins. When I hear the familiar sound of his truck engine coming to life, I keep my eyes trained on my bare feet, not trusting myself not to run after him.

• • •

I don't expect the cars spilling out from the driveway to the street. Even over the sound of the rain battering the pavement, I can hear music and voices hammering from the house.

"Are you ready?" Mara asks.

I turn and look through the darkness fanning across the interior of the car. Mara is watching me. Jodi is searching the floorboard for her purse and an umbrella, holding her blue hair out of her face with one hand.

"I don't know," I hedge, turning back to the house. I'm nauseated. An awful feeling is sloshing around inside of me. "Maybe just showing up like this wasn't such a great idea. They're obviously throwing a party and Cole didn't tell me anything about it…"

"Aimee!" Jodi's voice is authoritative and snaps my attention back to the car. "I have just spent the past two hours building you up to talk to Cole. Now I don't really care if he's sleeping or jacking-off or having a party. There's no way in hell that you are going to back out on me now."

"I know, but…" I'm a wimp.

"No buts," Mara insists, grabbing hold of my left hand. "I know what's going on with Cole's mom is scary, but it's a not an excuse to leave you hanging the way that he did."

"If you don't talk to him, it'll be like a wound that festers and gets infected and starts oozing yellowish puss all over the place," Jodi adds.

"That is disgusting."

Mara chokes. "Seriously, Jodi."

"I'm already lightheaded and you are not helping."

"You called me and asked me for advice but you're not willing to hear it."

"Technically, I didn't call you. I texted you."

Jodi tilts her head to the side and cocks one eyebrow up toward her hairline. "Aimee, stop disagreeing with me and get your ass in there before I pick you up and throw you over my shoulder."

I almost laugh. Jodi is barely five feet tall in heels. There's no way that she'd be able to throw me anywhere.

"Those are fighting words."

Her grin stretches wide. "Damn straight they are."

Cole

The burn feels good. Clamping my teeth together until my gums tingle, I press two fingers into my eyelids and swallow hard. Acidy heat radiates up from my chest and pours out of my nostrils.

Damn. That's good stuff.

Every sip takes me further away from shore. I'm out there, rocking with the motion of the water, floating under an open sky. I don't give a fuck if I drift like this forever. I don't give a fuck about anything. Wait. How does that old Papa Roach song go? *Cut my life into pieces.* Damn, I'm nauseous. *I've reached my last resort, suffocation, no breathing. Don't give a fuck if I cut my arm bleeding.*

That's me. Mindless. Suffocating. Not breathing. I'm not thinking about my mom or the way my little sister cried on the phone, or about Aimee's blue eyes. Nope. I'm too strung out to think about anything. *Do you even care if I die bleeding?* I pick up another glass from the table and I tip my head all the way back.

Get off of him.

Someone sounds pissed.

How many has he had?

I blink against the harsh sting of the light. Daniel is staring down at me pointing accusingly at the empty shot glasses tipped over and dribbling onto the scratched veneer of the coffee table. "How many shots have you had, Cole?"

My ears feel blubbery and my head feels too heavy for my body. I lean into the corded fabric of the couch cushions and shrug my shoulders. Shit. Nothing seems to be working right. "I lost count a while ago."

"I can't believe that Adam and Nate let you get like this." Daniel scans the room before reaching his hand down to me. "Get up. You're beyond fucked up and I'm putting you to bed."

I knock his hand away and try to speak. I'm going for *I'm fine*, but the words come out of my mouth muddied and broken. Breathing in through my nose, I close my eyes and rub a hand down the side of my face.

Did you hear what he said? Another voice. This one is even closer. *Go away, Daniel, he's just having a good time.*

I pry my eyelids open and turn my head to the side. Shit. Kate Dutton is perched on my lap, hanging her arms over my shoulder and yapping like a fucking cockatoo. She moves and her bony ass digs harshly into my thigh.

"Seriously," she's shouting over the loud music. "Leave him alone."

Daniel ignores her and directs his words at me. His face is fuzzy. "Don't make this mistake, Cole."

"Huh?" I'm groggy and my brain is sluggish and the noise isn't helping.

"Damn it." Daniel pauses. "Why don't you go sleep it off and we'll talk in the morning when your head is on straight? Think about Aimee."

Aimee. Fucking Aimee. A memory bobs to the surface. I picture her face the way it looked when I left her tonight and I want to throw up all over myself. *I'm an asshole.*

"Sure are," Daniel laughs and I realize that I've spoken out loud.

"Shit." My body throbs. I sit up and try to nudge Kate off my lap with my forearms. "Sorry, but you need to move."

Kate twists her blonde head around and glares at me. "Are you kidding me, Cole? You've certainly been enjoying my company for the last hour and now you're going to act like I'm disposable? How many times do you think I'm going to put up with that?"

I cringe. *What the fuck have I been doing?* The past few hours are fuzzy and distorted—the memories chugging and slipping away from me like an engine that won't turn over.

I know that when I got home from Aimee's place a few of Adam's friends were over here. The shit with my mom was hanging over my head and I just wanted to forget for a little while. I wanted numbness. *Oblivion.* I remember Adam cranking up the music and getting a bong down from the shelf and maybe there was some other stuff and... Fuck.

"Cole..." Kate leans in and tongues my neck just underneath my ear. Her mouth is wet and sticky against my skin and I have to swallow back the partially broken-down alcohol that pushes its way up my throat.

"Kate," I grumble as I wrap my hands around her wrists and hold them down against my leg. "I've got a girlfriend and you've got to go."

"Don't bother stopping on our account."

My head snaps up. It takes me a moment to fit all the slippery pieces together. Jodi is in my living room pointing the sharp end of an umbrella at me with ball-withering intensity. Mara and Aimee are standing just behind her. Aimee's hair is wet and her grey dress is spattered with rain.

"Aimee?" I'm dizzy. "Is it raining outside?"

But Aimee's not listening to me. She's staring at Kate. More specifically, she's staring at Kate's hands on my leg.

Shit. I try to stand but the room sways and I'm knocked back on my ass. "Aimee?"

She lifts her eyes to mine and I can't help my reaction. I flinch. Everything about her face is wrong. She's gaunt, torn-up like she's just been kicked down three flights of stairs. Her eyes are hollowed out, burning with hurt. I fucking hate it. And I hate myself for being the one who put that expression there.

"No," I say, pushing off the cushions and this time managing to get my feet under myself. I stiff-arm the back of the couch to keep my balance. "It's not what you think."

She makes an indignant chuckling sound. "Not what I think?" Her hands press back into her hair. "Do I look stupid? I don't even—I don't—" She sucks in a violent breath. "We never made each other any promises so don't bother with the stupid explanation because I don't need to hear it." She looks at Kate and lifts her hand. "You were right. He's all yours."

"Whatever, bitch," Kate rasps out.

And that's when all hell breaks loose. Jodi starts yelling and Kate's up off the couch and looming over her. Daniel and Mara both step in between the girls while Adam and some other guy that I don't know hoot their enthusiastic approval of a catfight.

Everything is leaking away from me—circling on the floor like sudsy water around a drain. Aimee grabs Jodi by the arm and pulls her toward the front door. She's shaking her head over and over.

"Wait!" I desperately stumble over the first few steps. Faces blur together, the walls shift. I trip but catch myself on someone's shoulder.

"Please!" What am I asking for? Forgiveness? Help? Time?

Ignoring the sound of my name from behind, I rip the front door open and crash outside. Wetness pricks my face and I look up and see raindrops spinning, spiraling to the earth. I wipe my forehead and peer out into the soggy night.

There.

Headlights.

Breathing hard, falling fast, I sprint over and pull on the handle of the passenger door. It's locked. I slam my hand against the glass. It's dark and I can't see her face through the muggy glass, but I can make out the outline of her head. "Aimee!"

Jodi lays on the horn and inches her car forward in a series of sharp jerks. I grapple with the handle some more but the wet metal slips through my fingers. "Talk to me!" I shout, moving forward with the momentum of car.

Jodi honks again and this time she doesn't let up. The car engine revs angrily. Frustrated, wrecked, panting, I let go and back away and watch from the curb as Aimee disappears out of my life in a fog of rain and red and white lights.

Twenty

Aimee

"You look terrible." Mara says. She's leaning against the doorway to my bedroom. Her hair is pulled up into a ponytail. In the grey morning light she looks pale and tired. Neither one of us got much sleep last night.

I rub my red, swollen eyes and prop myself up onto my elbows. "Thanks."

"You know what I mean." She glances down the hallway to the front door. "What are you going to do?"

"I'm not sure. My heart hurts."

"He's not going to leave until you talk to him."

Cole has been out on our front patio since midnight. He knocked and rang the doorbell for over an hour before he gave up and slumped to the ground with his knees pulled up to his body and his head bent to the crook of his arm. I think he fell asleep around two.

"I don't really know what to tell him."

"You tell him the truth," she says thoughtfully.

"Maybe I don't know what that is anymore."

"Then you make it up as you go."

• • •

Coffee. Caffeine and lots of it. It's the one thing that I'm sure of.

I pull two mugs down from the cabinet. Mine is chipped on the rim just above the handle. It's painted a streaky yellow with a badly sketched heart and uneven writing on one side. Jillian made it for me at one of those paint-it-yourself places the summer before junior year.

You talk too much.
You laugh too loud.
You're everything I've ever wanted in a friend.

And then on the bottom, she wrote:

I love you but I hope your boobs sag first.

I pour the coffees, top mine off with milk and sugar, and I carry the mugs and an extra glass to the front door. Cole's head is bowed to the wall so that I can't see his face. His hand is curved around his shoulder linking his arm to his chest. He barely moves when I sit down on the threshold.

"Cole," I whisper, lightly running my index finger over his temple and into his hair.

He stirs, rotates his shoulders and cranes his neck back. Disoriented, he yawns and blinks three times. I think he's going to ask me why he's waking up outside and why he feels like there's sandpaper scraping over the surface of his brain, but then I see the flicker of awareness spark behind his green eyes.

Before he can say anything, I shove a glass of water in his face. "Drink this."

Not peeling his eyes from mine, he takes it and drinks it down in two gulps. He sets the glass on top of the soft, black dirt just to the side of the walkway.

"Now coffee," I say.

With the barest hint of a smile, he picks up the mug and blows across the top of the coffee. After a few seconds, he takes a small sip. "I feel like I drank five gallons of battery acid last night."

"I think that you actually did," I say.

He looks at me for a moment, reaches into my eyes like he's trying to find something. "Nothing happened," he croaks. "With Kate last night. Nothing happened. I know what I'm like... I know what people say about me, but you have to believe me."

I gaze into the distance, past the brightly painted wall that borders the patio to where a car is backing out of a parking space on the street. Above our heads, a few blue scraps of sky wink from in between the passing clouds. If it weren't for the musky smell of wet asphalt, you'd never know that a storm came through last night.

"I believe you," I say, closing my eyes, trying not to see the image of Kate Dutton, disgustingly beautiful and blonde, sitting on Cole's lap, running her tongue over his neck. "I'm not going to lie. Last night, I was pissed and hurt and a million other things and I..." My voice fades out as I swallow hard and blink back my tears. I don't want to tell him how, last night, I cried until I was numb and Mara had to force me into a freezing cold shower to get me to calm down. "B-but after I had some time, I think I knew that nothing really happened between the two of you. Maybe it was the yelling and hitting my front door all night that convinced me."

Cole winces, reaches for my hand and turns it over in his. "I'm sorry, Aimee. I'm so fucking sorry about everything."

I stare at the way our hands are linked together, fingers weaving in and out of each other, his thumb rubbing circles in the center of my palm. "I know you're sorry but that doesn't make it all okay. It's not like yesterday just goes away if we want it to. I mean..." I struggle for the right words. I'm seriously reconsidering my own sanity right now. I think that I know what I need to say, but maybe I'm making a huge mistake. Maybe I should just shut up and throw my arms around his neck and kiss him. Maybe I should grab hold of him and never let go. "Even if you hadn't let Kate Dutton climb all over you and lick your neck, I'd still be hurt and upset."

"Fuck." He tries to turn my face toward his but I fight it. "Is this because of the stuff with my mom?"

"It's not stuff, Cole. It's *you*. It's all a part of you." I pull my hand away from his and I touch the leaves on the small plant that Mara bought the day that we moved into the townhouse. I can't think of what it's called but she told me that it symbolizes hospitality. "Do you remember when you told me that my scar was a part of me and that it mattered?"

He nods reluctantly.

"It's the same thing with your mom. She's a part of you. And even if you're angry or ripped up inside, you've got to understand that once she's gone you won't be able to go back. Not ever. All we get are moments, Cole. One at a time, like heartbeats. Once one of them is gone, that's it. No do-overs. No repeats. Every moment possesses its own kind of magic and what we do with it counts. It counts."

I think of Jillian and all the seconds that slipped away from us. *Do you hear that sound? It's the sound of the world ripping apart.* My mom and Mrs. Kearns and Mara and Cole that night last June. So many lines—connecting us, stringing together all of the moments, gathering them like raindrops in a bucket. "You could change your mind about something a hundred times. You could lay awake in bed and replay that single heartbeat over and over and over again, and you could imagine every other possible outcome, but it won't change what's true. Your mom is dying. *Dying.* That's forever. And if you let this chance get away from you, you'll always be too late. You could be twenty-five or thirty-two or seventy years old and you could change your mind, but your mother will still be gone."

"That has nothing to do with us."

"It does," I say, determined. "Because, deep down, in a way that matters, we're the same—you and me. You were right when you told me that I haven't faced things. We're both runners. We're both racers. That means that the minute the shit hits the fan we start moving in the opposite direction. It's what I've been doing since the accident and it's exactly what you did last night. Things went south and you ran. From your family and from me."

"I could have—"

"Just let me finish, okay?" My voice is a mixture of sadness and longing and I hate the sound of it. I feel scratched out, cold all over. "I'm not saying that just because she's dying you have to forgive your mom for everything. There are some things that you can't forgive and you're the only one who can decide that part of it. But I do know that you have to stop running. We both do."

"I just…" He closes his eyes and I see his throat bob with the effort of swallowing. "I don't know how to make myself talk to her."

"Maybe it's not something you make yourself do. Maybe it's something that you *let* yourself do."

He looks at me hard. A thousand years pass. The hard little knots in my stomach tighten.

"Aimee, please…" His voice cracks.

"Cole, we're not good for each other. It's… this…" I gesture between our bodies. "It's too much for me."

"Fuck!" He pulls on his hair and clenches his jaw. "Can't we just forget this shit and start over?"

"I don't think that real life works like that."

"Then how does it work?"

I shake my head and try to calm my thudding heart with a sip of coffee. "I don't know the answer to that yet."

Cole

I can't believe what's coming out of my mouth. "So this is really it?"

"For now at least," she says. I wish she would scream it instead. She's too calm. Just sitting over there—composed, drinking from her coffee cup. She picks off three star-shaped leaves from a potted plant positioned by the door. I watch her rip them up into tiny, jagged pieces and let them fall through the cracks of her fingers. I think they look like little pieces of green confetti decorating the grey cement walk and that seems all wrong.

I'm rattled. Angry. Sad. I honestly don't know what the fuck I am right now. I think about how I would rate myself on one of those pain scales that they have on the wall of a doctor's office. The ones with the cartoon faces. Happy and smiling on one end of the card. Droopy-eyed and crying on the other.

Hurts a whole lot.

Hurts worst.

I make a weird sound that might be a laugh or a sob. I'm not really sure. "Aimee, what the fuck does 'for now' mean?"

"I don't know…" She's quiet for at least a full minute and every passing second of her silence hits me square in the chest. "I think that we both need time to refocus.'"

"Refocus?" At least she hasn't pulled out the *just friends* card. I think that I'll lose my shit if she tells me that she wants to be my friend. I can do a lot of things, but I can't be *just friends* with Aimee Spencer. Not anymore. That ship sailed a long time ago.

"I know that it sounds stupid. It's a therapist's word and honestly, I'm not sure exactly what it means but I think that I need to figure it out." She puts her head down and lets the remainder of the torn-up leaves drop from her hands. "I've got—I've got *me* to work on and you've got *you* and until we can both stop running, we can't be together."

"Aimee, last night was…" I shake my head. "It was…"

"It was awful. What do you want me to say? I know that you were upset over your mom and everything was a mess, but when I saw you with that girl I-I couldn't even breathe."

"Aimee, I told you—"

"I know, and I said that I believe you and I meant it. But that doesn't change the way that I *felt*. Cole, I was obliterated. I had just opened up to you and when you pushed me away and turned to someone else… I-I felt like I was coming apart—disintegrating into so many bits and pieces. Afterward, when I started to think about that, I realized that it's no wonder I felt that way because the truth is that I'm already shattered. I have been all along. I've been using you and what you give me like a glue to keep all the parts of me in place and…" She hesitates. "And that's not okay. I've been counting on you to save me when I should have been figuring out a way to count on myself. Do you see that?"

If words could be a black hole, that's what this conversation would be. A hole I'm falling into. A vacuum sucking all the light out of existence.

My eyes are burning. It hurts to blink. "I hear what you're saying, but you can't sit there and expect me to agree with you. You can't ask me to clear your conscience. I want to be with you, Aimee. It's *all* that I want. Anything less than that sucks." I push my hands through my hair and pull at the ends. "So say what you have to say but don't ask me to understand or see things your way. You don't get my permission to break my fucking heart."

"Cole…" Her eyes are red and shiny. "If we can't get our own lives straight then we'll do worse than break each other's hearts. We'll tear each other apart. And maybe I could risk myself, but I can't risk you. I just can't"

"In math don't two negatives make a positive?" It's lame and I know it before I say it but I can't help myself. My whole world is going to shit and I need something… anything to hold on to.

Aimee gives me a sad kind of smile. "This isn't math, Cole. This is my life and this is your life and that means something. It means something to me." She chokes on that last part.

I need to be touching her, connecting the two of us by a solid line when I say what I have to say so I pick up her hand again and I stroke the tender part of her wrist where the thin blue veins cross over each other like road lines on a city map. "What would you say if I told you that I love you?"

She looks away but I don't have to see her face to know that she's crying now. Her shoulders are shaking and her fingers curl over mine so hard that her nails bite into my skin.

My voice is raw but I keep going, pressing my words inside her. "What would you say?"

Aimee lifts her head. She pulls her hand back and touches her scar with the tip of her middle finger. She won't look me in the eye. "I'd say that loving me is a bad idea."

So that's that.

Twenty-One

Aimee

Do *you hear that sound?*
The sound of muffled voices carrying over the patio wall. The soft shuffle of bare feet against cement. The crack of a door closing.

Do you hear it? It's the sound of the world ripping apart.

Cole

I'm not my dad. Being depressed isn't my style.

What's my style?

Being pissed.

So that's what I am. I'm pissed. I'm a lump of barely contained hostility. I can't see straight, can't think right. And deep down, I know that means that even if I'm not crying or playing dead, I'm just like every other schmuck that ever handed his heart to a girl and had her squeeze it between her fingers until it burst in a grotesque explosion of blood and torn up tissue.

Hour one: "Let me know if you're gonna upchuck," Daniel says. And he's being serious. I want to laugh and tell him to go fuck himself, but the thing is that I actually might throw up.

Hour three: I punch a hole in a wall at the house. Daniel goes to Home Depot to get a plaster repair kit.

Hour six: Adam leaves and comes back with a case of Natty Light. He puts the whole goddamn thing on my lap and tells me not to worry about getting him back because it was on sale.

Hour seven: I work up the nerve to look at my phone. There are four missed calls from Sophie and one from my mom's number. Oh, and I have a text from Kate. She's *just checking* on me. Fuck that shit. I smash the phone. I guess it's a good thing that I saved my contacts to the cloud or whatever.

I haven't counted time like this since my mom left us. It's like my balls are connected to the minute hand on the clock and with each passing second, they get twisted just a little bit tighter.

Seventeen hours.

Forty-eight hours.

Sixty-two hours and fourteen fucking minutes.

It's Tuesday and I get my ass up and haul myself to class. As I'm parking and walking the four blocks to Davis Hall, I tell myself over and over that I won't look for her in front of the Liberal Arts building, but let's face it, I look. It's not like I think that she'll actually be there, waiting for me with that ridiculously big bag looped over her shoulder. But still.

Lunchtime. We normally meet at that pita place anchored to the Union and she gets a Chicken Caesar pita (dressing on the side), and I get a Steak Philly (hold the onions). Today it's just me and the onionless Philly.

While I eat, my eyes dart between the tables and the door. I'm fucking pathetic. It's like one of those accidents that you pass on the interstate. You swear you won't look at the smashed windows and the caved-in metal. You promise yourself. You cross your heart and hope to die. But when the time comes, you just can't fucking help it, can you? That's me. Rubbernecking my own life.

I don't sleep at night. It doesn't matter that I ran ten miles this morning or that I put in an extra thirty minutes in the weight room after practice. If a million dollars were on the line, I couldn't fucking fall asleep. I toss and I turn. I shove my pillows into a hundred different positions. I try a scalding shower and then a cold one, but none of it helps. There's too much to think about, too much to obsess over. Memories of her vibrate against the walls of my skull, taunting me, shredding up the last of heart.

Blue eyes.

The tips of her long brown hair grazing my arm while I walk her to class.

The way that she'd sometimes skip ahead to the end of a book that she was reading to make sure that everything would work out. *I'm just checking,* she explained. *I can't go further unless I know.*

Her breath teasing my lips.

Loving me is a bad idea, she'd said like it was as simple as that. *Well, fuck you,* I think. *Fuck you.*

But I don't mean it. Not really.

I'm a pathetic sack of shit. It's no wonder that she doesn't want me anymore.

One hundred hours.

Five and a half days.

Nate and Adam talk me into a party they're going to at some chick's beach condo. I know that I should say no, but I guess that I'm just a glutton for punishment. I end up sitting on the porch by myself with the brassy clang of girly pop music filtering over me through the sliding glass doors.

I stare at my new phone. Sophie stopped trying to call me two days ago. Now she's emailing. This morning I scanned the latest email and picked up a few key words like: *glioblastoma* and *temporal lobe.* My thirteen year old sister is trying to talk to me about *palliative care,* whatever that means, and I'm too chickenshit to respond.

Until we both stop running...

I look at my phone so long that everything on the display screen starts to blur together. Taking a deep breath, I pull up my contacts and tap out a quick text before I lose my nerve.

I thought of a new one. Oliver Twit

Stupid, right?

I wait for a few minutes to see if she'll text me back. Surprise, surprise. She doesn't.

Some guy comes out onto the porch and asks me if I want a cigarette. *Why the hell not*, I think, lighting up and sucking that shit deep into my lungs.

I've got nothing to lose.

Six days.

A week.

Aimee

What would you say if I told you that I love you?

I think about those words as I'm staring into the dark of my room at night, trying to read the shape of the shadows. I play that question on repeat in my head with his voice tickling my ear and the memories pulling me under.

I close my eyes and take a breath. I hold it inside of my lungs and count to ten. And then I let it go.

• • •

"Aimee?" My mother's voice is strained, piqued. "Is everything alright?"

The unspoken rule is that I wait for her to come to me so I'm sure when my number showed up on her phone, she started to panic.

"Yeah um…" I look up and let my eyes drift over that crack in the ceiling of my bedroom. "I was, um, wondering if you still had the number for that doctor? The one that Dr. Galindo suggested?"

A pause. "I do," she says uncertainly. Then I hear shuffling and I know that she's looking in her purse for something, probably the doctor's business card.

She reads off the number to me and then we both hang on the phone for a bit, each of us waiting on the other. Or maybe we're just listening to the sound of our shared breathing.

"Thanks," I say eventually. "And, Mom?"

"What is it, Aimee?"

"Do you think… do you think that maybe you'd come with me sometime? Not to the first appointment, but someday? And Dad too? Because… I love you. And I don't think that I'm ever going to be the person that I was before the accident, but that doesn't mean that I want to stop being your daughter."

She's quiet for a long time. Finally she speaks and I can tell that she's crying. "I'd like that. I'd like that very much."

Cole

I text her a new title every day. After *Oliver Twit*, it's *Lice in Wonderland* and then *Laughter House Five* and *Life of I*.

I like to imagine that she gets my texts while she's sitting cross-legged in the middle of her bed in that little cream tank top, studying or putting lotion on her legs. I picture her trying to suppress a smile and failing miserably. And somehow, that one thought gets me through the day.

Sometimes I send her other things: a random song lyric that pops in my head, a picture of my sneakers right before I run in a heat against Nate. One morning I send over a shot of the awful kale and spinach smoothie that Daniel insists that I try for breakfast.

I tell myself that I'm not trying to be friends with her or anything like that. It's not like she ever responds so it seems more like sending messages out to sea in a bottle or writing in a journal than harassing an ex-girlfriend. It's hard to explain, but there's a sort of peace in it. And I know how stupid that sounds. I know that I'm figuring out ways to justify it to myself, but maybe that's not so terrible. Reaching out to Aimee in these little insignificant ways makes me feel something other than anger and self-pity, and today that matters more than my pride.

I finally call my sister back on a Tuesday when I know that she'll be home from school. I'm not up for a video chat yet, so I hold the phone up to my ear and I wait. Sophie answers on the second ring and, my voice a sopping mess of barely held together syllables, I tell her that I'm sorry.

The kid is cool. She doesn't give me a bunch of crap. She tells me that it's no big deal and that she loves me, which, of course, makes me feel like an even bigger piece of shit.

We talk about Mom for a while. Sophie tells me that she's on a waiting list to get into a hospice in a few months.

"What about treatment? Can't they try chemo or radiation or something?"

"Didn't you read my emails? She's past all that now."

"I-I'm…" I force myself to take a deep breath. I'm on the floor of my bedroom with my back pressed up against the closet door and my feet against the bed rail. "I'm so sorry, Sophie. You shouldn't be dealing with this on your own. I'm so fucking sorry."

"You shouldn't say fuck around me. It's crass." Her laugh is weak.

"Sophie..." My voice is serious.

"Cole…" Hers is equally as serious.

"I just—I just don't know what to say to you or to her or dad."

"It's okay. It is. *We're* okay. She's sleeping in the guest room," she says, sounding way older than thirteen. "At first it was weird, but now it's good. I think dad might be waking up from his coma." She pauses.

"And I know that it's not going to end well, but I think that we needed this. Dad needed this. It's like... like..." She's searching for the right word.

"Closure?" I offer up.

"Yeah. It's closure for all of us. I was mad at her for years, but now I kind of feel like—what's the point? I'm just happy to have this time with her to make things better." Sophie drops her voice. "Do you mind that?"

I'm taken aback by the question. "Why would I mind?"

"I don't know, Cole. You haven't wanted to talk to Mom since she left, and you still won't talk to her. It's always been us against her and now... Well, I don't want you to think that I'm not on your side anymore. You did so much for me and I—"

I cut her off. "Sophie, please don't even finish that sentence. I don't want you to think that way or carry around any of my bullshit for me. She's your mother. " Aimee's words come to me. "She's a part of you and I want you to have that."

"Me too." Sophie sighs softly and I wish that I could see her face because I know that she's smiling and I love that smile. "I was too young before. I didn't know her. I didn't know that her favorite dessert was lemon meringue pie, or that she sang in an a capella group in high school, or that she's afraid of heights. And I realize that those things sound silly, but... I don't know... I needed answers and now I have my chance to get them."

We talk a little longer. Sophie tells me about school and gives me the Aaron Miller update. Finally, she asks about Aimee.

"How do you know anything about Aimee?" I ask.

"I called the house phone looking for you and Adam told me."

"Then you know that it's over, yeah?" My stomach tightens. I don't want to talk to Sophie about this.

"But I don't know why. I don't know how you *feel.*" Now she sounds more like a thirteen-year-old.

"The *why* is because I'm an ass." I knock my head back against the closet door. "And I *feel* like I've been chewed up, swallowed, and then spit back up."

"Like regurgitated puke?"

I laugh because, disgusting as it is, regurgitated puke sounds about right. "Something like that."

• • •

One day, I think catch a glimpse of her walking across campus. My heart bucks and for a second I can't breathe right, then I'm rocketed in motion—running after her, carelessly pushing people out of my way. It turns out to be someone else. The girl is shorter than Aimee. She has dark brown eyes and a narrow nose that hooks downward at the end. She looks at me like I'm crazy and I wonder if she might be right.

A little while later, in a not-entirely-coincidental coincidence, I bump into Mara coming out of the campus bookstore. We exchange stilted hellos while I search her features for any traces of Aimee.

"How is she?" I try to sound casual, like my life doesn't depend on the answer.

"She's good. She's seeing someone."

The sentence steals my breath.

It knocks me on my ass.

Fuck me. So this is what being eviscerated feels like. My brain flashes to that scene in *Braveheart* where Mel Gibson is lying on the cross with his entrails in a puddle at his feet.

Mara catches the expression on my face and quickly puts her hand on my arm. "No! Not like the way that you're thinking. God no! I meant that she's seeing a counselor. It's a good thing. Good for her. Good for my parents." She narrows her eyes. "Good for you maybe."

"Huh," I say like the sun didn't just collapse and go supernova.

Life moves forward. Daylight comes. It goes. I've started to read at night. It helps me sleep. Maybe it does something to my brain, or maybe I like it because books remind me of Aimee.

Sometimes I dream about the two of us lying on our backs in my truck bed. I feel her hand in mine, her warmth pushing up against my body. Then the wind comes in and it picks her up and tries to carry her away from me. But I don't let go of her hand. I can't. I cling to that kite string like nothing will stop me. And when I wake up, I wish that I could keep dreaming.

On most days, Sophie and I talk. Sometimes she wants to tell me about our mom and I listen to that. Other times she talks about teenage girl stuff—school, boys, the dog—and I listen to that too.

"I emailed dad a few days ago."

We're on video chat and I can see her eyes get bigger. "You did?"

I nod my head.

"And?"

"It's good. I think we're both going to try harder," I say. "Sophie, I still haven't called Mom and I can't make any promises, but maybe. *Maybe*. I know that as your big brother I'm a miserable fuck-up and my only excuse is that I'm still working things out."

"Well, Cole… When we screw up on the court, our volleyball coach always tells us that as long as we're still breathing, we're still trying. And then he usually tells us to get over ourselves."

I laugh. "That's not bad advice."

"His other little tidbit of shared wisdom is to punch every day in the face." She shrugs. "I actually find that one a little more helpful."

What can I say? The kid is cool.

• • •

I tell myself that I'm not going to text her again. Then failing to take my own advice, I text her.

Who cares? It's not like she's going to respond.

One night I send her a picture of the sky after practice. More fake book titles.

It's okay because she never gets back to me.

Until she does.

Twenty-Two

Cole

I 'm in bed reading when my phone chirps. I expect it to be a text from Sophie. Or maybe it's one from Adam, detailing the myriad of ways that I'm a pussy for staying in on a Thursday night.

When I see her name, my entire world stops spinning.

What's it about?

At first I'm confused. What's *what* about? Then I realize that she means the book title that I sent her earlier—*Angels and Demos*. It only takes me a half a minute to come up with something.

It's a buddy comedy about a group of infielders from a California baseball team as they follow their passion to make it big in the music business.

My fingers itch as I type out a second text.

You're it.

A minute passes. Two. It feels like a million fucking years. Three minutes. Weeds grow over my feet. The polar ice caps melt a few dozen inches. Four minutes. My internal organs petrify.

My phone makes a sound and just like that, the world is back in motion.

Aimee

"That was a titillating lecture, don't you agree?" Jodi rolls her eyes.

"Dr. Hillard blew my mind like usual." I bring three fingers to my temples and rub vigorously. "After an hour of that, I think I need a caffeine boost."

"Me too. I actually want it to be pumped into my bloodstream intravenously." She fishes around the front pocket of her bag for her sunglasses. Slipping them over her nose to shield her eyes from the sunshine, she turns to look at me. "The Union?"

I nod once. "Union."

"Hey, I meant to tell you something," she says as we move down the sidewalk, dodging a couple of guys. One of them looks a little like Cole and I let my eyes linger on his blond hair and the straight line of his jaw.

"What?" It's amazing how a few months ago, when I wasn't looking for him, he was everywhere, and now I haven't seen him in weeks. Maybe it's the universe trying to tell me something.

"I saw Cole last night."

The sound of his name spoken out loud makes my heart do a somersault. I stop walking and spin around so that I can look at her. "You did?"

"Yep. Kyle and I were having dinner at that outdoor cafe on Southbay. They've got a fantastic mango tofu wrap that's the perfect balance of sweet and salty. Another plus is that you can get onion rings as a side instead of your standard fries. You know that I seriously love onion rings."

"Jodi," I say impatiently. "I'm figuratively tapping my foot over here."

"Okay, okay." She squishes up her mouth and pushes a loose curl back behind her ear. "There honestly isn't much to tell, which is probably why I didn't mention it first thing. I only saw him from a distance walking to his truck and all I can tell you is that he looked good."

Of course he looked good. He *always* looks good. "Was he alone?"

Jodi drops her head so that I can see her eyes over the sunglasses. "Yep. No shirt on so I think he must have been finishing up at the gym. Either that or he was modeling for a calendar."

I start to speak but change my mind and let Jodi babble the rest of the way to the Union. She fills the silence with a complete rehash of the compulsory sorority meeting that she attended two nights ago. I nod and grunt a little but, really, my brain is five minutes back, stuck in the tar pit that is Cole Everly, bare-chested and sweaty after a workout.

Once we've gotten our coffees, Jodi clears her throat and says, "I want you to tell me again."

"Tell you what again?"

"Go over it again." She rolls her hand in the air. "The texts, the photos that he's been sending… all of it."

I reach for a wooden stirrer from the opposite end of the counter. "Why? It doesn't mean anything."

Before Jodi puts the lid on her coffee, she dips her finger in and brings it to her mouth to test whether or not she needs to add more sugar. "Do you want it to mean something, Aimee?"

Do I want it to mean something? I take a few seconds to answer. "I don't know. Does it matter?"

She shoots me a knowing look. After that night, I told Jodi everything. And I mean *everything*—about Jillian, the accident, and Cole's mother. She needed to hear something so I gave her the truth. And the whole time that I cried and let her hold my hand, I was thinking about that time that I woke up and Cole was looking at me with sad, shiny eyes. *Didn't you have anyone else after Jillian died?*

"Ah." She tips her chin. "We're back to this again."

"Jodi, he's probably already met someone else by now. Guys like that… they don't just wait around."

"He didn't sleep with that Kate bitch, and I don't think he's interested in anyone else."

"How would you know?" I shake my head. "It's been *weeks*."

"Weeks, months! It doesn't matter. He told you that he loved you."

"Not exactly. He asked me what I would say *if* he told me that he loved me."

I can see that she's a little disappointed with my response. "Now you're just being obtuse."

"I'm not being obtuse. I just…"

Jodi doesn't let me finish. She's moving her head and her hands in ten different directions. "You can lie to yourself all you want, but I know the truth. I *see* it. Cole loves you and you love him." Her voice holds a certainty. "When you two look at each other your eyes turn into little sparkly red hearts."

"Jodi," I say. "That's not…"

"You're overthinking it. You're so busy worrying about what might go wrong that you're not giving it the opportunity to go right."

"No, I'm just…" I shake my head. "I think that I've lost my chance with him."

"Aimee, love is a choice, not a chance."

It takes me a minute to place my own words, the ones that I said to her after she met Kyle, when I was explaining why I didn't believe in insta-love.

"Oh." What else can I say?

She takes a sip of her coffee and touches my arm. "Now you get it."

• • •

"Hmmm… Have you thought very much about trust, Aimee?"

Have I thought about trust? Even for a therapist, I think it's an odd question.

I stare at Dr. Bernstein, sitting across from me in a chair covered in an ugly off-white fabric. She *looks* like a therapist. Glasses, hair pulled back from her face, the whole bit. And she makes a lot of *hmmm* sounds from deep in her chest. It's very doctor-ish and soothing.

"Trust," she says again, encouraging me with her eyes. Beyond her, the room falls away to a bright picture window that's full of sky.

"What do you mean?"

She uncrosses her legs and leans forward so that she's angled over the armrest. "When your parents came to the session last week, do you remember how we talked about trust? About it being a two-way street?"

Yes. Among a lot of things, she'd said that they needed to practice trusting me and that I needed to do the same for them.

I nod my head, trying to keep my thoughts straight.

"There's a certain level of trust between friends, isn't there?"

Friends? All of a sudden, I'm nervous. Something is seriously wrong here.

"And," she goes on. "I wonder if you've ever given any thought to the trust that Jillian broke the night of the accident?"

Jillian… I think my brain is snapping in two. Breaking. "What do you mean?" I can barely hear my own voice. I'm shivering, shaking. I draw an image out of my mind: Jillian and me standing against the railing of a bridge, our fingers entwined, the wind whirling our hair up around our faces. I think we were fifteen.

I will if you will…

"She didn't tell you that she'd been using pills." Her eyes are heavy and every word out of her mouth is a prick against my sensitive skin. "She told you that she was fine to drive, but that wasn't true, was it?"

Do you hear that sound? It's the sound of the world ripping apart.

"That's not... that's—she wasn't..."

"Don't misunderstand me. I'm not telling you what to feel, Aimee. I'm just giving you the tools to help you work through this and I think this is something that you should at least consider."

I can't think of how to respond to that. I have so many words inside of me and no idea how to say them so I keep my mouth clamped in a straight line and I rub my hands over my trembling arms. God, it's cold in here.

"One... Two... Three..."

After an eternity, Dr. Bernstein nods at the clock and closes the notebook on her lap. "Forgiveness isn't simple," she says like I don't already know that. "There's always a possibility that you aren't the only one who needs it."

Cole

It happens the way it began—with her bumping into me on a sunny day.

Later I'll be able to wonder about all the ways that we might have missed each other. I'll think about how the guy in the car in front of me could have made that light a mile back, or what would have happened if I'd decided to skip the Starbucks run before I stopped for gas.

But, in this moment, I'm not thinking about stars aligning or fate. Nope. I'm annoyed because the pay-at-the-pump machine isn't reading the magnetic strip on my debit card. Again.

"Fuck," I grumble, wiping the debit card against my leg and running it through the machine a third time. *Card Error.*

I start across the lot of the gas station, tucking the debit card in the fold of my wallet and the wallet in my back pocket. As I reach the swinging glass door, I see the girl coming. Her dark hair is pulled into a messy bun. She's got a lopsided walk, her back is to the outside world, and she's pushing against the glass with her bony hip. I just don't realize who the girl is until after she's caught her foot on the grated metal threshold and her bottle of orange juice is dripping down the front of my shirt.

"Agh!"

"Oh my God!"

"Sh—" That first split-second of recognition hits me hard. It feels like an earthquake is trapped inside my body. My skin rumbles with the impact.

Power lines go down.

Trees are uprooted.

Homes are destroyed.

Cities are leveled.

Her hands fly to my chest right before her eyes find my face. "Oh my God." *Wait for it.* "I'm so s—"

There. I watch the words evaporate right off the tip of her tongue. She goes white and then pink like a human mood ring. Her mouth flaps open and her black eyelashes flutter against her cheeks.

"Hi Aimee."

Her eyes dart between my face and my orange-juice-soaked shirt. She pulls away and covers her face with her hands. "I am so sorry. I am such a klutz," she whispers, peeking at me through her fingers.

I gingerly pull the sticky fabric away from my chest. "It could have been hot coffee. Just tell yourself that."

"I can't believe—" She falters, shakes her head. "I have no idea what to say right now."

"A simple hello could lead to a million wonderful things."

That gets her hands off her face, which is nice because I want to look at her. I want to examine all the details that make her up and then compare them to my memories to make sure that I haven't forgotten anything important. Hair, eyes, shoulders, that freckle on her cheek.

"What are you doing here?" She squeaks.

"Getting gas." I state the obvious. "You?"

"Same." I follow the movement of her head to where Mara is leaning over her car. She waves and I wave back. "We're skipping class today to head home early for the Thanksgiving break. M-Mara wanted a granola bar and I had a craving for orange juice and, well… you can figure out the rest."

Silence. We're awkward. *This* is awkward.

I cough. "Of all the gas stations in all the towns in all the world…" Aimee blinks at me and I know that she has no idea what I'm talking about. "*Casablanca*," I offer up.

Aimee shakes her head. "I haven't seen it."

"Well you could knock me sideways. I'm shocked."

She laughs and as it fades, it turns into a smile. A real smile. It's the one that I remember. So beautiful that it puts the sun to shame. I tell her this and she smiles and blushes some more.

"So, um, are you going home for Thanksgiving?" She asks eventually.

I lean back on my heels and squint my eyes against the sun hanging at the top of the sky. "Nah. It's too far for such a short trip. I have to be on campus by Saturday morning for track team stuff." I take a shallow breath. "So, how are things with your family?"

"Oh, good actually. We've been talking and clearing up a lot of the misunderstandings, and I think things are better."

"Good."

"Well, it was, you know…" She waggles her shoulders and gets a look on her face. "… nice to see you."

"Yeah, of course," I say, mimicking the look and scratching the back of my neck.

Silence.

She points to her sister. "I should go."

"Me too." I step to the right the same time that she steps to the left and we end up smacking into each other.

"You first," I say, moving out of the way and grabbing the handle of the glass door to keep myself from touching her again.

"Thanks," she breathes. "Um, bye, Cole."

If she looks back, I'll say something. If she doesn't, I'll let it go.

I wait.

I wait some more.

She looks back.

Just once, right before she gets to Mara's car. It's a small swing of the eyes over her shoulder—so quick that if I weren't already looking for it, I would miss it.

Still counts.

"Hey, Aimee!" I shout.

She turns fully, wipes a hand across her beautiful face.

I'd like to say something profound or great, but if those words are inside my head I can't find them. All I can come up with is this: "I'm finally reading the *Harry Potter* books. "

"You are?" I can tell that she's genuinely surprised. "Why?"

I move my head to the side like *why-do-you-think.*

"Which book are you on?"

"Three."

Her eyebrows go up even further and a fragile smile tips the corner of her mouth. "I think that's my favorite one. Do you like them so far?"

I spread my hands. "I'm not a douchebag, am I?"

She looks at me and it's not so much the fact that she's looking at me—it's the *way* that she's looking. Hope stirs in my chest. And when she breaks into laughter, it grows wings and takes off into the sky.

Twenty-Three

Aimee

"**W**here are you off to?"

I crane my neck over my shoulder. My dad, home early from work, is coming down the stairs cradling a magazine under one arm and a kayak paddle under the other. I don't ask.

He pauses on the fourth step. "Aimee?"

"I'm actually going down to the pool for a swim." I finger the strap of the black bathing suit peeking out from under my tank. "It kinda feels like time."

He flinches in surprise at the words *pool* and *swim,* but just barely. He takes the next stair as he works out what to say. "That's… that's tremendous, Aimee."

Tremendous? Who says words like tremendous? "Yeah, um…" I stand and stretch my legs, pressing my slick palms into my thighs. "Try not to make a big deal, okay? I didn't mention it to Mom."

Dad smiles. It's the conspiratorial, it's-us-against-them smile that he used to use with me. "Of course. No big deal. No deal at all." He wipes his hands in front of his body to emphasize that he gets it. "Do you want a ride, sweet pea?"

"No, that's okay. I'm going to take my bike because I actually have a couple of stops to make first."

The smile slips a bit. "Oh, alright."

"But hey," I say, heading toward the garage. "Would you mind checking the air in my tires for me?"

Dad makes me wait while he fiddles with my bike for a few minutes and I feel twelve again. Then he follows me down the driveway and once we've reached the end, he hugs me for a long time. We don't use actual words but it feels strangely like a conversation. As I peddle away, I decide that it's not perfect but at least it's a start.

My first stop isn't far so I don't have much time to get psyched up. I tell myself that it's like swimming in a race. You don't think, you just *do*.

Don't think, just do. The words move inside of me like fast water, propelling me down the road, around the curve. Panting, pushing, I drop the bike at the crest of the hard-packed shell walkway, take the familiar front steps two at a time, and ring the bell before I can stop myself. *Don't think, just do.*

"Do you know how many times I've played the what if game with myself?" The words are fizzing in the air before I can register the lines on her face. "What if we hadn't gone that night? What if we'd gotten a ride with Brian?" My voice breaks and tears begin to roll down my cheeks. I can barely make myself look at her but I keep going. I came here to talk to Jillian's mother and that's what I'm going to do. "What if I had known about the pills? *How* could I have not known, right? She was my best friend and I thought that was the kind of thing that we told each other. Maybe she'd gotten good at pretending... I-I don't understand any of it and still, I wake up every morning and think: What if I could go back to that night and choose all over again? *What if?*"

Mrs. Kearns takes a step forward then stops. "But you can't."

"Right. I can't." I think of Jillian, taking my hand, jumping into the void. And I think of her taking my keys out of my hand, laughter creasing her eyes. *I'm fine.*

"Aimee…"

"I'm sorry. I just… God! I miss her so much that it hurts. And sometimes it hurts so much that I'm convinced she's trapped inside of me trying to beat and claw her way out of my chest." I pound my fist against my breastbone. "And I don't even know if that's what I want… because, because… if she gets out—if the memories stop haunting me—I'll be alone. Really and truly alone."

"Oh, Aimee," she says and her voice holds more sadness than anger. "It's *me* that wants to go back. What if I had been stricter? What if I'd gotten her into ballet instead of swimming? What if I were the type of mother to search her daughter's room? Would I have found the pills then? What if I could go back and live an entirely different life? Would one single choice make a difference?" She closes her tear-soaked eyes. "And, honey, I'm the one who should be telling you that I'm sorry. You were just a kid—a kid that I loved and then turned my back on for one mistake and all the other things that you couldn't control. Do you know what Jillian would do if she were here right now?"

Unable to look her in the eye, I give my head a little shake.

"She'd slam a door in my face and not talk to me for over a week." Mrs. Kearns finds my hand, winds her fingers into mine. Her skin is warm and smooth. "You aren't to blame for Jillian's death. You never were."

I'm so overwhelmed that I can't lift my voice above a whisper. "I didn't know about the pills. I didn't know."

She doesn't respond, but she nods her head like she believes me, and she pulls me into her arms and squeezes me hard against her body. "Come inside," she says against my hair. "Please."

So I do.

• • •

One thing I know from watching all those movies with Cole is that real life doesn't work out the way that it does onscreen. In real life, you rarely know the right thing to say and the best parts aren't condensed down to a manageable script that wraps up at the two-hour mark. The director never calls cut. There isn't a period at the end of the last sentence. There's a question mark.

If my life were a movie, fresh from seeing Mrs. Kearns, I would go to the tabernacle of Jillian's grave and I would sprawl out on a pallet of lush green grass under a sunlit blue sky. I'd talk out loud for hours, telling her all of the things that she's missed. The breeze would pick up along with a stirring musical score. A white bird of some sort might take flight from a nearby tree and I would just *know*, in some secret place inside of me, that Jilly and I are okay.

Real life doesn't work quite like that, does it? It's jumbled up and it's messy and there are too many thoughts, too many *feelings* curling around inside of you. You can't unwind them and say for certain, "this is this, and that is that."

It's not like that.

It's like *this:* grass, scorched and brittle under my sneakered feet and sweat pooling in the butt of my bathing suit from the bike ride over here. Real life is me slapping occasionally at the no-see-ums circling my ankles as I silently stare at the stone tablet that marks the spot where my best friend's ashes are buried. Real life is me searching for answers but winding up feeling more lost than ever.

Looking around, the only thing that I know for sure is that she's not here. Not in this place. There's no way Jillian Kearns would stick it out for eternity in a humdrum Florida cemetery full of browns and greys and a bunch of decaying old farts. Not a chance. She'd go where the action is.

I will if you will.

I tilt my face to the sky and something that Mrs. Kearns told me earlier comes back to me.

"When you girls were about ten or eleven, I was driving the kids to school and I asked them who they would be if they could be anybody. I don't remember Daniel's answer. I'm sure that he said he'd like to be the President or some famous athlete with a massive endorsement deal." She pushed my hair back from my face and sought out my eyes. *"Do you know what Jillian said?"*

I shook my head.

"I'll never forget it because it was such an odd thing to say. She told me that she'd be you. You, Aimee." She cupped her hand to the place where my heart beat under my skin. *"Maybe you aren't wrong. Maybe she is inside of you. But I don't think she's making a racket because she's trying to get out. I think she just wants to make sure you know that she's there."*

Cole

I can't explain what's happening inside my head. It's like trying to describe in one concise sentence how and why *Terminator Salvation* went so very wrong. It's more like, *where do I begin?*

If I had to bottom line it? Then I'd say that I'm fucking sick and tired of getting in the way of myself.

I'm not sure exactly *what* I'm supposed to do next, but I'm pretty sure that I have to do something or I'll just get swallowed into the bottomless vacuum of dead space that's been carved out where my heart should be.

So, on Wednesday night, I dial the numbers one at a time and then I bring the phone up to my ear.

When she answers and I hear her voice—live and unscripted—for the first time in three years, I make myself take a breath and I say, all casual like, "So, there's this girl…"

My mom, to her credit, doesn't miss a beat. She doesn't get gooey on me. She doesn't breathe heavily into the mouthpiece, or start to cry, or heave the phone across the room.

Nope.

Like she doesn't have a terminal brain tumor, like we talked yesterday, like there isn't a giant elephant sitting on top of her, she says, "There always is. What's her name?"

Aimee

"I, for one, think that you should just call him."

I look up from my book and see Mara staring at me anxiously. She slides onto the stool next to me and props her elbows on the dark grey granite counter.

"Call who?" Mom tosses two halves of a cracked eggshell into the garbage can. She's making a batch of pumpkin-zucchini muffins for the morning.

"Cole," Mara answers. "I think that she should call him and tell him that she misses him."

Mom nods thoughtfully. "He was a very attractive young man."

I put my hands up and duck my head to the counter. "Ugh. I'm not—I can't even have this conversation with you guys. Honestly."

Dad walks in the kitchen. "What are we not talking about?"

"No." I adamantly glare at my mother and my sister. "Definitely not."

Ignoring me, Mom says: "Cole. Mara thinks that Aimee should reach out to the boy and settle things."

"Mmm..." Dad nods his head once and sits down at the kitchen table.

"Ugh!" I moan. "We're not doing this."

Mom points a wooden spoon at me. "Remember that Dr. Bernstein told us that communication is key."

"Then let's communicate. Let's talk about something else... *anything* else!"

Dad pipes up. "I read an article in *Men's Health* about kayaking and—"

Mara cuts him off. "I saw Daniel on campus the other day and we talked about the situation."

That whips my head around. "You *what?*"

"Daniel Kearns?" Mom asks as she measures out a half-cup of vegetable oil.

"Yep. If you remember correctly, we do know each other from high school." Mara clicks her tongue and shakes her head. "Anyway, Daniel agrees with me. And the two of us have decided that if you and Cole don't talk soon, we're going to have to pull a parent trap number and force you together."

"You're not my parent, Mara," I say, twisting my hair over my finger.

Mara flares her eyelids. "You know what I mean. Daniel told me that Cole is still completely heartbroken."

Mom's forehead creases and she frowns. "Poor thing."

"Mom, it's not—" A loud noise interrupts me.

"Wha—"

You would think, with the way the members of my family react to the sound of the doorbell, that we're Colonials and this is the eve of the British invasion.

Mara yelps. Mom drops the wooden spoon she's holding.

"What *the?*" That's dad, checking the digital clock above the stove, furrowing his brow.

Mom titters, moves the mixing bowl back to the center island opposite the sink. "Don't answer it, Carl."

"Why?" I interject, stepping off the barstool more out of instinct than curiosity.

Mom runs the wooden spoon under the tap, wipes it on the bottom of her apron and shrugs delicately. "Could be burglars."

"Burglars ringing the doorbell?"

"You never know…"

Dad ignores her and strides to the foyer with me on his heels. The doorbell sounds again.

"Coming!" He bellows, flipping the lock with his left hand.

"Shhhh!" Mara is pushing herself into my back.

"Shhh, *what?* I don't understand why we're all so jumpy." I glance over my shoulder and see Mara and Mom both creeping up behind me, back-to-back, shoulders curved forward like quotation marks.

"Oh." Mom's changing expression is my first warning. Mara's gasp is my second.

Nerves escalating, pit in my stomach gaping open, chills prickling over my skin, I swivel my neck around and look.

One. Two. Three. Breathe.

It's Cole.

I can't quite believe it, but of course it's Cole.

He really is standing here—just this side of my front door with his blond hair looking blonder and his green eyes looking greener and his muscly body looking more muscular than ever.

I'm hyperaware of every single breath, every flutter of air that passes in the space between us. Cole moves his mouth slightly and I feel an answering tingle nip below my navel.

My mom is the first to break the magical spell and speak. "Cole, how nice to see you." She comes forward, tugging on my hand as she passes by.

Her words seem to spur the rest of the Spencer clan into motion. Dad starts in about his new kayak (what is with him and the kayak?), Mara blathers something about midterms. Mom nods appropriately and does a lot of smoothing of her clothes.

This is surreal. I'm almost afraid to blink my eyes, but I do, and my faith is rewarded by the fact that he doesn't just… evaporate. He's still standing here in my house, with his weight on one leg, hands tucked deep into his pockets, talking to my family like a normal human, all while keeping his eyes on me.

An awful thought hits me and my hand snaps to the rat's nest that is my unwashed hair and my eyes dart down to the old camp shirt that I found and slipped over my head after I got home from the pool.

Nice.

"Um."

Everyone turns and looks at me expectantly. I try again. "D-do you guys, um, mind if Cole and I go outside for a second?"

Cole

The longer we just stand here staring on her front porch with a frail wind kicking up around our feet and the stars flickering above, the more the pressure builds.

"How'd you…" Her voice trickles away.

"Daniel. He gave me your address." I can tell that she's about to ask another question but I don't give her the chance. I drove down here because I have something to say and I'm going to say it. "I want to ask you a question, but first, can I just talk for a minute?"

Aimee nods her head like she's on autopilot. She's got her eyebrows pulled together and her mouth pursed into a pucker and I can see that her whole body is practically shaking. I'm not sure if that's a good sign or a bad sign.

I draw in a breath and let it out. "I called my mother earlier."

"Oh." She pulls her arms around her body. "What happened?"

"I don't know," I tell her honestly. "We're not alright but… we'll see. It was actually her that told me to come here to see you. She pointed out that girls are big into the romantic gesture thing. I told her that you weren't like most girls, which is true. But then I started to think that maybe she had a point." I remember our first official date. Aimee said that she liked flowers and I realize that I probably should have brought her flowers or chocolates or bacon covered donuts or something. Ah, fuck it. All I've got is me and I'm going to keep talking even if it kills me. "But before I get into the whole romantic gesture, I need to tell you that you were being an idiot when you ended things."

She makes a sound and her eyes change.

"Don't look like that. It's the truth. Pulling away from me was a bad call. I don't need space to figure things out or get my shit together. I don't need time or a shrink or a priest. I need you. I need you like I need air. And don't think that I'm a codependent bastard who wants to smother you because it's not like that. It's not. The truth is that we make each other better. *You* make me better. Aimee, you make me *want* to be a better man."

She looks down, pulls on the bottom of her t-shirt. "Cole, I—"

"I'm not done yet." I blurt, pushing my hand back into my hair. "I actually stole that line from a movie but you didn't know that, did you?"

She shakes her head and bites her bottom lip. Fuck. That lip.

"See? I know you, Aimee Spencer. I know you inside and out, and you know me. Shit. You're crammed so far under my skin that it's like my feelings can't even take one step without tripping over a part of you." I shuffle toward her. *As long as I'm still breathing, I'm trying.* "I want to be with you. And that might be selfish of me, but I never claimed to be selfless or a good guy. Maybe the circumstances aren't perfect and maybe we don't make sense all of the time, but as long as my heart is going and I'm still breathing, I'm going to try for you. I've got to fucking try because that first day... Aimee, you weren't the only one that fell." I take a long breath, attempting to control the maelstrom of words moving through me. I focus my gaze on her—on that one freckle on her cheek. "Now I have to ask you a question."

Her voice is soft and uneven. "Okay."

This is it.

One. Two. Three. Four. Five. Six. Seven. Breathe.

No thoughts.

No worries.

"After all of it... the good, the bad, the in-between... If I told you that I love you, what would you say?"

Aimee

Love is a choice.

Cole is standing statue-still looking at me hard. His question reverberates in my ears. *If I told you that I love you...*

"I'd say that loving me is a bad idea." All we've got are moments so I don't make him wait long, maybe just a second or two. "And then I'd tell you that I love you too, and I'd probably throw in a sonnet or something else equally as cheesy."

His eyes shift and he gets this look on his face. God, I love that look. "Yeah?"

My shrug is matter-of-fact like I'm not on the verge of unraveling into a boneless puddle. Cole Everly drove to my parent's house and has placed his heart in his palm and passed it over to me. I'd say that it's a feat of nature that I'm still able to keep myself upright. "This is hypothetical, right?"

Cole keeps his gaze locked on mine as he takes another step forward. Now he's so close that I can see my reflection shine on the surface of his eyes and feel the warmth coming off of his body.

"Definitely hypothetical," he says, reaching out to touch my hand. One by one, he lays his fingers against mine, telling me with his touch what he feels.

"Well, then..." I glance down at my bare arm. It's covered in raised bumps and I'm pretty sure that my entire body is trembling like a Chihuahua. "Yes, I would. Probably Shakespeare. You know, like, 'shall I compare thee to a summer's day' or something."

"Shakespeare?" His voice is tinged with wonder. He lifts his other hand and cautiously brushes my hair away from my face.

"Shakespeare," I confirm, swallowing hard.

We look at each other for a long time, barely touching, feeling the heartbeats move over us and through us. I think about those lines, the ones that tangle in the space between, winding, stringing us together. I think about the rhythm of Cole's heart and the predictable whoosh of his hot breath moving over my skin. And I think about Jillian knocking against my ribcage to let me know that she approves. *Do you hear that sound?*

"Come here," he says as he slides his hand to the back of my neck and pulls me into his body.

"Fina—" I don't get to finish because Cole is kissing me, searing me, handing over the words with his tongue. I fall into him—well, I guess I fall. I'm certainly not holding myself up anymore. I register Cole's arm wrapped tightly around my waist and his other hand coasting down the side of my body, pulling my left knee up. *Oh God. Oh God.* As he continues to greedily shape his lips to the contours of my mouth, I tip backward until my shoulder blades are pressing into the cool wood of the front door.

"Holy shit." I don't even know which one of us mutters it.

Breathing hard and fast, he breaks away from my mouth and presses his face against my hair. "Your parents are right behind that door and if I don't stop now, I'm not going to stop."

His thumb drifts up the edge of my t-shirt to trace the line of my spine. I inhale the scent of him and it's like remembering the lyrics to a song that you forgot you knew.

"Mmmm," he sighs huskily, mirroring my thoughts. "Chlorine. I love the smell of chlorine."

Cole

I ended up eating Thanksgiving dinner with Aimee's family. When her mother realized that I didn't have plans, she insisted that I stay over. *In the guest room,* her dad was quick to point out.

And I'm not going to lie. Thanksgiving was a little awkward. Daniel stopped by to thank Aimee for going to talk to his mother. Then he stayed for pie. It was weird. But it was weird and wonderful and all ours.

"You know," I say, glancing over at her. We're in my truck driving back to her place. "If you keep looking at me like that, you're going to ruin me."

Staying out of her bedroom last night was a testament to my will-power. Every inch of my body was burning. I think I may have actually left a pile of ashes back in the guest room bed.

"What do you mean?"

"That," I point with one finger. "Right there. That lip bite. I think you're aware that it drives me wild and you're using it against me. We're not even going to make it to your bed."

Aimee blinks innocently. "What... *this*?" She sucks on her bottom lip. "Does it bother you?"

I growl. I actually growl.

Right before we sat down for Thanksgiving dinner, I pulled Aimee into the hall and whispered into her ear all the things that I planned to do to her when I had the chance. I think that I may have even licked her neck. I can't be sure since things tend to go a little blurry when I'm that close to her.

The good news is that she didn't hesitate to announce to her family that we were heading back to school early to... "um, study." I swear that her dad looked a little nauseous and I don't really blame him. The things I plan to do to her tonight...

"I'm not kidding," I say to her.

And I'm not.

Aimee

Cole's right. We don't even make it to the bed.

He's on me before I can kick the front door shut. His fingers are at my waist, fighting with my zipper, eagerly peeling my panties down my legs.

I think I make a sound as we hit the ground, but I'm distracted by the weight of his body pressing into mine in all the right places. I grab the back of his shirt and pull, digging my fingers into the flesh of his lower back.

"I need..." I whimper. God, I sound insane, like I'm being pulled apart at the seams.

Cole kisses me, captures my breaths with his mouth tells me that he needs me too. *Like air,* he reminds me.

Later, when we've managed to remove all our clothes and make it to my bed, I ask him a question that's been niggling at my brain. "So what was the movie?"

I'm on my stomach and he's next to me, propped with two pillows behind his back. He's holding my right hand in front of his body, drawing lazy circles in the valley between each finger. "What?"

"The one that you quoted to me earlier."

Cole shifts and the sheet falls so that the top of it cuts a line right through that vee in between his hips. God. *"As Good as it Gets,"* he says.

I pull my hand away and starting just above the edge of the sheet, I slowly crawl my fingers up his chest like a spider. "Haven't seen it."

He chuckles and I watch my hand move with his body. "It's basically about this OCD guy who meets a woman and gets his life turned completely upside down."

"Oh, so do you think that's true?"

Cole grins and pulls me fully on top of him so that he can see my face. "Is what true?"

"That this is as good as it gets?"

He thinks about it. "Honestly, Aimee? I'm not sure that my body can handle much better than this." He touches his hot mouth to my neck and I shiver.

I scoot a little lower so that my face is level with his navel. I run my tongue over his smooth skin and he moans.

"I'm not done," I whisper, pulling away to trace the words into his thigh. Our words. *This is real.*

"You know," I continue. "I think you *can* handle better. You're young. You're an athlete. I've heard that runners have great stamina."

Cole's breath is coming fast now. He's struggling to keep his eyes open and trained on me. "Huh," he manages. "Why don't we prove that?"

So we do.

Epilogue

"A Feast for Cows. It's a book about different factions of warring bovine, each one intent on seizing control of the pasture."

She tucks her face into the crook of his neck and laughs softly. He feels the moisture of her mouth against his skin and instinctively tilts his jaw into her. The pilot's voice comes from overhead and they both pull apart and look forward to where the flight attendants are doing the safety spiel at the front of the cabin.

Cole makes himself take a breath. Unfortunately, the lady jammed up next to him prescribes to the idea that full-on bathing in perfume is perfectly acceptable. He chokes, sputters, looks at his girlfriend with wide eyes and flared nostrils.

She rolls her eyes and peeks over his shoulder at the older woman in the twill brown pants and loud orange-patterned blouse. The plane is packed. It's just before the holidays so he guesses that people are making visits to loved ones, going home. *Home.* That's where he and Aimee are headed. Home to Nebraska. Home to his dad and sister. Babs. His mom. The unknown.

Nervous energy churns deep inside of him, but at least he's not running and at least he's got Aimee with him. He picks up her hand and turns it over so that he can trace the lines etched into her palm.

First they've got two stops. One in Atlanta and then one in Dallas, so realistically they won't make it to his house until nearly midnight, and that's counting on all the flights being on time. But his dad is footing the cost of the tickets for both of them so Cole's not going to start complaining about the flight plan now. He's not going to whine about having to spend more time with Aimee, even if it means being stuffed in a shiny metal tube and sent hurtling through the sky. No fucking way.

"Back to the game. I've also got *Harry Otter.*" He taps his head with his free hand. "Now you're two behind me."

Aimee lets her eyes slide to the top of the plane cabin and back to Cole's face. "Okay, wiseass. How about… *Fight Cub.*"

The engine whines beneath them as the plane punches down the runway. He feels the slight pressure of her fingers tightening around his. "Uh-uh-uh. That's a movie."

"No… it was a book first."

"Huh."

The look on her face can only be described as smug. "So, you don't know everything after all?"

He seeks out her eyes and smiles. "Apparently not."

"Well, wonders never cease." She leans back into her seat and grips his hand to her chest as they pitch upward. "You know, we could play the game with movies too. Let's see… *Aging Bull, The Fat and the Furious,* and… *Finding Emo.* That one's about two guys who both fall in love with an emo chick. They band together to find her when she goes missing and an unlikely bromance develops."

The dimples deepen. He can feel them cutting into his cheeks. "This could go on forever, yeah?"

The world slips away beneath them. The greens and browns are replaced by a blue so complete and true that it almost steals his breath.

Aimee lifts one eyebrow. "Is that going to be a problem?"

Acknowledgements

L ately I've been getting asked one particular question.
What's the best part about writing?

I could say something really deep but, if I'm being honest, the best part is staying in my pajamas until two in the afternoon. Shallow, right?

Now... The *second* best part? That's you—the reader! And I'm not just stroking your ego so that you go online and write an awesome review or find me on Facebook and like my page (wink, wink)—I'm being serious.

I know that your time is short and your to-be-read lists (if they're anything like mine) are long, so if you've shared in Cole and Aimee's journey—I thank you. This is a figurative hug from me to you. You are the reason my kids will get popsicles tonight and you are responsible for all the pajama wearing, which makes you pretty much my favorite.

That being said, my life is full of folks that deserve a thunderous round of applause, and though it's probably ridiculous to attempt to single people out, I'm going to try...

My husband, Dave, read *Harry Potter* for me while we were dating all those years ago and is not a douchebag. He puts up with the laundry and the moods and the dogs sleeping in bed with us. What more can I say?

I'd like to thank my friend, Brittany Walters, for graciously allowing me to use a version of her story about having a bird shit in her eye. As with most of her tales, it made me laugh so hard that I almost peed my pants.

While writing the *In This Moment* I played the book name game on Facebook with my friends and I want to thank the always witty, Ben Westermann-Clark and Tripp Ruding for letting me paraphrase their fake book blurbs.

I was lucky enough to have an extensive group of beta readers this time around. These women cheered for Aimee, swooned for Cole, and gave me direction and a reality check when I needed it. Here they are (in no particular order): Jackie Hillman, Stephanie Dean, Ana Boza, Summer LoDuca, Nelle Minich, Cindy Smith, Erica Cope (author of *Lark*), Mimi Sall, Michelle Flick (author of *The Owens Legacy*), Elizabeth Hilburn, Peggy Warren (Le' BookSquirrel—blogger and reader and person extraordinaire), Renny Shuster, Jennifer Lyons Smyth, Kristy Shuster, Sarah Baldwin and Heather Doughton (that's my mom).

I'd also like to thank Komal Kant (author of the *With Me* books) for reaching out to me, answering so many writer-ish questions, being a reader and friend, and hooking me up with other indie authors in my genre. I am indebted.

Lastly, my family members (this includes pets) deserve a parade or some sort of grand gesture. They are tremendous. They make me better. They make me *want* to be better.

Until next time... Cheers!

Music Notes

Music is a big part of what I do. Sometimes a song will inspire me or get me in the mood to do a scene. Other times, I actually find myself using the words of the song. In this book, I think I've quoted lyrics twice.

I'll be the bottles on the beaches
You'll be the waves that wash them all ashore.

If you're curious, the song is "No Nostalgia" and the band is Agesandages. And they really are out of Portland, Oregon. (As are the maple syrup and bacon donuts from Voodoo.)

I also quoted a Papa Roach song called "Last Resort." The beat, the words, everything, matches up with how I wanted Cole to be feeling that night.

Cut my life into pieces,
I've reached my last resort.
Suffocation, no breathing,
Don't give a fuck if I cut my arms bleeding.
Do you even care if I die bleeding?

There's one more song that I feel deserves a mention. I listened to "What You're Thinking" by Passenger (featuring Josh Pyke) almost every day that I was writing. The lyrics, the melody, the rhythm... I think they flow through this book. I can't imagine a better song for Cole and Aimee's story.

If you're itching for more, I actually have an entire IN THIS MOMENT playlist. You can find it through my website www.autumndoughton. com or on Spotify.

About the Author

M y first love is reading. My second love is pizza.

Currently, I live in Gainesville, Florida and I write books. Fun books for you, your sister, your best friend and your hairdresser. I think of writing as a sort of therapy, and the results tend to be feel-good odes to my youth, which is exactly how I like it.

When I'm not working or chasing after my two daughters, two dogs, two cats, three ducks and one lovely husband, I can be found skulking around the movie theater or local bookseller. Generally with chocolate somewhere on my person, because I never leave home without a treat.

Find me on Facebook, Goodreads, or through my website: www.autumn-doughton.com

43983640R00162

Made in the USA
Lexington, KY
23 August 2015